THE TIES THAT BIND

"I want you to do something for me," Essence said.

"What?"

She moved back a little farther. "Raise your arms over your head."

Titan squinted.

"Come on. Hold them up."

Titan lifted his arms.

With her eyes remaining on his, Essence pulled Titan's shirt over his head. His eyes darkened.

"What are you doing?" he asked softly.

"You'll see." Slowly, she reached down and pulled her dress over her head. "I want you to feel my heart. Feel it beating inside me." In her black lingerie, she snuggled close to him. "All the hope that I have. I want to share it with you."

She could see the desire mounting in his eyes as Titan's arms went around her. "Slowly. Slowly," Essence whispered. "Try to feel my heart. Feel what it's saying."

Essence felt Titan's arms tremble as he controlled his natural impulses. They sat as still as statues, feeling one another—each heartbeat, each breath, until their heartbeats and breathing were in sync.

"I can't believe you've got me doing this," Titan said, his voice raspy. "Woman, you're something else."

"I am when I'm with you," Essence replied. "Because I want you to know me, Titan. I want you to know who I really am." She looked down. "How I think. What I believe." Essence looked into his eyes again. "Because it's my belief that allows me to have hope." She paused. "I want you to have hope, too."

Titan's arms tightened about her again. "Hope for us?"

"If that's meant to be," Essence replied softly. But her inner voice cried yes, and so did her eyes.

BOOK YOUR PLACE ON OUR WEBSITE AND MAKE THE ARABESQUE ROMANCE CONNECTION!

We've created a customized website just for our very special Arabesque readers, where you can get the inside scoop on everything that's going on with Arabesque romance novels.

When you come online, you'll have the exciting opportunity to:

- View covers of upcoming books

- Learn about our future publishing schedule (listed by publication month and author)

- Find out when your favorite authors will be visiting a city near you

- Search for and order backlist books

- Check out author bios and background information

- Send e-mail to your favorite authors

- Join us in weekly chats with authors, readers and other guests

- Get writing guidelines

- AND MUCH MORE!

Visit our website at
http://www.arabesquebooks.com

THE TIES THAT BIND

Eboni Snoe

BET Publications, LLC
http://www.bet.com
http://www.arabesquebooks.com

ARABESQUE BOOKS are published by

BET Publications, LLC
c/o BET BOOKS
One BET Plaza
1900 W Place NE
Washington, DC 20018-1211

All Kensington Titles, Imprints, and Distributed Lines are available at special quantity discounts for bulk purchases for sales promotions, premiums, fund-raising, and educational or institutional use. Special book excerpts or customized printings can also be created to fit specific needs. For details, write or phone the office of the Kensington special sales manager: Kensington Publishing Corp., 850 Third Avenue, New York, NY 10022, attn: Special Sales Department, Phone: 1-800-221-2647.

First Printing: September 2002
10 9 8 7 6 5 4 3 2 1

Printed in the United States of America

To Na'imah and Ali,
The brightness of your being forever shines. Know that. Live it, and celebrate your life.

Chapter One

Essence Stuart held the doorknob with one hand and wiped away tears with the other. It was her house, but now every time she stepped into the bedroom upstairs, Essence dreaded what might lie inside.

Her chest quivered as she opened the door. She tried to control it. Essence didn't want her mother to see. She feared that, with the sight only a mother has for her child, Sadie could see beyond the strong front Essence presented. But Essence's shoulders sagged when she realized there was no chance of that. Sadie's frail body lay motionless on the modest full-size bed. The rich brown eyes Essence loved so much were hidden beneath thin, dark eyelids.

Quietly, Essence sat in the cushioned chair. Over the past few days, this chair had become her bed, her dining table, and the place from which Essence was watching her mother die. Daring such a thought created a tightness close to her heart. It seemed like an impossible notion. Not that Essence expected her mother to live forever. No one did. What was impossible was accepting that the tireless woman she had known all of her life would simply stop—be no more. All of Sadie's energy, her life force—which cooked, cleaned, danced, sang, worked exhausting hours, cried, laughed, and most of all loved Essence—would be gone.

She closed her eyes. Perhaps not gone, if any of the religious or spiritual teachers, or even philosophers, had a clue. It meant Sadie would simply not be here for Essence to hug and touch, not here for Essence to look into her eyes without words because words were not necessary. The thought created tears behind Essence's eyelids.

"Essie."

Essence's eyes opened when she heard her mother's thin voice. She leaned in quickly. "Yes, Mama."

In slow motion, Sadie lifted her hand and wiped away Essence's tears. "Don't cry, Boo. Don't cry."

Essence turned her face into her mother's hand and held it there. Finally, she shook her head. This was all too much. Everything seemed caught within the lump in her throat. Essence feared if she spoke a tidal wave of tears would be released. Yet her heart overflowed, and her love for her mother was greater than her fear. "What am I going to do without you, Mama? It's always been the two of us. We've been through so much together."

"And we will go through this ... together. You'll just keep going, Essie. I've got another path to take." Sadie gathered her strength. "I have no doubt the Essence I know, the one who's always found the strength and courage to move forward, will have the ability to weather my passing."

"I don't want the strength, Mama. I want you to stay here, with me." Essence couldn't stand to hear her mother speak of dying. She struggled under a wave of grief.

Sadie pressed on. "You've always been a good daughter. I want you to know I know that. Minding me and taking to heart anything I felt was important. And Essie?"

"Yes." Essence sniffed.

"We haven't come across anything more important than this."

Essence closed her eyes again. "I know." She opened them only to see Sadie's face contorted with pain. "Are you hurting?" she inquired, tossing her own suffering aside.

"A little." Sadie searched Essence's eyes. "But I fear not as much as I've hurt you, Essie."

"Hurt me?" Essence was dumbfounded. "You've never hurt me. You gave me all you could give, Mama. I'm twenty-nine now, and when I look back over my childhood, I don't know how you did it: raised me while you worked two jobs without any outside help or support. You gave me a loving, stable home. I couldn't ask for more."

Sadie's smirk was almost a grimace. "That's not what you said at twelve when you got your first job."

"Nope, it wasn't." Essence's smile created more tears. "I didn't understand then. But now I know I'm better for it, because I learned the value of work and money early in life. And I also learned money isn't everything."

"No, money isn't everything. But I could have made it easier on us." Sadie paused again. "My pride wouldn't let me. Just like it wouldn't let me tell you about your father."

"My father." Essence was shocked. She collected herself, determined to focus on her mother. "Oh, Mama. I—" She started to reassure Sadie.

"This is not the time to sweep the truth aside or to cover up our feelings. There's been enough of that, and I think you learned how to do it so well from me."

Essence could see Sadie's chest rising and falling. She placed a comforting hand on her mother's arm.

"I know through the years you've wondered about your father," Sadie continued. "You had to. It's only human. But I couldn't bring myself to tell you about him." Her dim eyes probed Essence's bright ones. "And through the years, because you never asked, I told myself it didn't matter. The truth is my mind accepted that excuse, but my heart knew better."

Essence looked down at the green-and-blue comforter that covered her mother's bed. Yes, she had wondered about her father, wondered who he was. Why wasn't he a part of their lives? Was it because he didn't care to be? Or was he even alive to care?

"Essie."

Wistfully, Essence looked up. "Yes."

"I want you to do something."

"Anything you want, Mama."

Sadie closed her eyes and sighed. "There's a key taped in the bottom of the jewelry box your grandmother gave me." She spoke slowly. "Bring it over here. And bring the round leather box that's tucked in the left-hand corner of my top drawer."

A box and a key? Essence didn't know what to make of Sadie's request. For a moment she studied her mother's face. Somehow it appeared more relaxed, relieved even.

"Go get them, Essie," Sadie said without looking at her.

Essence followed her mother's instructions. Her movements were almost involuntary. Didn't deathbed revelations occur only in the movies? Still, somehow, this strange turn of events felt fitting to Essence. From the moment she'd discovered her mother had terminal cancer, life had seemed to be coated with a fictional veneer. Essence found the tarnished gold key and the deep green box. She returned to the cushioned chair.

Sadie stared at the box in Essence's hand. That made Essence stare at it, too. With a touch of apprehension, she wondered what was inside, and how it would change her life.

"I remember the day I bought that box." Sadie's voice was full of the past. "I pictured myself giving it to you on your fifth birthday. I told myself that would be the perfect time. You would be just old enough to understand, but young enough not to be bitter. But your fifth birthday came and went, and I kept my secret. Then you got older in real life and in the daydream where I saw myself giving you the box and the key. Funny"—Sadie turned a smile that was no smile at all—"I never saw you opening it under these circumstances. But isn't that like life? You never know what's ahead."

Sadie continued to talk. Her voice became a low, monotone backdrop as Essence slid the tiny key inside the lock.

It turned as if the box had been bought yesterday. When Essence lifted the lid, two star sapphire cuff links sparkled.

"Those were your father's," Sadie told her.

Essence looked at her mother, then back at the cuff links.

"He didn't mean to give them to me. He left them behind on the night I got pregnant with you."

"So, you never saw him again after that?" The words came, but Essence felt disconnected from them.

"That was the last time we were together in a personal way. I've seen him many times. I couldn't help it. He's everywhere."

"What do you mean?" Essence looked confused.

"He had just started his political career when we got together. I fell in love the first time he smiled at me." A ghost of a real smile touched Sadie's mouth. "I was lost to him after that. Fascinated that a man like your father would be interested in me."

"Did you stop seeing each other because you got pregnant with me?" It was a difficult question, but Essence had to know.

"You were part of the reason. But it was more than that. He was married." Sadie paused. "It's one thing to have a woman on the side. It's another to have one who claims to be having your baby."

Essence looked straight into her mother's eyes. "So, who is he, Mama?"

Sadie's thin eyelids closed as if she had to gather her strength to continue. Finally, she replied, "Cedric Johnson."

Essence's stomach dropped. "Cedric Johnson! Brenda and Shiri's uncle?"

Sadie nodded. "It's very complicated, isn't it? Cedric being your best friends' uncle was another reason it was hard to tell you. Ohhh." Sadie sighed heavily. "Brenda's and Shiri's families had practically claimed you. Many, many a day you were at their house when I had to work. They fed you and guided you when I couldn't, and I just couldn't bring myself to tell Pamela and Doris, tell their mothers, that their beloved brother was your father." Her

eyes sought understanding. "Not after all the things they'd
said to me in private, berating the man who abandoned a
wonderful daughter like you. So, there I was, knowing they
were talking badly about their own brother, the pride of
Birmingham, Alabama's black community. One of our city
councilmen."

Cedric Johnson is my father! The words repeated in
Essence's head. "Oh, my God. I sat near him during a
wedding." Essence's eyes widened. "And as a kid I thought
he told some of the best jokes at the Johnson family Christmas parties." An audible intake of breath followed. "The
Johnsons think the world of him. And so does everybody
else."

"I know. I know. And there was a time I did, too." Sadie
licked her dry lips. "Then when I found out I was pregnant,
and Cedric denied that you were his baby, I was so hurt.
Shocked." Her speech slowed. "But I pulled myself
together, and I told myself I didn't want anything else to
do with him. I wanted him to see I could make it on my
own. That I didn't need him or anybody else." A dim light
appeared in Sadie's eyes. "I moved on and time passed, but
then fate stepped in. You, Brenda, and Shiri became good
friends. And for a while I had many a sleepless night over
that, picturing all kinds of things. Because of my secret, I
imagined Pam and Doris turning their backs on you if they
ever found out about your father. And that the whole Johnson
family would hate us for dragging their beloved Cedric into
a big mess."

"Oh, my God." Essence grabbed her mother's hand.

"But do you know what gives me a strange kind of
comfort?" Sadie asked.

Essence shook her head.

Sadie closed her eyes again. "I never, ever, loved anyone
like I loved your father." Her voice filled with life, more
life than her body had exhibited for months. "He gave me
you."

*She still loves him after all these years. My mother still
loves Cedric Johnson.*

''But, Essie.''

''Yes, Mama.'' Essence's emotional needle struck over-load.

Sadie locked eyes with her daughter. ''I don't want what was a peaceful life to be the center of a scandal at death.''

''Ma'am?''

''I mean, I told you about your father because you've always had the right to know, but I want to be buried, Essie, without a cloud hanging over my head. Please.'' Sadie touched her daughter's hand. ''You can do whatever you want about your relationship with your father after I'm gone.''

Essence didn't know if she could hold back all that she was feeling. It was like someone had thrown open the door to a locked room inside of her ... a room that had been forbidden all of her life. But now that it was open, she was being told not to walk through it.

Essence looked at her mother. Her eyes were closed again, and she appeared frailer than ever. That's when Essence gave in. She knew Sadie would not be with her much longer, and there was no way she would not honor her request.

''You don't have to worry about that, Mama. I won't breathe a word of this to anyone.''

Chapter Two

After Sadie's burial, Brenda and Shiri looked out Essence's living-room window. The airport shuttle was late.

"What is she doing up there?" Brenda whispered with her hand on her hip.

Shiri shrugged.

Brenda stepped over to the staircase. "The van will be here any minute, Essie. We don't mind coming up there to say good-bye if you don't want to come down."

"No, no. I'm on my way," Essence replied from the room in which Sadie had passed away.

"Okay," Brenda called, then continued in low tones. "That girl is acting really strange. I don't like leaving her like this."

"We just buried Mama Sadie," Shiri replied. "What do you expect?"

"I know that. But there's something else going on. I can feel it," Brenda insisted. "I don't think she should be alone."

Shiri looked up at the second floor. "I've got to make some headway at work. I'll be taking off early for the reunion day after tomorrow. I've got to put in that last day."

Brenda crossed her arms. "Well, I'm on vacation, so . . . maybe I can stay a little longer."

Both heads turned toward the window when a horn sounded outside.

"Essie, it's the—"

"That's the shuttle," Essence said, descending the stairs. Shiri opened the door and waved at the driver.

"Shiri and I were talking." Brenda put her arm around Essence. "And we think maybe I should stay a few more days with you."

Essence shook her head before she spoke. "No, I'm fine. Don't worry about me."

"Essence, you're just . . ." Brenda looked at Shiri for help.

"We don't think you should be alone right now," Shiri added.

"But that's exactly what I need to be: alone," Essence replied. "I need to be alone to sort out my feelings . . . my thoughts."

"I really don't mind," Brenda pushed. "I'm on vacation and—"

Essence made a face. "Sure, you don't mind. I heard you and Shiri talking about Wes and J.D. I know you can't wait to get back to them."

"Yeah, we were talking about them, but being here, if you need us, is more important," Shiri assured her.

Essence hugged Brenda and Shiri. They had been lifelong friends, and now Essence knew, in truth, cousins. "Nobody needs to stay with me." She looked away. "There's a lot on my mind, but eventually I'll be fine." Essence looked at them again. "It helps to know Mama was really ready to go. I believe she's better off now; at least she is out of pain." She felt a sudden urge to hold them, to tell them they were blood, but the circumstances held Essence back.

The driver tooted the horn again.

Brenda opened the door and stepped outside.

"Are you coming to the family reunion?" Shiri asked.

Cedric, my father, will be there. "I don't know," Essence replied.

"Well, when you make up your mind, give us a call." Shiri started up the walk behind Brenda.

"Love you," Brenda called.

"Love you, too," Essence said as she watched them climb into the van and drive away.

Essence closed the door, ascended the stairs, and sat down in front of the computer again. A picture of her father in a dark suit, white shirt, and perfect tie dominated the monitor. She read the headline in the *Birmingham Post Herald*. CITY COUNCILMAN VIES FOR STATE SEAT. Essence read the remainde of the article. It validated her biological father as a qualified candidate. "He wants to be a state representative, and he has a good chance of winning," Essence spoke out loud. "But how can Cedric Johnson be about doing so much good when he never reached out to me and Mama?"

She looked over at the bed. Essence could still see her mother lying there, small and still. As if they were on a switch, tears cascaded down Essence's cheeks. "And he was the love of her life. I know he was, just by the little bit she said. But now Mama's gone, and the mighty Attorney Johnson didn't send a flower, a card, nothing." Grief was quickly replaced by anger. Essence read the last line of the article. " 'Cedric Johnson is a partner in the Birmingham law firm of Johnson, Levi and Smith.' " Essence's eyes narrowed. "Well, I'd like to know what you have to say for yourself, Attorney Johnson. You're going to have to explain to me how you can be a crusader for good for an entire city, when you couldn't even do right by your own child."

She opened a search engine on the Internet and entered the name of the law firm. Without hesitation the name, address, and phone number appeared on the screen. Essence copied them down and logged off. As soon as the phone line cleared, Essence dialed the Birmingham number.

"Johnson, Levi and Smith," a mature voice said.

Essence froze.

"Johnson, Levi and Smith. May I help you?"

"I'd like to speak to Attorney Johnson, please."

"May I ask who's calling?"

"Essence . . . Stuart."

"One moment please."

Essence's adrenaline pumped during the silence. She had actually called him! She was actually going to speak to her father, knowing who he was! Where Essence had been angry moments before, she was now apprehensive. *Oh, my God. What am I going to say?*

The woman returned to the line. "I'm sorry, Attorney Johnson isn't available right now. May I take a message?"

As untrue as it was, Essence felt as if her one and only opportunity to talk to her father had slipped away. "But this is important."

"Is it an emergency?"

"Not really."

"If it isn't an emergency . . ." Essence could hear the woman's puzzlement. "Are you a client?"

"No, I'm not. But believe me, Attorney Johnson will also feel this is important." Essence's stomach wrenched. It said she wasn't sure.

The receptionist wasn't convinced. "Well, ma'am, can you tell me the nature of the call?"

"It's personal."

"Personal?" All kinds of questions were housed in the word. "All right. Hold on."

The line turned silent again. Essence closed her eyes and began a silent prayer, but this time the secretary returned to the line very quickly.

"I'm sorry, Ms. Stuart," The woman said in a take-charge voice. "I'm going to have to take a message."

"Tell Mr. Johnson Sadie Stuart's daughter is calling," Essence blurted.

"I'll give him the message. Sadie Stuart. Is there a phone number?"

"No, I don't want you to give him a message." Essence

knew she sounded desperate. She attempted to calm herself.
"Please, just one more time. Tell him."

There was a pause.

"One moment."

Essence's hand covered her mouth. *What if he still doesn't take the call? What if he doesn't remember my mother?* The thought that her mother might not have meant anything to Cedric Johnson, although she had feelings for him to the end, made Essence shiver. Suddenly, she heard, "This is Attorney Johnson."

Chapter Three

The tone of Cedric Johnson's voice wasn't what Essence expected. It was cool, impersonal. Somehow she had expected something else. What? Essence didn't know. "Hello."

"Yes. This is Attorney Johnson."

Essence swallowed. "Mr. Johnson, this is Essence . . . Stuart." She waited a split second to see if he would respond, but he didn't. "I'm Sadie Stuart's daughter." Her inflection said, *Why are you making me say this again?*

"Yes. I remember Sadie. We were good friends." The words were sterile. "That was a long time ago, but I do remember her. Did she refer you to me for some emergency legal assistance? The receptionist said you sounded rather anxious."

"No. No, I don't need any legal help," Essence said through an emotional fog.

"Is Sadie in some kind of trouble?"

"My mother died, Mr. Johnson. We had her funeral yesterday."

"Died?" Essence could hear his shock was genuine, and so was his condolence. "I am so sorry to hear that."

Essence remained quiet.

"So, I can imagine this is a very difficult time for your family," Cedric continued.

"It was only me and Mama," Essence replied. "She was an orphan. But perhaps you knew that. . . ." Her voice trailed off.

"I see," Cedric replied awkwardly. He recovered with a more professional tone. "Do you need legal advice concerning your mother's property?"

"No, I don't. Mama was very efficient. She took care of her life and me very well until I grew up and got out on my own."

"Yes, I guess Sadie would have." Threads of past connections wove through his words. "And what do you do for a living, may I ask?"

"I'm a massage therapist," Essence replied.

"That's good."

Cedric's reply was empty. To Essence, *that's bad* could easily have been said in its place.

There was a distinct pause.

"Well, thank you for telling me about Sadie. I assume that was your reason for calling."

"Yes, it was part of it." Essence felt like she had been detached.

"Part?" His voice turned cautious.

Essence drew a deep breath. "Yes, part. The other reason I called was to tell you my mother told me . . . you are my father."

"What?"

"A few days before she died, my mother told me you are my father." Essence stressed the last words.

"You must be mistaken." His words were icy.

"No. This is not a mistake." Essence's voice was soft but strong. "She was literally on her deathbed, and this is what she told me."

Deafening silence took over the telephone line. It was Cedric who broke it.

"Well, I'm sorry, Ms. Stuart, that you think that I am your father, but I can assure you I'm not. I have been a happily married man for the past thirty-four years. I am very visible in this community as a city councilman—"

"I know who you are, Mr. Johnson." Fatigue laced her words. "I've read about all the good things you've done for Birmingham and how you plan to run for state representative."

"You read right," he replied in a clipped fashion. Cedric's next statement had an obligatory tone. "Once again, I'm sorry that your search for your biological father has taken a wrong turn. I hope you have better luck next time." There was a brief pause. "I've got to get back to work now, Ms. Stuart. You truly have my condolences."

Essence held the phone, speechless in the face of his strong denial.

"Good-bye."

Essence continued to hold on. She heard him hang up. Slowly, Essence replaced the phone on the stand. "How dare he call my mother a liar. And he practically hung up on me." She was stunned by what had transpired. Cedric Johnson had outright denied her mother's deathbed confession, and had dismissed her as quickly as he could. Essence sat in stunned silence for an indeterminate time. "You won't get to ignore us so easily, Mr. Johnson. Not this time." Her anger rose.

Essence grabbed her appointment book and turned to the coming weekend. "I guess I will be going to the Johnson family reunion after all." She dialed the first number of the massage client she planned to reschedule. "And when I'm done with you, *Daddy*, you're going to acknowledge that I'm your child and that my mother was good enough for you to lay down with."

Essence turned suddenly and looked at the bed. "Mama?" For a moment she felt her mother's presence, but the room was empty. She turned back to her appointment book and looked up another number.

* * *

Cedric Johnson pushed back from his desk. He had an instant headache, and his stomach was doing weird things. Cedric couldn't say he had thought about Sadie through the years, because he hadn't. For him, their relationship had been purely sexual. But Cedric remembered how Sadie had exhibited a kind of innocence when it came to their relationship. She'd seemed to see it through rose-colored glasses, see him through rose-colored glasses, as if he were perfect, and could do no wrong. Unlike Vivian, his wife, who knew his flaws and wouldn't let him forget. Sadie might even have been in love with him. Cedric stood. He began to pace.

That was one of the reasons Cedric bolted when Sadie told him she was pregnant and planned to have the baby. He'd known she was serious and Cedric thought if he left her high and dry she would do what was best—right in his opinion—which was get rid of it. He couldn't have a baby outside his marriage. What would his constituents have thought? What would Vivian have done? Her confidence and, he believed, her love for him had already begun to wane.

When Cedric never heard from Sadie again, he'd believed that that was what she'd done: gotten rid of the baby. As time passed, he questioned if Sadie had ever been pregnant. As he dealt with one woman after another, the memory of Sadie's sincerity faded.

Cedric closed his eyes. The women had been so easy to come by. Some, Cedric believed when they'd told him he was the best man they'd ever had. Something inside of him needed to hear it. But most weren't so convincing, and he'd begun to distrust the women with whom he slept. Still, Cedric couldn't stop. It was like an addiction, an addiction that took a heavy toll on Vivian.

Cedric rubbed his temples. But he and Vivian had gone on with their lives, moving out of the old neighborhood to greener pastures—yet not so green Cedric couldn't use the folks from his stomping grounds as the foundation for his constituency.

The intraoffice phone line rang.

"Yes?" Cedric said.

"There's a Martin Simpson holding for you."

Cedric looked at the blinking light. "Take a message."

"All ri—"

"And hold all my calls, Diane. I've got some important business to take care of."

"Sure," she replied.

Cedric watched both telephone lights go out. He sat down again, picked up the telephone, and dialed. Edgy, he loosened his handmade silk tie. The phone rang several times.

"Hello."

Just the sound of James Valentine's familiar voice helped Cedric to exhale. "Hey, man. It's me."

"How ya doin'?" James replied.

"I'm hangin' in here."

"What do ya mean? What's up?"

Cedric could visualize James's eyebrows rising. "Ma-an, I don't know if my past has come back to haunt me or what."

"Your past?"

"Yeah." Cedric sighed. "I just had this phone conversation, and I don't like how it's got me feeling."

"Why don't you tell me about it? That's what old friends and campaign chairmen are for."

Cedric laid his head on the back of the chair. "I tell you, this—"

"Just say it, Cedric."

"All right." He paused briefly. "There was this woman—"

"Aww, Cedric," James groaned. "Let me sit down. I thought you put all that behind you when you decided to get serious about these politics. And . . . when Vivian threatened to leave you."

Cedric flinched. "I did. I did put it behind me. I'm talking about a long time ago. And the truth is ... well, I don't know what the truth is.''

"So what? This woman called you today?''

"No. Her daughter called me. The woman's dead.'' Cedric rubbed his temples again.

"Dead.'' James repeated the word with a dreaded hush. "Is she trying to connect you with her death?''

"No. No, man. It's not that bad.'' Cedric sat up in his seat. "The daughter claims that I am her father.''

"Ohh.'' Cedric could hear James's relief. "Okay. Now, that's a piece of cake compared to what I was thinking.''

There was a pause.

"Did you mess around with this woman's mother?''

"Yes. Yes, I did,'' Cedric admitted.

"I see.''

Cedric could hear James's thoughts churning. "Okay, so you did. You messed around with a lot of women,'' James piped up. "But that doesn't mean you fathered any children by them. Let me ask you something. Do you think this woman is your child?''

"That's what I meant when I said I didn't know the truth,'' Cedric replied. "To be honest, it's possible. But after nearly thirty years of having no contact with Sadie, the woman's mother ... I just feel ... if she knew I was the father, she would have gotten in touch with me before now.'' A twinge of guilt surfaced as he recalled his last conversation with Sadie. "Taken me to court or something.''

"You got that right,'' James said. "And I think this young woman's timing is rather interesting, don't you? Seeing that you just announced your intention to run for state representative.''

"Yep. I thought about that,'' Cedric said.

"How old is this woman?''

"I don't know.''

"Where does she live?''

"I don't know,'' Cedric replied, frustrated. "I didn't think to ask. She could be here in Birmingham.''

"Well, what do you know about her?'' James pressed.

Cedric reviewed the conversation with Essence Stuart. "Basically, I know she's a massage therapist."

"A massage therapist?" James made it sound like a talking orangutan. "Is she a real one, or is she using that as a cover for something else?" His insinuation was clear.

"I don't have a clue," Cedric replied. "That's why I called you, so we could mull this thing over. See how I need to handle it."

"All right, I know just what to do," James announced. "Hold on. I'm going to get Titan on three-way."

"Titan? Wait a minute." Cedric shook his head. "I don't know about bringing anybody else into this. Especially Titan. He's your son, but . . . you know how special Titan is to me. I mean, I just don't want him to start looking upside my head and thinking bad thoughts about me."

"I hear you. But Cedric," James said, "Titan is thirty-three years old. He's no child."

"Thirty-three. God, time goes by," Cedric replied. *I don't feel much older than thirty-three.* He touched the top of his forehead where his hair had receded a bit. *But I know I'm not thirty-three anymore.*

"Titan would be perfect for this. We need to know more about this woman," James stressed. "Her claim that you are her father could really mess with the campaign. Hell, it could even jeopardize your current position."

"I know that." Cedric didn't want to think about it.

"Look, man," James said. "You called me because you know I've got your back and we need to find out if this woman is legit. Titan's a private detective."

"I thought he did research for a law firm in Memphis."

"He does," James replied. "Research and investigative work. And you don't have to worry about Titan. He loves you. Nothing's going to change that."

"I hope you're right." Cedric thought of Vivian. "I've already disappointed one person who is very important to me. I don't want to add anyone else to the list."

"I am right," James assured him. "Plus, I have to give it to my son. He's good at this."

"All right." Cedric dropped his chin. "See if you can reach him."

Cedric waited, looking out the window. Several thoughts vied for his attention. Part of him believed Essence Stuart was his child. Cedric had always wanted a little girl. He had a son, Cedric Jr., but a little girl would have made his family perfect . . . almost perfect. Vivian had refused to have another child. He took a deep breath. But it didn't make sense that Sadie had never pressed the issue, never demanded child support or anything. Any woman in her position would have. Wouldn't she? For a brief moment, Cedric recalled how Sadie used to look at him. She'd looked at him with all of her. Her eyes would become soft and yielding, just like her body, in a way he remembered well. Cedric had searched for the same thing in the other women, longed for it to return in Vivian. Cedric knew Sadie had been a good woman. But there was nothing he could do about it, or wanted to do. He was married and loved his wife, despite their problems. Still Cedric knew, in all his life, he had never dealt with a woman like Sadie, and he never would again.

Cedric closed his eyes. That warm, special woman was dead. Life in its cruelty had left her, just as it would leave all of us. Cedric's recent fiftieth birthday loomed like a specter. *But I'm not dead,* he fought back. *Yet my political career . . . hell, my marriage, my family, all of it could be if it gets out that I had a child by another woman. The wholesome family image James and I created wouldn't survive it.*

"Cedric?" James's voice called him back.

"Yes, I'm here." Cedric's tone was deeper.

"Ce-edric," A rich voice boomed. "It's been a long time since I've heard your voice."

"It's been too long." Cedric brightened. "How ya been doin', Titan?"

"Can't complain," Titan replied. "But I hear it's not the same for you."

"No, I—I can't say it is." The circumstances dampened the reunion.

"When I got Titan on the phone, Cedric," James jumped in, "I told him what happened, and he says this will be an easy job."

"It will," Titan assured them. "First, I'll do a routine check on the woman, and it might take a little bit of digging, but you can be sure I'll find out what you need to know. Now, how fast the hard-core evidence appears will depend on how deep she's into the business," Titan said matter-of-factly. "If she's in real deep, it will be right there. But if she's been careful, it could take a little longer."

"The business?" Cedric questioned.

"Yes. Pops told me you suspect she might not be a legitimate massage therapist."

"Oh." Cedric's stomach flipped.

"Chances are," Titan continued, "she and her mother saw you on television, and Moms may have bragged about 'knowing' you. You recently announced you're running for state rep, and her daughter saw this as a grand opportunity to make herself some quick money."

"Or she's already gotten a little cash from your competition, Donald Stafford, and is working both ends of the deal," James added. "I wouldn't doubt that Stafford is dirty enough to pay somebody to throw a wrench into our political machine. Because guess what?" James slipped into his campaign chairman lingo. "He's the incumbent. And if he doesn't pull off some kind of miracle, he knows you've got him beat."

"Now, that's true." Cedric paused. "But what if Titan finds out I am Essence Stuart's father?"

Titan jumped in. "Pops told me this Stuart woman's mother is dead."

"Yes . . . that's right." Cedric felt strange hearing the hard, cold fact.

"And after this Essence Stuart was born, about thirty years ago, her mother never confronted you?" Titan questioned.

"Never." Cedric was glad to be able to answer the question truthfully.

"Well, from being a private detective in these streets, and from what I know about human nature, I would say she was either an extraordinary woman, or Essence Stuart is not your child." Titan paused. "But I don't think an extraordinary woman would raise a daughter who is most likely a prostitute operating as a masseuse."

"Makes sense to me," James said.

"It does make sense, doesn't it?' Cedric eagerly accepted the possibility of his own innocence.

"Yes, it does," Titan replied. "And it's probable. I've seen it over and over again."

"So, when will you have the information, Titan?" Cedric asked.

"It won't be until next week. I'm going to visit my grandmother in Kissimmee, Florida, this weekend."

"That's near Orlando, isn't it?" Cedric replied.

"Yes. Just south of there."

"My family is having a family reunion in Orlando this weekend. You should come."

"Noo. I don't think so. But thanks for the invitation. I—"

"I insist," Cedric said. "This way I'll get to see you. I haven't seen you in a long time. And I'd like to show you how much I appreciate what you're doing for me."

"Well." Cedric heard Titan sigh. "Since you put it that way, sure, I'll come."

"Great." Cedric smiled for the first time since Essence's phone call. "We start registering on Thursday, but the activities really start this Friday. It's at the Orlando Wyndham Resort. We have stuff going on straight through Monday."

"In that case, you'll probably see me Friday morning," Titan replied.

"Great," Cedric repeated.

"Well, seems like we've got the ball rollin'," James chimed in. "Good. So, I guess that's that. I'll see you later,

Cedric. And I'll talk to you, Titan, when you get back from Mama Cecilia's.''

"All right, Pops. Good talking to you, Cedric. I'll see you in a couple of days."

"Later, James," Cedric replied. "Same here, Titan." He waited until the lines went dead.

Cedric sat for a moment and breathed the first deep breath he'd had since Essence Stuart's call. He glanced over his appointments, then pressed the intraoffice line on his telephone. "I'm free now, Diane. You can send Mr. Williams in whenever he arrives."

Chapter Four

Titan Valentine rounded a corner of the quiet hotel hall-way just as a woman closed the door to her room. He watched as she started down the hall then stopped. For no apparent reason, she began to gesture as if she were talking to some-one. Her movements were graceful, and her voice, although he could not discern her words, held a rich vibration. The woman started to walk again and Titan decided he liked the way she moved. He could see her hips swaying beneath the long, loose dress she wore. The soft cobalt blue–and–fuchsia material lapped against her body, and Titan wondered if she wore a slip, or any underwear at all. Silently, he walked behind her at a distance. The more Titan watched, the more he wanted to put a face with the movements, although his pace remained even, unhurried. Like most people, he had learned sometimes the fantasy was far better than the real thing.

In truth, Titan didn't put much energy into pursuing women. He loved them, but since he'd become a private detective, his exuberance toward the female sex had burned carefully. Titan had decided women could be vindictive with just cause or no cause at all. They could complicate a man's life so thoroughly that they shut him down mentally, emotionally, and financially. Titan had seen it many times, and he was in no hurry to be in that predicament.

As Titan drew closer to the woman, he could see the wavy pattern of her thick shoulder-length hair. It reminded him of threads of high-gloss black ribbon. Until then, she had been deeply engaged in her soliloquy, and as Titan advanced within a few feet of her, his body reacted as if they were touching. It was strange, intriguing. She must have felt something, too, because she turned. Dark, startled eyes stared back at him.

"Were you talking to me?" Titan asked without cracking a smile.

She looked embarrassed. "No. I wasn't." Her eyes never left his face as he matched his stride with hers. "How long have you been back there?"

"Long enough," Titan replied.

The woman looked down, but not before Titan saw concern cross her features.

"Just kidding," he reassured her. "But now, from your reaction, I wish I had been able to hear."

She stopped and Titan did, too. He had never had anyone search his eyes like this woman did now. Her gaze was almost hypnotic. As if compelled, Titan felt aware of nothing else, only her eyes open to life, yet mysterious, as if something was hidden behind a veil.

The door beside them opened abruptly and a gang of noisy Boy Scouts poured into the hall. She was distracted as one door after another opened in the hotel corridor. In short order, there were boys running and yelling everywhere.

"What's your name?" Titan asked as a Boy Scout ran between them, followed by several others in hot pursuit.

"What?" She placed her hand near her ear and moved farther away to give the chasers more room.

"Your name," Titan repeated. He caught a glimpse of an interesting smile before his cell phone rang. Automatically, he pulled it out of his pocket. It was a client who had tried to reach him the day before. Titan held up his hand to tell her to wait as he stepped into an area buffeted by a drink and snack machine. But the woman simply smiled again and continued down the hall.

Essence made her way through the crowd of boys in the hotel corridor. God, he was handsome, she thought as she left the man behind. *I wonder who he is . . . if he heard my name. At any other time I would have waited, but right now I've got something more important to do.* She pushed the look in the man's eyes, and how it made her feel, to the back of her mind.

Essence looked at an arrow that pointed to the pool. "Are you ready to meet your father face-to-face?" she asked under her breath. For a second she was uncertain, but then she thought, *I'm as ready as I'm ever going to be.* Essence lifted her chin and continued on her way.

When she arrived at the glass door that opened to the pool, bundles of orange and purple balloons bobbed outside, announcing the Johnson family reunion . . . her family reunion. It was still hard to believe. All these years, Essence had been among her own people, her blood kin, yet had never known it. So many times when she, Brenda, and Shiri were younger, people would ask if they were related because they looked alike. Essence recalled how they would say no, telling the truth as they believed it then. But as the years had passed, they'd begun to tell people they were cousins. Essence remembered how it had given her a sense of comfort, a sense of belonging to something larger than her mother and herself. Little did the friends know that by saying they were cousins, they'd been actually telling the truth.

"Essence!"

Essence knew that voice before she turned to acknowledge it. "Hey, Mama Doris."

"It is you," Doris said. "I wondered if you were coming." She put on an admonishing face. "You know, since you've gotten older, you've stopped coming to our family gatherings.'' Doris tilted her head. ''I thought perhaps you'd outgrown us.''

''Never,'' Essence said. She hated the tears that welled up in her eyes.

''Oh, sweetie. I didn't mean it.'' Doris hugged her. ''Forgive me for being so thoughtless. I should have known this is not the time to tease you. You've got so much on your heart already.'' Doris released Essence. ''I guess we've been in such a festive mood around here. I forgot myself. I'm truly sorry.''

''It's okay,'' Essence replied, but she appreciated the apology.

''I hope you liked the flowers. I'm sorry Pam and I couldn't come to the funeral. We had just flown down here and . . .''

''You don't have to explain, Mama Doris. Brenda and Shiri told me.'' Essence squeezed Doris's thick waist. ''I didn't come here to grieve. Mama was sick for so long that I actually did a lot of that during the months before she passed away.''

Doris nodded, but she looked uncomfortable.

''Now it's time for me to go on just like Mama wanted me to,'' Essence continued. ''Just as I promised her I would.''

''That's just like you, Essence. You've always been such a wonderful daughter.'' Doris hugged her again and gave her a peck on the cheek. ''Well, c'mon in.'' She opened the door. ''I'm sure everybody will be glad to see you.''

Essence followed Doris onto the deck. It was a hub of laughter and conversation, against what Essence thought was a perfect backdrop, instrumental music. The two had only advanced a few feet when a bony but strong hand grabbed Doris by the arm.

''What's that he's playin'?'' Rosie Kincaid pointed toward the DJ. ''They better get some music playin' up in here. That ol' laid-back stuff.'' She popped her fingers. ''We need something that's moving.''

''So Auntie Rosie, that's not hip enough for you?'' Doris replied.

"No, it's not. That's for folks who want to sit back and be cool." Rosie waved her hand in a catchy fashion. "I ain't got time to be cool. I've got to use every moment that comes my way."

Essence laughed.

"Oh, you think I'm funny, huh?" Rosie put her hand where her hip used to be. "You better hope you can say the same *if* you reach eighty."

"I'm not laughin' at you, Auntie Rosie," Essence explained. "You make me feel good. That's all."

"Auntie?" Rosie looked confused.

"You don't know who this is?" Doris pointed.

"Should I?" Rosie peered at Essence through tricolor-rimmed glasses.

"It's Essence Stuart. Brenda and Shiri's little girlfriend."

"Law-wd, is that you, Essie?"

"It's me, Auntie Rosie."

"Well, the saints be praised. The last time I saw you, you were like a stick." She tightened Essence's dress to fit her frame. "Now look at you. I ain't never seen no stick curved like that."

"Auntie Rosie, you gonna wrinkle her dress." Pamela stepped up and released Essence. "How you doin', baby? You okay?" She held Essence by the arms.

"I'm fine, Mama Pam." But Essence thought, by the look on Auntie Rosie's face, that the older woman wasn't.

"Look here," Rosie snapped. "Don't be tellin' me what to do, Miss Pamela. You can boss everybody else around, but you don't have no control here. If you weren't my sister's child, I would have told you some things about yourself long time ago."

"Auntie Rosie, what are you talkin' about?" Pamela crossed her arms.

"You know what I'm talkin' about, and if you don't, you should. That's part of the problem. Always tryin' to take over everything," Rosie mumbled.

"Essie!" Brenda called. "You made it."

Essence smiled at Brenda, but the exchange between Pamela and Rosie had her ear. It didn't seem as if Pamela was going to take her aunt's words sitting down.

"What are you talkin' about?" Pam repeated. "I do what needs to be done, and if anybody's got a problem with that, then they need to take some responsibility for their feelings, *and* do some of the stuff that needs to be done around here."

"All right, you two," Doris jumped in.

"You come over here with us." Brenda tugged at Essence's arm. "I'm sure a few more words will fly before those two work it out." She stopped and leaned back. "You look . . . better, Essie."

"I do?"

Brenda nodded.

"Thanks. And you look great in that black-and-white swimsuit."

"You like it?" Brenda's eyes brightened.

"It's tight, girl," Essence replied.

"It surely is." Shiri met them. "And where is your swimsuit, lady?"

"Hey, Shiri." Essence gave her a squeeze.

"I'm so glad you came," Shiri said.

"Me, too." Essence glanced around the pool.

"Did you bring a swimsuit?" Shiri reiterated.

"Noo."

"I've got another one if you want it," Shiri pressed.

"Noo, I don't want to swim," Essence replied.

"You never did like the water," Brenda said.

"Not like you two mermaids." Essence smirked. "I guess nobody ever told you two black folks don't like to swim."

"Who's swimming? I'm just out here for show," Shiri replied.

"I know that's the truth," Essence said.

"And speaking of a show"—Brenda looked over her sunglasses—"who's that?"

"It surely isn't Wes," Shiri quipped.

"I may be in love, but I'm not blind," Brenda replied.

"You've got a point there," Shiri said. "I might be interested if J.D. didn't have me so wrapped up. So that leaves you, Essence." She nudged. "What do you think?"

Instantly Essence recognized the man from the hallway.

Chapter Five

Essence watched the man maneuver on the outside of the crowd. His style was poetic, from his clothes to his walk, and the way he glanced around . . . as if he understood everything and everybody.

"Hel-lo. Earth to Essence," Shiri said close to Essence's ear. "I guess you don't have to tell us what you think. It's quite obvious," she teased. "And ohhh! He's looking right over here. It appears our girl, Essie, has made an impression from across a crowded pool," Shiri joked behind a strategically placed hand.

"Who says he's looking at me?" Essence looked back boldly.

"Well, I don't know about you, but I still have twenty-twenty vision. And not only can I see who he's looking at, but the vibes he's sending out might create a tidal wave in the pool at any moment."

"Well, it's all for the best," Brenda said. "Essence is probably the only one of us who can get involved with him and not be toying with a semi-incestuous relationship."

"You're probably right. We've got some good-looking folks in the Johnson family," Shiri boasted.

Essence's eyes widened. "So, is he a Johnson?"

"There's a good chance he is. I know Mama, Aunt Doris, and Aunt Karen really went all out to reach some relatives that we've never contacted before," Brenda informed her. "So he might be one of them. But he doesn't seem to be with anybody. If I were his woman or wife, I wouldn't let him get too far out of my sight."

Brenda and Shiri laughed.

Essence couldn't. To her it wasn't funny at all. It was possible this man was a relative of hers. *If that's true, God, what an awful trick to make me feel such an attraction for someone I can never have.*

A disjointed burst of applause sounded from the other side of the pool. Essence turned and saw a good-looking couple walk toward the group responsible for the noise. A man with wonderful gray-flecked hair reached out and started shaking hands and giving hugs, while the woman held back in a rather reserved fashion. Other people started moving toward them, and the man appeared to grow in stature under the admiration.

"You can count on Uncle Cedric to make an entrance," Shiri said with ill-concealed pride.

"That's so true," Brenda joined in. "But we have to give it to him, time hasn't hurt Uncle Cedric one bit."

"That's . . . your uncle Cedric?" Essence asked in a kind of blank way, but her heart beat a little faster.

"Yes. That's the representative-to-be." Shiri just couldn't hold back. "You don't remember Uncle Cedric, Essence?"

"Vaguely," Essence replied as she studied her father, who by now had a small crowd in the palm of his hand.

"I guess it has been a long time since you've seen a lot of the family," Brenda said. "I think the last thing you attended was a Christmas party the year after we graduated from high school."

"Was it?" Essence responded automatically as she watched Grandma Lela and finally Granddaddy George greet their son. George Johnson's gravelly voice floated across the pool.

"Here he is. State Representative Johnson. My son." He patted Cedric on the back. "A chip off the old block."

Essence watched Cedric laugh and hug his father.

"Yes, Essie," Shiri interjected. "What's up with that? You shouldn't stay away so long," she chastised. "You know we're family." Her voice softened. "And with Mama Sadie gone, I hope you know you can depend on us."

Essence looked from Shiri to Brenda. "Yes, we are." A sudden urge to tell her best friends that they truly were family surfaced. She looked down. "Did you two tell everything?"

"Huh?"

Essence looked into Shiri's confused face. "I mean, have you ever had anything you didn't tell or share between us?"

"Nothing I can think of right off the bat," Brenda replied.

Shiri shrugged. "Not really. You?"

Essence looked them in the eyes. "Yes, there have been . . . things."

"Things as in plural?" Brenda looked surprised.

Essence swallowed. "Yes."

The lightness they'd shared a few moments before was gone.

"Like what?" Shiri looked as if she had been deceived.

"Like when we were growing up." Essence couldn't bring herself to blurt out the truth about their favorite uncle. She started somewhere else. "I never told you how I worked to help my mother pay the bills." She paused. "We were poor compared to you all. I didn't tell you because I didn't want you to see me as different."

"I knew you did some baby-sitting," Shiri said.

"I did that and odd jobs, too. I had a job, at the cannery on Sundays."

Shiri's eyebrows went up. Then she looked a little embarrassed. "I didn't know you felt like you had to work."

"I did have to. We needed the money. But also, I wanted to help my mother." Essence had to look away. "You both had a father and a mother. I didn't. So life was different for me, but I tried not to show it."

"But we wouldn't have treated you any differently, Essie, if you had told us the truth," Brenda assured her.

"Of course we wouldn't have," Shiri echoed.

"Maybe. Maybe not." Essence couldn't hold their gaze.

"What do you mean, maybe, maybe not? We wouldn't have," Brenda replied. "And that was so long ago, why are you bringing it up now?"

Essence wanted to say why, but it was so difficult. "Because we're different. Look at us. You and Shiri fit right into society. You're a doctor." Essence lifted her head high, then looked at Shiri. "And you're a petrochemical engineer. I'm a massage therapist."

"And?" Brenda looked bewildered.

"Don't you see?" Essence needed to separate herself from them. Make herself unique so that they could expect the unexpected. "I go about life differently. I use herbs and oils and do womb meditations."

"You do what?" Shiri's face screwed up.

"Womb meditations. I place my hand over my belly and I meditate on the feelings that come from that part of me. I ask my womb questions."

Brenda and Shiri looked at each other.

"Okay. So you've always been a little weird," Brenda said. "But we love you anyway."

"Thanks." Essence felt frustrated by the direction the conversation had taken, but at the same time grateful for Shiri and Brenda's sincerity. "I'm having difficulty saying that—"

"Don't worry." Brenda grabbed Essence and hugged her. "I've heard that sometimes when someone close to you passes away, you can feel very much alone. So I want you to know, no matter what you say or do, we will always be here for you. Oh, no." Brenda's tone changed completely as she looked over Essence's shoulder.

"What is it?" Essence said, alarmed.

Brenda stepped back and shot Shiri a look. "Aunt Karen is going over there to Vivian."

Essence turned to see.

"Why doesn't she just let Aunt Vivian make the first move?" Shiri moaned. "She knows how Vivian is, and Aunt Karen is a little high-strung herself."

"Aunt Vivian?" Essence questioned.

"Vivian is Uncle Cedric's wife. She's one way one day, and there's no telling how she'll act the next. The truth is, she has never really fit into the family."

"Why not?" Essence turned her attention to the fashionably thin woman with her hair slicked back in a smooth ponytail. She couldn't help but compare her classy style to her mother's simpler one.

"I don't know," Shiri replied.

"Don't tell that lie," Brenda retorted. "Something went down between Vivian and my mama and Aunt Pam, when they were younger, and they have not gotten along since. At least that's what I heard. Something about them covering up for Uncle Cedric."

"That's right. That's what you heard," Shiri checked Brenda. "But we were too young to know what was going on, and nobody has ever really told us the story. So, the truth is, it's hearsay," Shiri continued. "I say that Aunt Vivian has never fit in because she doesn't want to. She's always felt like she was better than everybody else. Had to make sure she and Cedric Jr. dressed better, that they lived in a better neighborhood and in a bigger house, and drove some kind of prestigious car. She was like that as long as I can remember. Of course, she put it all off on Uncle Cedric, but I don't think so. I think it was her doing."

"Were she and"—Essence had difficulty defining her father—"Cedric happy?" She watched Vivian step back when Karen approached. "Are they happy now?"

"Who knows?" Shiri replied.

"I don't think they are," Brenda said. "They might have been a long time ago. But I don't think they're much of anything now. But you know how Uncle Cedric is. He's a good man. He's been a good father, and I'm sure he's probably been the best husband any woman could find."

"I think so, too," Shiri confided. "I think she may have

given him a hard time by wanting everything, wanting everybody to bow down to her.''

The conversation between Vivian and Karen was short. They watched Vivian walk away and take a seat by herself.

''But how do you know that?'' Essence's desire to tell her cousins the truth faltered under the weight of their admiration for their uncle. ''You never know what goes on behind closed doors. Maybe he did some things that helped make her the way she is.''

Shiri shrugged, but Brenda wouldn't give a bit.

''No, I don't know what goes on behind closed doors. But I know my uncle.'' Her voice filled with love. ''And he wouldn't do anything to hurt anybody. His life has been about helping people. He's helped a bunch of folks in the family. And from what I hear, lots of people in the community. Uncle Cedric is just like that.''

Essence looked away. This family loved Cedric Johnson, loved her father, and she believed they would fight tooth and nail to protect him. Brenda had made that plain. How could Essence ever tell them the truth without destroying the only people who remained close to her? She felt she couldn't. That's why today, Essence would keep it between the two of them. This wasn't about destroying a family. This was about Cedric Johnson facing the truth, and acknowledging the relationship he'd had with her mother. Although Essence tried to ignore it, a little voice inside cried, *Acknowledge me.*

Cedric waved at them from across the pool. Brenda and Shiri waved back.

''It's about time you got here,'' A man in the pool yelled at Cedric. He wiped the water from his face and hair. ''Folks are going to start replacing CP time with CJ time.''

''All right now.'' Cedric pointed a menacing but playful finger. ''Don't start.''

''Who's that?'' Essence watched the man duck back into the water.

''Cedric Jr.,'' Shiri replied. ''You probably never saw him that much, if at all. Shoot, we didn't see him.'' She put on a nasally voice. "Vivian insisted he go to a private boarding school out East."

That's my brother! Essence watched Cedric Jr. splash water on a boy around ten. There was so much to consider. It was difficult to know where to start. Essence felt overwhelmed as she watched Cedric Sr. approach the man she'd met in the hotel hallway.

"Well, it seems somebody knows him," Shiri said. "And of course it would be Uncle Cedric."

They watched the men share a manly hug and some pats on the back before their heads bent together in conversation.

"I guess there's no better time than now." Essence exhaled.

"What?" Shiri questioned.

"I think there's no better time than now to introduce myself," Essence rephrased the statement.

"Oh, so you want to be introduced, huh?" Brenda smiled. "We'll take you over there and reintroduce you to Uncle Cedric, and I'm sure he'll introduce you to his friend."

"No," Essence said quickly, then tried to smooth it over. "No, I want to do this on my own."

Brenda and Shiri looked at each other. Then Shiri said, "I don't think she wants us in on the introduction. I think Essence wants all the attention on her."

"Really?" Brenda looked at Essence in an exasperated fashion.

"What can I say? Shiri is right." Essence was grateful for the explanation. "I do want all the attention on me."

"Bold, isn't she?" Shiri said, acting as if she were ignoring Essence.

"The heifer. I think she gets bolder with time," Brenda quipped.

Chapter Six

Essence began the long trek to the other side of the pool, and everything she planned to say vanished as she walked around the pool. Logic was replaced by raw feelings that surfaced, exposed themselves, then evaporated before she could get her mind around them. *Oh, God! Oh, God! What am I doing? What am I going to say?* She tried to get a grip on the situation . . . on herself.

"Hello, Miss Essence.

Essence felt a tug on her arm. She turned. It was Karen Johnson. Essence reached out and hugged her. "Aunt Karen. How good to see you."

"Good to see you," the most outspoken Johnson sister replied. "How are you holding up? I'm assuming pretty good, since you're here."

"I'm doing okay." Essence glanced at her father and his companion, who stood several yards away. They appeared to be in deep conversation.

"Good," Karen replied. "Maybe we'll get to talk later."

Essence nodded and continued on her way. As she got closer, her steps slowed, of their own volition. Essence stopped when she stood within a few of feet of the two men.

"Hello there." Cedric reached out to shake her hand as if he had known her forever. "How you been doin'?"

"Fine," Essence replied, but she was confused by his reception. Did he remember her? She didn't think so. Maybe Cedric remembered her face and not her name. Or perhaps, being the consummate politician, he'd never known it.

"Hello again," The man beside him said.

"Hello," Essence replied.

"You two know each other?" Cedric asked with a shimmering smile.

Essence couldn't help but marvel at her father's captivating way. Even now he was a handsome man, and it was obvious how her mother could have fallen for him.

"We met earlier," the man replied. "But she refused to tell me her name."

"I did tell you my name." The man's pull was distracting. She looked at him. "Perhaps you couldn't hear me."

"That's quite possible," he said, searching her eyes.

Essence felt herself being drawn within them.

"I saw you standing over there with my nieces," Cedric interjected. "And you look so familiar."

"Brenda, Shiri, and I are old friends," Essence said.

"So I probably have seen you around," Cedric surmised. "For a minute I thought you were one of my nieces."

"No, I'm not."

"But you've got to be a Johnson. Only we have women as pretty as you," Cedric quipped.

For a moment Essence couldn't speak.

"It seems like we've got a mystery lady on our hands." The man's lips did not smile, but his eyes did. "Let me introduce myself. My name is Titan Valentine."

Cedric chuckled. "Every time I hear your name I can't help but think of when your mother and father named you." He shook his head. "I told them, I hope this boy can live up to a name like that, because if he isn't a favorite with the ladies, the women are going to be mighty disappointed. Do you think the ladies are disappointed? Miss . . . uh . . . ?"

"Essence. Essence Stuart."

If she had slapped her father, he couldn't have looked more surprised. The shock quickly turned to contained anger.

Essence looked at Titan. His face was like a mask.

Finally Cedric said, "You've got some nerve coming here."

"Actually, I was invited by Brenda and Shiri." Essence kept her cool, but she was injured by Cedric's remark. "But I've been to other Johnson get-togethers. Christmas parties. Family reunions."

"Say what?" Cedric appeared more offended. "So, what are you saying? You and your mother have been lurking around for years waiting for the right opportunity to start a scandal."

Essence felt as if she had been prodded with a hot poker. "My mother is not here. Can not be here. And I'd appreciate it if you left her out of your accusations." Her eyes burned. "This is my doing. Not my mother's. She had all the right in the world to confront you, but she chose to live her life another way. She wasn't going to beg you, and you can believe I'm not asking you for anything now."

"Well, what in the hell do you want?" Cedric's voice rose. "I don't know what you expected, coming over here like this."

Essence saw Karen look in their direction. "You are the one who is making a scene."

"Your being here is a scene." Cedric's mouth trembled as he tried to control himself.

"I have every right to be here." She let the words sink in. "Like I said, I was invited."

"Let me tell you something." All pretense of the charming family man disappeared.

"Yes." Essence tried to keep the tremor out of her voice.

"There's nothing I can do about Brenda and Shiri being your friends. But if you've got even an ounce of what's right in you, you will not approach me again. As a matter of fact, you will leave this reunion and my family alone."

Essence noted how several people would glance at them, then look away. She lifted her chin. "I am your family, and if you were half the man these people think you are, you would have acknowledged that a long time ago.'' Essence paused. ''And no, I'm not leaving. I wouldn't give you the satisfaction.'' She started to turn, but looked back. ''And if you really want to keep your image, you better hope I stay, because everybody in hearing distance is wondering what the hell has angered the great Cedric Johnson to the point where he has lost his shiny facade.''

Essence walked, she hoped, not too fast and not too slow toward the door. But she couldn't feel her feet against the concrete. Essence couldn't feel anything. Cedric had yelled at her. He'd done and said everything he could outside of physically pushing her away. She was numb with the pain.

It was only when she made it inside that she closed her eyes and started to run. They opened abruptly when she collided with George Johnson.

''Wait a minute, daughter. Wait a minute.''

''Oh, I'm so sorry,'' Essence apologized as her eyes started to tear. ''Are you okay?''

''Am I okay?'' he repeated with a throaty chuckle. ''Of course, I am. Are you?''

''Yes, I'm fine.'' Essence looked away.

''Well, you don't look like it.'' George attempted to look into her averted face.

Essence pulled herself together. ''But I am.''

''Yes, I think you are. Or at least you're going to be.''

She watched George Johnson's wiry brows slowly descend.

''Well, I'll be a monkey's uncle,'' he said.

''Sir?''

''I ain't seen nobody look so much like that picture in my life.''

Essence wanted to leave, but she couldn't. ''What picture?''

''The only picture I have of my mother when she was a young woman. I tell you, you look like a young Martha Johnson.''

Essence's eyes began to sting again. ''Really?''

"Yes, you do." George attempted to take her by the hand. "C'mon back in here with me. I want Lela to see ya. She's gonna say the same thing."

"I can't." Essence pulled back. "Not right now."

George looked puzzled.

"I've got to go," Essence explained. "Maybe another time."

"All right." He accepted the rain check.

Essence hurried down the hall. She turned toward her room, but changed her mind. She needed to get away, really away. So Essence headed for her car.

"I can't believe the nerve of that woman coming over here like that." Cedric felt embarrassed under Titan's keen gaze.

"But you have to say, she was pretty up-front, wasn't she?" Titan replied.

"Up-front?" Cedric repeated. "Downright brazen if you ask me."

Titan lifted a glossy eyebrow. "It seems like she felt she had cause to be."

"Well . . . I don't believe she does," Cedric dug in. "And don't you think if she was on the up-and-up she would have told me while she had me on the telephone that she planned to come to the reunion? But she didn't say a word about it."

"That's something to consider," Titan agreed.

"Yes. She's a slick one." Cedric was glad for the foothold. He felt like a drowning man, grabbing at anything he could to stay afloat. "She comes over here looking all respectable, but I believe she got more tricks up that long dress of hers than a country dog has fleas." Cedric was shocked at his own vehemence. He eased into another subject. "So you met her earlier."

"We saw each other in one of the halls. She appeared to be practicing a speech of some kind."

"Practicing a speech? Now, see there." Cedric pointed.

"I bet she was polishing what she was going to say to me to make it look natural."

Titan nodded, slowly.

"So, as you can see, son," Cedric continued, "I need your help. This woman's got the ability to really mess me up, and I need you to find out everything you can about her. I can feel she is definitely going to be a thorn in my side."

"I'll do my best, " Titan replied, although he was secretly impressed by Essence's performance, sincere or not. Titan intended to find out more about Essence Stuart for Cedric. He had a few questions of his own. Titan had to admit, he was disappointed to find out his mystery woman was the so-called masseuse, Essence Stuart. No one had made him feel that way in a long, long time.

Chapter Seven

Drained, Essence sat on the bed and listened to two messages left on the hotel message service by Brenda and Shiri.

"Where are you, woman?" Brenda demanded during the second message. "You come to our family reunion and then you disappear."

"Yeah. We're going to talk about you when we catch up with you," Shiri said in the background.

"Call room one-twelve," Brenda advised, then asked Shiri, "What's your room number?"

"One-fifty-one."

"Or one-fifty-one when you find time."

"That woman," Essence could hear Shiri say as Brenda hung up.

Essence dialed room 112, then lay back on the pillow. She thought about delaying the inevitable, but decided against it. Essence wanted to sleep, and she didn't want the telephone ringing while she was doing it. "Hey there." She mustered up the energy to face the music.

"Hey there, yourself. Where you been?" Brenda asked.

"Out and about. I did some shopping." Essence spoke with her eyes closed. It was the truth. She had bought some stockings, but the majority of the time had been spent thinking and getting lost in the crowd at CityWalk, where she'd tried to escape from her own thoughts by watching a movie at the cineplex. Still, it was a flimsy bandage for the wound created by her conversation with Cedric by the pool.

"That's right, you come up here to shop sometimes," Brenda remarked. "What did you do? Hit some of your favorite spots?"

"Sure did," Essence said. "But I wore myself out." She paused. "I think I'll take a nap."

"Are you going to ride with us to the family dinner?"

"Where is it being held?"

"At Fishbone's Restaurant. Six o'clock."

"No, if I come I'll drive. If not, you'll see me at the dessert dance."

"All right. I'll tell Shiri."

"See you later," Essence said and hung up. She nestled deeper into the bed.

An hour and a half later, Essence zipped up the fitted black dress and looked in the mirror. The neckline plunged to an almost decadent level, and she thought, how appropriate. By now the Johnsons, who had overheard her exchange with her father, were drawing their own conclusions and spreading them around. Essence was certain they weren't in her favor.

"So, why are you going to the dance?" she asked, continuing to look in the mirror. "You were probably on the menu at Fishbone's, and even Brenda and Shiri might be against you by now."

Essence stared into her own kohl-traced eyes before she applied a bronze-colored lipstick. "You're going because you have a right to be there. Because you are not in the wrong. Cedric Johnson may have closed you out of his life, but he will not control yours." She pressed her lips together. "I only hope Brenda and Shiri will give me a chance to explain." She took a deep breath. "Ready?" Essence smoothed her hands over her hair, which was sculpted back and up. She nodded, picked up her purse, and walked to the door.

Essence entered the room. Several people glanced at her, but basically they gave looks of approval. A few heads bent together in a gossipy fashion, but all in all, Essence felt her reception was no different from any other and she felt relieved. Essence didn't know if she could take another gut-wrenching scene so soon.

The bald-headed DJ was playing an old-school tune, and a few Johnsons were on the dance floor, showing their age.

She wandered toward the dessert table, and after a moment of study, Essence put several sweets on a plate. Now she wished she had gone to Fishbone's, but at the time she simply hadn't had the energy. Nibbling on a lemon tart, Essence saw Shiri and Brenda sitting at a table with their mothers. She crossed the floor and sat down. "Hey."

"There she is," Shiri greeted her. "We were just talking about you."

"You were?" Essence's brows rose.

"Yes, we were," Doris replied. "I was saying you really missed a good dinner. I asked Brenda and Shiri if you were coming to the dance."

"I wanted to come, but I was too tired," Essence replied. "Still I didn't want to miss this." She took another bite of lemon tart. "But I've got to say, I surely wish this was a plate of food instead of desserts."

They talked about who had gained weight, who had recently married, and who had divorced. Concern was expressed for an elderly uncle who'd had a stroke, and surprise and relief over a nephew who'd finally made it out of high school. Essence listened to the Johnson family happenings with a new interest. They were her family now, and it felt good to belong, but disheartening that none of them knew it.

Essence found herself constantly glancing at the door,

expecting her biological father to walk through at any moment. She realized the expectation had her on edge.

Another song ended, and they watched the dancers leave the dance floor. Seconds later a familiar tune blared, and the dance floor began to fill up again.

"Come on, you all," Shiri encouraged. "Let's do the Electric Slide."

Pam was already on her way, and Doris started removing her shoes.

"I'm going to finish this." Essence took another bite of cake.

They looked at Brenda.

"Don't look at me. You know I'm not getting out there." She looked away.

Shiri batted her hand and said, "You're nothing but a party pooper."

"But that's all right," Brenda retorted. "I'm waiting for Wes."

"I'm waiting for Jake but that don't stop no show. You're a party pooper. Always have been. Always will be." Shiri left and joined the electric sliders as they made a unified turn.

Essence and Brenda chatted as the group on the dance floor grew larger. Auntie Rosie was the last to join in, but she managed to keep up with style. By the time the song ended, Karen was using her hand as a fan.

"What you fanning for?" Auntie Rosie said, coming up from behind her. "See, you young folk can't even keep up with an old woman."

Karen rolled her eyes. Essence saw her bite her lip to keep quiet.

"You sure did give us a run for our money, Auntie Rosie," Shiri quipped.

"Don't humor her." Karen wiped her forehead with her fingertips. "She needs to act her age."

"And how would I act? Like you?" Rosie challenged.

Essence watched Brenda turn her head so Aunt Karen

wouldn't see her laugh, but it was the expression on Shiri's face that caught her attention.

"Don't look now," Shiri said, "but that good-looking man that you and Uncle Cedric were talking to just walked in, and he's making a direct line over to our table."

"His name is Titan Valentine," Essence replied.

"Titan Valentine," Brenda echoed. "Ooooh-wee. What a name. And just the man to go with it."

"Valentine. That sounds familiar." Karen looked at the ceiling. "What's James's last name, Pam?"

Pam looked bewildered.

"You know, James. Baybrother's friend. He works with him now as his campaign chairman. Isn't it Valentine?"

"I think it is," Pamela replied.

The conversation around Essence went in one ear and out the other. She wanted to turn around, but she just sat there. If Titan hadn't had a front-row seat during her conversation with Cedric, she would have reacted differently. But Essence was uncertain about what he was going to say. Would he mention the confrontation in front of everyone? If Titan did, that would open the door to questions Essence was not ready to answer.

"Hello. How is everybody doing tonight?" Titan's baritone voice emanated from above her head.

A chorus of pleasant *fines,* and *doin' goods* erupted. Essence's might have been the softest of all.

"That's good to hear," Titan replied. "I must say, it makes my job a bit difficult choosing between you lovely women, but I believe I would like to ask Essence to dance."

Essence looked at him for the first time. A slow tune was playing, and she was on the verge of refusing when Titan offered his upturned hand. Essence glanced at Brenda, who gave her a look that said, *You'd be crazy to turn this one down.*

Against her better judgment, Essence replied, "Sure," and rose from her chair.

As they turned toward the dance floor, Karen asked, "Is James your father?"

"He sure is," Titan replied, moving aside so Essence could lead the way.

"We thought so," Pamela piped up. "There's a strong family resemblance between the two of you."

"Is that right?" Auntie Rosie smiled. "Well, I must ask the magic question: Do you have any brothers?"

Karen made an exasperated sound, but Rosie ignored her. Titan simply smiled. "No, ma'am. I don't."

"Well, from the looks of you, your parents should have had some more sons," Rosie flirted.

Titan continued to smile. "I think my father wanted to, but after three children, my mother had had enough."

"Shame. Shame," Rosie replied and took a bite of cheese-cake.

Chapter Eight

Essence entered Titan's arms when they reached the dance floor, but stopped at a comfortable distance. She had to admit, it felt good being held. Essence took it a step farther. It felt good being held by a man. It had been such a long time, and there was a kind of strength there. She stopped short of thinking of security. Perhaps that was because Essence had never known the security of a father's arms.

From Titan's reaction, it was clear he had his own ideas. He tightened his embrace, and Essence had no choice but to come closer ... so close their bodies became one. She attempted to ease away without being too obvious, but Titan placed his foot between her feet, making their union more intimate than ever.

What in the world ... ? Her brows descended as she felt more pressure on her back. They danced until Titan's moves turned erotic in a way that only Essence could feel. She could hold back no longer.

"For a first dance, don't you think you're moving rather fast?"

"What do you mean?" he asked calmly as the singers crooned "Betcha by Golly, Wow."

Essence knew he knew what she meant. What she didn't know was why he felt at liberty to hold her this way. And on top of that, he baited her. Could he be accustomed to women accepting his actions? "You picked a slow song for our first dance, and I must admit, I'm not accustomed to dancing with a stranger . . . like this."

"Stranger? Do you consider us strangers?" Titan asked. "I don't."

Essence wondered what Cedric had told him about her. She replied, "I know your name. You know mine. I think that would categorize us as strangers."

"But I know much more about you than that," Titan said.

Essence leaned back to look into his face. "What did Cedric Johnson say about me?" She knew she sounded defensive. She couldn't help it.

"Was there a need for him to say anything?" He searched her eyes. "I drew some conclusions from the conversation you two had. It's obvious you have some ideas about him that he doesn't share."

Essence leaned forward again. "That would be putting it mildly."

"I'm a mild man," Titan said, scooping his body in a fashion that disrupted Essence's breath.

"I don't believe that for one minute."

"Do I detect a bit of distrust here? That's no way to start a relationship."

"I didn't know we were seeking one." Essence's voice was thinner than before.

"But I would say we're definitely starting one, wouldn't you?" Titan tried to look into her face.

"Perhaps." She couldn't believe she'd said that. Essence looked away. There was a flutter below her navel. "Although you say we're not strangers"—she tried to get a hold of herself—"I say, how can you start a relationship with a woman you know nothing about? You're obviously friends with Cedric, and you heard how our conversation went— how do you know you can trust me? Aren't relationships built on trust?"

"Some are." Titan let his hand trail over her back. "And getting to know you will be easy to handle."

"Easy? How?" Essence arched slightly.

"I'll take this opportunity to find out more about you. Ask you penetrating questions about your life."

"I see." Essence wondered if there were any other reason Titan had chosen the word *penetrating*.

"Where do you live, Essence Stuart?"

She closed her eyes. "In Tampa." A heat was forming between their bodies, and Essence could feel Titan's response. She was more certain than ever the word *penetrating* had a double meaning. She tried to keep her words steady. "Don't you think I'm finding out more about you than I need to know at this point?"

There was a pause. Titan hadn't intended for this to happen. As a matter of fact, he could barely remember the last time he had lost control. Was it back in high school? *And for it to happen with this woman* ... He almost grimaced. *I knew I was attracted to her from the very beginning, but this* ... The more he thought about it, the bigger the problem got. *Still,* he relaxed a bit, F*rom what I've heard about her, she shouldn't mind. Perhaps she even welcomes it.* He pressed himself against her, slightly. "Don't turn the tables on me. I'm the one who's asking the questions, remember?" His voice was a bit raspy. "What do you do in Tampa, Florida, Essence Stuart?" Her name sounded enticing.

"I'm a massage therapist."

"A massage therapist. Mmmm." The throaty noise vibrated. "Are you good at what you do?"

"I've been told I am."

"Well ... perhaps I'll have the pleasure of finding out. How about coming to my room tonight and giving me a late-night massage?"

Essence's brow wrinkled. She leaned back and looked at him. "What did you say?"

"You say you're a masseuse." Titan didn't blink as he returned her gaze. "I'd like to sample your ... talents, in a private massage ... tonight."

Essence was dumbfounded. What made him think that she was willing to go to bed with him? Because that was what he thought. It was right there in his eyes, along with a bit of contempt. How did he make such a leap? Essence couldn't help but conclude that Cedric had something to do with it. She stopped dancing. "What is up with you?" Her eyes narrowed. "What do you think I am?"

"A massage . . . therapist." The innuendo was plain. Titan intended it to be, but for some reason, he hated it.

That's when Titan realized Essence's lifestyle perturbed him. But in truth it wasn't the lifestyle. What got to Titan was that Essence was the one living it. Living the life of a woman totally defined by money. Didn't she realize she had the qualities that could be special to some man? He fought it, but Titan thought, *Special to me.*

Essence stiffened as she nodded slowly. "Oh, I see." Their eyes remained locked as her arms went to her sides. "I don't know where you got your ideas, Mr. Valentine, but you won't get a private, late-night massage from me."

Essence wasted no time. She took a step back and Titan didn't stop her. She wanted to say more, to read him the riot act, to tell Titan she was offended. Essence wanted to say, based on that moment when their eyes first met, from somewhere deep inside, she expected more, wanted more, but instead she left him standing on the dance floor without a second glance. Emotionally, Essence couldn't take anymore. When she reached her table, Essence picked up her purse. "I think I'm going to turn in."

"Already?" Pam asked.

"Yes. I've had enough for one day."

Pamela looked at Titan who remained on the dance floor. She gave one of those looks, but she didn't ask any questions. "Okay. We'll see you tomorrow."

"Good night," Essence replied. She waved at Shiri, who was hitting the dessert table with Jake. Brenda was wrapped tightly in Wes' arms, oblivious to everyone on the dance floor.

Titan followed Essence with his eyes. It made no sense.

Why would a woman who used massage as a cover for her activities with men be offended when he propositioned her? And she was genuinely upset. Titan was certain of that. He was also certain there was a kind of live chemistry connecting him and Essence Stuart.

"What did you do to Essence to run her out of here like that?" One of the women from the table asked as Essence walked through the door.

Titan had been so intent on watching Essence leave, he hadn't seen the woman walk up. He could tell she was really curious. "What's your name again?" He smiled.

"I'm Pamela Reid. Cedric's sister."

"Yes," Titan replied.

They shook hands.

"I'm as baffled as you are," he lied. "Maybe you can give me a hint."

"I don't have a clue. But I know you must have done something because Essence is one of the most levelheaded people I know."

"Really?" Titan studied the woman. He could see her resemblance to Cedric.

"That's right." Then her brows furrowed. "But, of course, she did bury her mother a few days ago, so I'm sure that's heavy on her heart."

Titan looked at the empty doorway. Suddenly, he felt bad about his brazenness. "Did you know her mother well?"

"I knew Sadie, but—" Pamela paused, then sighed— "she worked so hard that there was never time for her to really get to know anybody. And she seemed to want it that way, if you know what I mean."

"I think I do," Titan replied.

"But Essence was one of the best daughters a woman could have. She was a very spirited child, yet tenderhearted. Always taking home stray animals and . . . she had a big imagination. Really big." Pamela chuckled. "She could think up some games for the three of them to play, let me tell you."

Titan couldn't help but smile a little. He found it easy to

imagine a little Essence holding a stray puppy. There was something about the woman—a naturalness. "And what do you think of Essence the adult?"

"I haven't seen her much recently," Pamela spoke the realization. "As a matter of fact, it's been a couple of years since I've seen her. But Essence, Brenda, and Shiri stay in touch. They're always planning something." Pamela pointed. "That's my daughter, Brenda, sitting down with her friend, Wes. She's a doctor. And her cousin, Shiri"— she pointed again—"is an engineer."

"What does Essence do?" Titan noticed how his stomach tightened.

"You know, I'm not sure." Pamela chewed her bottom lip. "She didn't get her degree like Brenda and Shiri did, but she's been making out real good from what I understand. Living nicely and, as you can see, looking real good."

"Yes, I can see that." Without trying, Titan visualized just how good.

"Well, tell your father Pamela Johnson Reid said hello." They shook hands again.

"I definitely will," Titan replied as Pamela walked away and he found himself walking toward the door. *So, Essence Stuart was the best daughter a woman could have.* Titan felt a kind of excitement over that. Maybe not excitement, but hope, although he tried to ignore it. Then his mind kicked in again. *But I know a lot of good girls who have crossed the tracks. And I've probably seen them all. Why?* His lips curled cynically. *Money. Power. Drugs. A man, even. I wonder which one it was for Essence.* Titan walked into the hall and continued to mull over his conversation with Cedric's sister. *And it seems she's been able to keep how she makes her living very low-key. Keeping secrets seems to be easy for her, and I bet using those secrets to her advantage does as well. Boy, I'm sure the Johnsons who think so highly of her would be surprised to know what she really does for a living.* Titan stuck his hands in his pockets. *Cedric has been my father's friend for a long time, and he's done a lot of good things in Birmingham. Things that he is known for.*

*Wouldn't he be man enough to tell the truth if Essence Stuart
was his daughter? Right now I'd have to say yes. The odds
are all stacked in his favor.* Titan entered the hallway where
he'd first seen Essence. *But I have to admit, Ms. Essence is
quite an enigma. And . . . she has an ability to fool people.
To win them over to her side. To make them want to believe
in her.* Titan stopped in front of the door out of which
Essence had come. An image of a young Essence tenderly
stroking a baby rabbit entered his mind. *Damn!* he thought.

Chapter Nine

Someone knocked on her door and Essence grabbed her robe. *It's nobody but Brenda or Shiri*, she thought, struggling with the left sleeve. She had her hand on the doorknob when she looked through the peephole. Her hand dropped when she saw Titan Valentine. *What is he doing here?* It only took Essence a second to figure that out. "Yes." She used her most authoritative tone.

"I'm sorry for knocking on your door this late," Titan began. "But I figured you left a few minutes ago, so I knew there was a high possibility that you would still be up. And I didn't want to wait until morning."

"Wait for what?" Essence continued to look through the hole.

"To apologize."

"Really." She tried to read his body language. No luck there.

"But of course this is no way to do it."

"I agree," Essence said. "It's very late and—"

"I'm not talking about the time," Titan cut in. "I'm talking about apologizing through the door."

"Oh," Essence replied. She watched him. He stood perfectly still, waiting for her answer.

"Well . . . may I come in?"

"I don't know why you should," she replied.

"Because I obviously offended you, and I'm truly sorry for that. And I really need to see that you have accepted my apology. I'm not usually so crude."

Essence looked down. *Why shouldn't I let him in? What can he do to me? Everybody's seen me with him, and if he tries anything crazy, I'll make sure he pays.* She looked through the peephole again. *I'll let him in for a few minutes, then I'll put him out of here.* She opened the door and Titan stepped in.

Essence closed the door and tightened her robe. She intended to remain where she stood, but Titan had already moved farther into the room. Essence followed him, making a face. *I will not feel uneasy in my own space,* she bolstered herself. *I will not.* "So, you came to the conclusion that talking that way wasn't a good idea." She entwined her wrists and locked her hands in front of her. They created a protective layer over the thin silk robe.

Titan didn't answer her right away. She watched him look around the room. He glanced at her things before he looked at her and replied, "I want to apologize. I didn't mean to upset you. Sometimes I'm not the most tactful person."

There was something mechanical about the way he spoke.

"You could have said that through the door," Essence replied.

An eyebrow rose. "I could have, but like I said, I wanted to see your face when I said it."

"Okay. You saw it." Essence had had enough of Titan's game. And the truth was, she did feel uncomfortable. It was much more intimate in the small hotel room, and Essence was vastly aware of her almost nude condition under her robe. "Well, I guess I'll go to bed now. I'm tired."

Titan just stood there, looking. His gaze was quite disturbing to say the least, like hot, exploring hands. Finally he said, "You're still not satisfied, are you? Something within you always wants more. What are you really looking for, Essence?'' Titan realized how much he wanted to know the answer.

''I should ask you that question,'' she replied.

Titan's eyes continued to bore into her before he looked down. ''What is it that you want out of life?''

Essence shook her head. *Did I miss something? Or maybe he's had one too many.* ''Look. I don't know what you're trying to do, but this isn't the time or place for this kind of discussion.'' She paused. ''And I think you missed your cue. I was trying to politely tell you it's time for you to leave.''

''I just got here. Why are you so anxious to see me go?''

It was Essence's turn to look away. She couldn't tell him the real reason: that he put her on edge, created a kind of bodily craving. Her instincts warned that it would only take one touch. . . . ''Like I said, it's late.'' Essence looked back at him. Her eyes blinked over and over, attempting to veil the lie.

''You're uncomfortable,'' Titan replied. ''Don't worry. I don't bite.''

''That's what you say,'' Essence replied softly. She walked to the door, not daring to look back. Finally, she heard Titan move toward her and she prepared to let him out. Essence reached for the doorknob, but Titan placed his hand on top of hers. He removed her hand from the knob and turned it palm up.

''What are you doing?'' All the control left her voice.

Titan guided Essence's arm to her side as he leaned forward. Essence watched him warily, unable to resist the breeze-like kiss. It was brief, but so titillating that Essence couldn't help but offer her lips for another. Before she knew it, the mistlike kisses were dappling her face and lips, light and refreshing. As Essence marveled at the feeling, a kind of roar began in her ears. She wondered if it was her blood rushing through her veins.

Titan leaned Essence against the wall, which became a brace that kept her standing when her knees wanted to give way. Or was it Titan's arms holding her tightly that kept her upright? Essence wasn't sure as their breaths mingled until their breathing became panting, and he pressed his mouth against hers in a deep kiss.

From the sounds Essence made, an eavesdropper would have surmised there was more going on between them as she rubbed the muscles of Titan's back. They were hard, tight, and they quivered as if Titan were trying to restrain an uncontrollable force. Essence couldn't remember anyone ever feeling so good. When Titan withdrew from the kiss, Essence hung her head to the side, reacting to the sweet ache that remained and exposing the curve of her neck. That was something Titan couldn't resist, and the heat of his suckling lips burned her neck, then the skin cooled as his mouth moved on, easily marking a path to her shoulder. It was exquisite—every flick of his tongue—every movement of his lips. The pleasure of it lodged in Essence's throat, and she arched her back. *Remarkable,* she thought. *Remarkable and so wonderful.*

When Titan loosened her robe, just for a second Essence thought of stopping him, but she didn't want to. She wanted the pleasure. She wanted the freedom to feel it, to allow herself to feel something more powerful than sorrow and death.

As Titan sampled the tips of her breasts, Essence reveled in the sensations. "Uh-uh," she muttered. His head shook as he licked each breast in a barrage of tongue salutations. Titan seemed to be on fire when he kissed her again. Essence could feel the flames. The gentleness was gone, replaced by a desire that could only be quenched one way. Titan's hand moved in the direction of fulfillment, and when his fingers found their target, there was no turning back for either of them. *Why turn back? Why turn back when I want him so badly,* Essence thought as she opened to it all, her body seeking the pleasure he sought to give. Her mind chose to ignore that it was far too much too soon.

It had been so long since anyone had touched Essence there. So long, and she melted against Titan's hand, seeking his mouth and his tongue with her own. It was Essence who held on the tightest now, Essence whose arms were like bands trying to hold him to her. When Titan's pleasuring hand stilled, Essence's desire was so high, her mind fogged, overpowered with the need.

"Don't stop," she cried, at her loss.

"I don't intend to," was all she heard him say, and Essence realized why her arms were the only ones holding tight. Titan had found a way to free himself. Expertly he put on a condom and he bent low before he entered her. Immediately, Essence released in a hail of pleasure. She emitted the sound of a woman deep in an orgasmic clutch, sparked simply by Titan's entry.

But it was far from over, and the ride from there was pure and steady. Essence could tell when Titan was coming to his moment. She expanded, wanting it all. When Titan gave it with a "my God!" Essence allowed herself to feel the heavenly release once more.

Only then did the roar in her head subside and the cloud of passion lift from her vision. Essence's sight was crystal clear as she looked past her bare breasts, past Titan's fully clothed body, to her crumpled robe on the floor. *What have I done?* she thought as her body continued to tingle. When Essence mustered the nerve to look into Titan's face, she could not see into his eyes. The truth was, she could not see what he was feeling behind them. It was guarded under hooded lids. Despite that, he kissed her. But this time when his mouth met hers, it felt like a practiced kiss . . . a kiss that acknowledged the goal had been met, and it was time to move on.

Titan adjusted his clothes and backed away. Essence remained against the wall, paralyzed by what had taken place. He bent down, picked up her robe, and offered it to her. Essence accepted the flimsy garment from Titan's hand. He stood and watched as she put it on, and although it provided some cover from his probing eyes and the air-conditioned room, it did not have the power to warm the cold spot at the pit of her stomach.

"Good night, Essence," Titan said, opening the door.

Essence had no idea how he looked when he said it. She could not bring herself to look into his face, and she did not return his parting words. Once he was in the hall, Essence closed the door and walked to the bed with her hands covering her face. "Why did I do that? Why?" She wanted to kick herself. She wanted to scream. Instead, she dialed Shiri.

Chapter Ten

The phone rang several times. Essence was on the verge of hanging up when Shiri answered.

"Hello." Her voice was hurried.

"Shiri?"

"Essence? Girl, what's goin' on? You called at the perfect time. Jake just went out to get us something to drink."

"Oh." Essence tried to put some lightness in her voice. "Well, I'll just talk to you in the morning."

"No, you won't. It's one o'clock in the morning. What's going on? I thought you'd be in bed by now."

"I wish I had gone straight to bed. Ohh, Shiri." Essence's frustration spilled over.

"What is it?"

"Girl, you won't believe what I just did."

There was silence, then Shiri said, "This has something to do with Titan Valentine, doesn't it?"

"Yes. Ughh. I don't believe this." Essence was almost talking to herself.

"I knew it. I knew it. You were in such a hurry to leave the party, and he left shortly afterwards. Did you invite that man to your room?"

"No, I didn't. But he ended up in here anyway."

"Oh, my goodness." Essence could hear Shiri chuckle.

"It's not funny," Essence insisted. "And I don't feel like laughing."

"Well, it may not be funny, but I have to say it's about time."

"About time? Shiri! I barely know this man."

"He-ey. Evidently, there was a real strong connection."

"Ughh!" Essence repeated. "I can tell you've got J.D. on the brain. Strong connection or not, I've never done anything like this before. You know that." Essence's distress mounted.

"Essie. Calm down," Shiri compelled her. "I know you've never done anything like this before. But maybe you've had all kinds of stuff mounting up inside of you where there was no way for you to hold back. And you've got to take things into consideration."

"What's that?" Essence asked softly.

"You just lost your mama. People do strange things when someone close to them dies." The phone line went quiet. "You're entitled to whatever you've done. Don't beat yourself up about it."

"But, Shiri . . ."

"C'mon now. Where is all that stuff you espouse?" Shiri challenged Essence. "Like things happen for a reason. And for the two of you to hit it off so quickly, you must have known each other in a previous lifetime or something."

"I know all that. Although," Essence replied, "I haven't actually thought about it that way. I haven't had the time. But oh, my God, I've never had anyone seduce me like that." She paused. "Although there wasn't much seducing. I couldn't help myself. He was on his way out, and the next thing I know . . . boom." She sighed into the phone.

"Hey. Sounds pretty good to me."

"Pleeze. You're head over heels, so you can't see things any other way."

"It's not a bad place to be," Shiri chimed.

"But it's not the same. You didn't give up the milk the first day you met J.D."

"Nope, but now we're trying to make up for lost time."

"Ohh, my." Essence sighed again.

"Lighten up, girl. Lighten up!" Shiri insisted.

"I guess I just have to let this all sink in, so by the time I see him tomorrow, I'll be centered again. Right now I feel like I don't know if I'm coming or going."

"You will feel better by tomorrow," Shiri assured her. "And when you do see him, smile like you got exactly what you wanted."

Essence paused. "I think I did."

They snickered.

"There he is," Shiri sang. "Someone's knocking at the door, so it must be Jake. I've got to let you go."

"Replaced by J.D.," Essence taunted her.

"You're right. Until you can do what Jake does, there ain't no competition."

"All right," Essence replied. "See you tomorrow."

Shiri was already hanging up.

Essence sat on the side of the bed and looked around. Boy, was she was thirsty. "I need something to drink." She stood, smoothed her hair, and tightened her robe. "I think I'll grab some juice from the machine." She continued to think out loud as she dug for coins in her purse. "Shiri's right. I'll be better by tomorrow. God, but it's going to be hard not to act embarrassed when I see that man." She picked up the card key and slipped outside.

The drink machine was just up the hall. Essence stepped into the alcove, deposited her money, and selected some apple juice. She was about to reenter the hall when she heard voices.

"You have drank entirely too much, Cedric. I don't know what's wrong with you, but I am past putting up with your craziness."

"I don't know what you're talking about," Cedric replied. "I'm fine."

Essence's eyes widened as she positioned herself beside the machine, out of sight.

"You are not fine," the woman retorted. "Nobody else may be able to tell when you've had too much, but I certainly can."

"What are you talkin' about? Why don't you go on to the room, Vivian. I'll be there in a second. I want to stop right here and talk to Titan for a minute."

"Do you know what time it is? He's going to think you're crazy."

"No, he won't."

"It's after one o'clock in the morning, Cedric," Vivian insisted. "Don't you think he's asleep?"

"Karen told me he left the party not too long ago. I'm sure he's still awake."

"And I'm sure he wants to see you this time of morning," Vivian snapped.

There was silence before Vivian started up again.

"And if we had gone to the family party like we should have"—she was obviously upset—"maybe you wouldn't have drank so much. What got into you today?"

"Just go on. Would you, please? I'll be there in a minute." Cedric's tone remained even despite the pressure Vivian applied.

"Cedric . . ."

"I promise," he pleaded. "Give me a couple of minutes."

Why would Cedric be going to Titan's room this time of morning? Essence waited to hear what would be said next.

"Okay," Vivian finally said in a tone that held a threat.

Essence continued to listen, but the hall went silent. Slowly, she moved from her place beside the drink machine. Suddenly, there were several raps on a door not far away. Essence waited.

"It's Cedric," Essence heard Cedric say.

A door opened. "Sorry, man," Cedric continued. "You weren't asleep, were you?"

Essence could hear a very low, "Not yet."

"I don't need to come in, but I heard you were dancing with Essence Stuart."

Titan paused. "Yes . . . we danced."

"Good. Good," Cedric replied. "I can see you know how to take care of business."

Essence's mouth dropped open.

"Perhaps you should come inside," Titan suggested.

"No. It's late, and I don't want to keep you up."

"All right. We'll talk in the morning," Titan said.

"Okay." Cedric sounded reluctant to leave. "But did you find out anything?"

Find out anything? Essence couldn't believe her ears.

"No more than what you've told me. It's always good to know I'm working with the right information."

"Yeah. I can imagine," Cedric said.

There was another pause, as if Cedric were waiting for more.

"I'll let you know how it goes." Titan attempted to bring the conversation to a close.

"Good. Good. That's my Titan. You've got this private detective stuff down pat."

Private detective! Essence was stunned.

"I'll talk to you tomorrow."

Cedric's parting words combined with a number of frantic thoughts in Essence's mind.

"You mean later today." Titan emphasized the time.

Cedric gave an embarrassed laugh. " 'Night, Titan."

"Good night."

Essence didn't move. The implications, followed by an understanding of what she'd overheard, immobilized her. Then anger ignited, and she stepped into the hall, hoping Cedric was still there. She wanted to confront him . . . confront both of them. She'd let Cedric know he didn't have to hire a private detective. Her life was an open book. Essence turned in a circle, looking from door to door, wondering which one was Titan's. She yearned to tell him where to go. But a mental image of her crumpled robe on the floor and her body leaning against the wall out of breath pulled the plug on Essence's anger, and it was replaced by torrents of shame. The cold feeling returned to the pit of her stomach. This time it was accompanied by nausea. Essence held her stomach and hurried to her room. *I provided Titan with an unexpected fringe benefit on this job. He was setting me up to get information for Cedric, and I gave him more than enough. God, how low can they go? How low can I go?* Essence wallowed in the feelings surrounding the difficult situation. Yet, in the midst of them, it was still hard to believe it was happening. Finally she decided *I don't want to be around people who can do something like this. This is horrible, and I don't want any part of it.* She stood looking at the closed curtains. *I don't care if I ever see either one of them again. And I definitely don't want to claim a man like Cedric Johnson for my father.*

Chapter Eleven

Titan sat on the side of the hotel bed and rubbed his eyes as the sun peeked around the closed curtains. He listened to the telephone ring for a third time.

"Hello," the familiar accented voice said.

An unexpected feeling of relief swept through Titan at the sound of his grandmother's voice. "Hello, *Grandni*. It's Titan."

"Titan! *Mon chou!*"

He chuckled. "Mahmah, if anybody heard you, they'd think you were speaking to a tiny child."

"Big or small, you are still my sweet. My grandson. You'll always be that."

It warmed his heart to hear how much she cared. Titan couldn't remember a time when he didn't feel Cecilia-Marie Balan's unconditional love. "What you doin'?"

"Me? I'm about to go into my garden and pick some okra and tomatoes. I still love my gardening, you know."

"I'm sure," Titan replied. "How can I ever forget the times that I stayed with you and ended up picking beans, peas, squash ... you name it?"

"You picked them, all right, but you didn't like it."

"Nope. I guess I'm just not cut out to be a farm boy," Titan said.

"I don't know. You liked the animals, especially the little ones," Cecilia replied.

"I don't know too many people who don't like baby animals," Titan said, but his thoughts went to Essence.

"Where are you calling from?" Titan's grandmother cut in.

"I'm at a hotel in Orlando. I'm thinking about heading out early and coming your way. Could you stand that?"

"You tease me. You know I would love to see you early, late, anytime."

Titan sighed. He had slept through the night, but it didn't feel like it. "Well, I thought I'd warn you."

The conversation paused.

"What is that I hear in your voice?" Cecilia-Marie asked. "Ma'am?"

"In your voice. That sound. Something's wrong."

Yes, something is wrong. I saw Essence in a dream. Nothing but her face. I can't get her out of my mind and I don't like it. "No, nothing is wrong. I'm just ready to get out of here. To distance myself from the rat race."

"Poooh," Cecilia-Marie sounded. "There is something wrong. I know there is. But if you don't want to talk about it now, that's okay."

Titan could imagine Cecilia's expression from the tone in her voice. "So, you have decided to trade in the craziness for your loving *grandni*," Cecilia-Marie continued. "It's a good idea. One you can do at anytime."

"Merci, Maman."

"Ohh, I love it when you speak my native Haitian tongue. Your tongue."

"Dad would argue that point."

"And what does he know? It is your tongue, and it's in your blood. So, when what you call that craziness gets to you, know that your ancestors' blood runs richly through your veins. You don't have to seek your maman or anyone. You hold the source of peace inside of you."

I do? Titan stared at the door to his hotel room. *I wish I could find it now.* "You remember the two weeks I stayed with you when I was ten? Dad and a friend of his drove down and dropped me off."

"Sure, I do. My mind is still good. My body needs some work, but my mind . . . *bon.*"

"Speaking of mind," Titan said, "you gave my father a piece of *your* mind before they left that day."

"You heard that? I didn't know you heard that."

"I was hiding in the bathroom. You can really hear what's going on in the second bedroom if you put your ear in the right spot."

"Ah! Shame on you," Cecilia-Marie said. "I didn't want you to hear it. That's why we left the room."

"I know. And that's why I went to listen."

"Children," Cecilia-Marie muttered. "Such a mess." She spoke up again. "That was the only time I ever spoke to your father like that. I didn't like him running around with that friend of his. He was too good-looking and too slick for his own good. What was his name?"

"Cedric." Titan looked down. "Cedric Johnson."

"Yes. That was it. He said all this flowery stuff to me, but I could tell he was raring to go. When a man is that anxious to go do something, it has got to do with a woman, and probably not the right one, if he's married." She paused. "So, I wanted your father to remember he was a married man, and had been a good husband to my daughter up until then. He didn't need any unhappy married man to lead him astray."

Titan's brows furrowed. "How could you tell Cedric was unhappy?"

"I could feel it and see it in his eyes. No matter his flashy smile and happy talk. You know your maman."

"Yes. I do." Titan recalled the time when the weatherman had said there would be no rain for weeks, and his grandmother had prayed for rain. It had been a cloudless day. It had rained that evening. "I think Pops might have been a little scared of you. Still might be."

"No need to be scared of me. Just because I listen with all of me and I am open to God's miracles. Yes, I know things, feel things that would come to anybody else who approached life the same way. You have never been afraid of your maman."

"Never. Been amused by her, yes. Afraid? Never."

"Amused?" Cecilia-Marie laughed.

"I'll see you some time before noon," Titan said with his eyes closed.

"Good. I'll be waiting."

Titan hung up the telephone. He was more than ready to leave Orlando. He'd told Cedric he would see him today, but Titan was in no mood for that. He was in no mood for socializing at all. He walked in the bathroom and turned on the shower.

Years ago, after a one-night stand, neither the woman nor the sex had crossed his mind the morning after, but that were far from true today. Both Essence and what they'd done were heavy on his mind.

Titan stepped into the shower and let the water rain down on his head and face. He hesitated when it came to labeling what had taken place between them. For some reason, he couldn't bring himself to call it any of the four-letter words that could come so easily. They just didn't fit the feeling. Inside, Titan felt like it was more than that, and he didn't know why. His mind argued against it. It just didn't make sense. Still, something deeper within knew it made all the sense in the world. Essence had opened to him in a way that surpassed all those four-letter words, that surpassed just sex. *When a woman melts into your arms so deeply, becomes one with you so willingly that you don't know where you end and she begins . . . it's beyond the physical. You can't call it those words that are tossed around so carelessly.* Titan scrubbed himself until he tingled. *Maybe I'm just getting older and I'm feeling things more deeply than I've ever felt them before. Maybe it wasn't Essence; maybe it's just me. Either way, getting with her was not a good idea. But I did it to prove a point to myself. To prove that she was available to anyone.* He turned off the shower. *But what we experienced had nothing to do with commerce or money. It was . . . it was . . . I don't want to think about it anymore. Whatever it was, I'm heading out of here. I promised Cedric I would investigate Essence, and that's what I'm going to do—rom a distance.*

Chapter Twelve

Essence guessed, by now, Brenda and Shiri were aware that she had left. Shiri had probably put two and two together and determined Essence's departure had something to do with Titan Valentine. Shiri would only have a small piece of the picture. *I'll call Brenda and Shiri and let them know where I am.* Essence watched a burgundy car pass her on the highway. Several large, gray plumes that had seemed far away minutes ago were closer on the horizon. She held the steering wheel with both hands. *I don't belong at that family reunion, and even if I do, it just doesn't feel right anymore. I no longer care if Cedric Johnson ever acknowledges me. And he surely doesn't have to acknowledge my mother. For him to do something like that. To have me investigated like some criminal.* Essence eased off the accelerator when she noticed the climbing speedometer. *I pray I only have a few genes from that man.* She wiped away a tear she hadn't realized was coming.

Essence noticed the faint smell of smoke. She tried not to think about Titan. She had enough on her mind without that. Essence could blame the other hurts on her biological father and the inevitability of death, but she could only blame what she'd done with Titan on herself. *And I played right into his hands. Why did I let him into my room? Why?* She forced herself to exhale. *Well, I did, and there's nothing I can do about it now. He probably thinks I'm the biggest slut on this side of the Mississippi. I might as well have taken him up on the offer he made me on the dance floor. What's the difference? Getting paid for sex on the first night or giving it up for free to a man who couldn't care less.* Essence wiped away another tear. *God, why did it have to turn out like this? I hadn't felt anything for anyone in such a long time; why did I have to be attracted to him? A man who's working for my . . . FATHER, trying to dig up dirt on me?*

Now the smell of smoke was obvious, and there was a gray color surrounding the car. Essence realized the plumes were products of brush fires and not pending rain. She tried not to inhale the acrid air. Brush fires had become a regular part of the Florida landscape, and Essence figured they weren't very far away.

Traffic slowed somewhat as the smoke thickened, but the cars were still moving at quite a clip. Essence forced her thoughts to remain on the deteriorating driving conditions. She turned on her right blinker. She decided she'd be more comfortable in the slowest lane. Suddenly, there was an awful noise ahead. It was a bang and a pop combined. Then there was another, and another. Essence stomped on her brakes. Red lights appeared in several places ahead, like eyes beaming through the smoke-filled air. The closest set was yards away. Essence rose out of her seat as she continued to apply pressure on the brakes. "Oh, Jesus, it's not going to stop! It's not going to stop!" The car stopped with a jerk. Essence dropped into her seat.

She sat there, shocked, her leg shaking uncontrollably from the effort. Raindrops fell on the windshield, and the sound of them echoed within the car. Essence looked into the rearview mirror. She screamed as a pair of headlights barreled down on her from behind, then stopped just in the nick of time.

Essence was not hurt, but she knew from the sound of things only moments before, there were others who weren't so lucky. "There must be a pileup. I wonder how many cars were involved." She took a deep breath, then stopped midway. The air was full of smoke and gasoline. Gasoline was falling on the car, not rain.

She jumped out of her car and ran to the curb as gasoline spewed from the truck beside it. Essence watched the truck driver scramble out of the cab, escaping the dangerous situation. She could see a red car in front of the truck and someone lying on the ground.

Not far away, Essence heard a small child crying at the top of its lungs, while a woman in an unsteady voice attempted to comfort her. She couldn't see beyond the red car, but from the sound of things, there were many people in similar predicaments. Essence didn't know what to do, so she walked toward the sound of the crying child. The only sounds of significance other than moans and uncanny, frantic voices were sirens—sirens that were on their way.

"Is she okay?" Essence knelt down beside a woman cradling a little girl. There was blood on the child's arm and face.

"Sure she is." The woman patted the child and tried to smile, but when she looked at Essence, there was fear in her eyes. "Are you a nurse?"

"No, I'm not. I'm sorry." Essence wished she were. "But as you can hear, help is on the way."

The woman looked back at the child and began to rock ever so slightly. "It's going to be okay," Essence reassured them. She squeezed the woman's shoulder, which created tears in the woman's eyes. Hurriedly, she wiped them away.

The girl stopped sobbing. "Are you crying, Mommy?"

The woman replied by lowering her head. Her hair mingled with her child's.

"Don't cry, Mommy. I'm okay." The child tried to comfort her mother.

"We're both fine, baby," the woman replied. "The doctor

will put some bandages on our cuts and we'll be as good as new.''

"You're such a brave girl," Essence said to the child as new intermittent flashes of red, blue, and white lights colored the scene. She touched the girl's hair. Blood appeared in her hand. "How old are you?" Essence asked.

"I'm five," the child replied in a small voice.

"A brave five. You want to do me a favor?"

"What?" Her watery eyes held pain.

"I want you to take care of your mama while I go find some help. Okay?"

The child gave a small nod.

Essence got up from the curb. She walked past the vehicle that had almost rammed into her car, toward the nearest flashing light. It was a police car, straddling two lanes. A policeman stood by it, directing traffic with a powerful flashlight.

"Officer."

"Yes?" he replied, but continued what he was doing.

"There's a little girl who's hurt." Essence pointed when he finally looked at her. "Her mother's sitting on the curb, holding her."

"She'll get some help soon," he replied. "An ambulance just arrived, but it's farther up. A couple more are on their way." He shouted at a gawker. "Keep moving. Keep moving. Is the child conscious?" he asked Essence.

"Yes, she's conscious," Essence replied. "She doesn't look like she's badly hurt, but there's blood on her forehead. I think it's coming from her head."

"I suggest they wait right there until the other ambulances arrive. One of them will be placed at this end of the pileup."

"How many cars are involved?"

"Ma'am, I have no idea at this point, but I've got a job to do here." He continued to wave the flashlight. "You need to get back over to the curb and out of the way."

"Yes. I'm sorry," Essence replied. She understood, but at the same time his strict manner hurt. Essence turned away.

"Essence!"

She looked. Someone had called her name. There was an odd mix of human need born of tragedy and distrust when Essence recognized Titan in one of the passing cars.

"Are you okay?" he called.

"Got to keep moving, sir," the policeman commanded.

Essence shrugged in a motion of surrender. "Yes." She could have said more, wanted to, if the circumstances had been different. But as it stood, Essence simply walked away. For a moment she wondered what Titan was doing on the highway, but that quickly passed. Essence had the woman and the injured girl on her mind. She had to tell them help was definitely on the way.

Titan drove forward as he was instructed, but his eyes remained on Essence. There was blood on her face as she disappeared into the smoke. Titan wanted to keep going just as the policeman instructed, but he couldn't. He had to find out more, to help if need be ... to help Essence, if she needed it.

He drove, waiting for the perfect opportunity. When Titan found it, he pulled over and parked. Quickly, he got out and walked in the direction in which Essence had disappeared.

Emergency medical technicians were pouring onto the scene. Titan watched as in a practiced manner, they got to work. He tried to avoid the bent metal and the broken glass as he passed dazed drivers and passengers, and people whose conditions were beyond that. Titan looked at each face, but none were Essence's. He stopped near the policeman who had told him to keep going. An ambulance was parked several yards away, and Titan watched a woman grab a medical tech's arm as he descended from the vehicle. "Please. Over here," she said. It was Essence. But before Titan could reach them, she was pulling the man forward. He followed them to a mother and child seated on the curb.

"I told you help was on the way." Essence stood to the side so the emergency worker could do his job.

The technician bent down beside them. He touched the child's face and then her head. Blood appeared on his hand, but not much.

The technician looked at the mother. "How did she get over here?" He quickly followed with, "You shouldn't have moved her."

"But she was hysterical," the mother replied. "She kept screaming that we had to get out of the car. I didn't know what else to do."

"In a situation like this, you should have waited for professionals to make that decision," the medical tech stressed.

The little girl looked from her mother to the technician. "But the big lady said we had to get out."

"What lady?" The technician inquired. "Has someone else already looked at her?"

"No," the mother replied. "What lady, Alicia?" the mother asked.

"The big lady. I think she was an angel. She was bigger than him." Alicia pointed.

They all turned and looked at Titan. Titan looked at the child and then at Essence. Their eyes locked.

"She glowed and had big, big wings. They were so soft, like Pepper." The girl smiled a little. "She wrapped her wings around me as my head hit the glass."

"What are you talking about, honey?" The mother searched her little girl's eyes.

"The angel, Mommy."

Titan stepped forward and squeezed Essence's hand. She looked at Alicia before she pulled away.

"Angel?" the mother repeated with awe and hopeful disbelief. "But you were wearing your seat belt. Your head couldn't have hit the windshield."

"I loosened it," Alicia said. "I dropped Pepper on the floor, and I wanted to get him."

"Pepper?" Essence questioned. "Who's Pepper?"

"My teddy bear."

"Alicia! You unbuckled your seat belt? I told you never to do that, sweetie." The mother tried not to scold. "When that car hit us from behind you could have . . . oh, my God!" She grabbed her head.

"I promise I won't do it again, Mommy. I promise. Never," Alicia pleaded.

"So, you're telling me you weren't wearing a seat belt?" The technician dabbed at the cut near Alicia's hairline.

"No, sir," Alicia replied guiltily.

In silence, the technician cleaned and bandaged Alicia's forehead and swabbed her arm. "Where's your car?" He looked at the mother.

She pointed to a nearby green compact. The trunk was totally smashed in, and gasoline from the spewing truck poured into the vehicle through the shattered rear window.

"If you two had stayed in that car with gasoline pouring in like that, it wouldn't have been good." The medical tech took Alicia into his arms and stood. "Well, all I've got to say is, if an angel wasn't protecting you, somebody else was."

"It was an angel," Alicia said. "I saw her."

The technician simply nodded. "Ma'am, we're going to need to check her out at the hospital."

The mother rose unsteadily to her feet.

"Follow me. I'll get you situated," the technician said.

"What about you?" Titan looked at Essence. The medical tech looked at her, too.

"What about me?"

"There's blood on your face." Titan tried to touch her. Essence moved away. "Are you hurt?"

"No." She touched her own face. "I was trying to comfort Alicia. It must be her blood."

"If that's the case, we'd best be on our way," the technician prodded.

The woman looked at Essence. "Thank you."

"You're welcome," Essence replied. She leaned toward Alicia. "Bye. Remember what I told you about your mom. Take care of her."

"I will." Alicia nodded before they walked away.

Chapter Thirteen

Titan and Essence stood alone. Titan scanned the smashed vehicles and continuing chaos. He finally said, "This is a bad situation."

"Like many others," Essence replied. She knew Titan was looking at her, but she refused to look back.

"Where is your car?"

His *concern* irked her, but she had no energy to do anything about it. Essence crossed her arms. "What do you want?" Titan's expression changed. She recognized the guarded looked. It was the same one he'd worn before he'd left her hotel room.

"Just finding out if you need any help," he replied.

"From you?" She paused dramatically and gave him a scathing look. "No, thanks."

"I'm going to have to ask you people to clear the area if you don't need any medical assistance," a policeman interrupted them.

"I don't need any medical help, but my car is in the middle of all this." Essence pointed. "It's got gasoline all over it."

"I understand, ma'am, and there's no way you're going

to get your car out of here anytime soon. What about you, sir?'' The officer moved right along.

''I'm parked over there. I pulled over to see if I could help.''

'' 'Preciate your attitude.'' The policeman wasted no time. ''But the best thing you can do right now is leave the area. Ma'am, is there someone you can call for a ride?''

Essence thought of Shiri and Brenda. Lately, they'd dealt with enough when it came to her. She didn't doubt, one day, when they found out who her father was, they would have to deal with even more. So she couldn't bring herself to take them away from the family reunion. ''No, there's not,'' Essence replied.

''Do you two know each other?'' The policeman motioned between them with his index finger.

''Sort of,'' Essence hedged. She knew where the policeman was headed.

Titan simply replied, ''Yes.''

''You wouldn't mind giving this young lady a ride, would you, sir?''

''Wouldn't mind at all,'' Titan said.

''Good.'' The officer herded them along with his arms. ''So, let's go.''

Essence and Titan started walking.

''My car's over there.'' Titan veered to the right.

Essence followed. She felt she had no choice. Suddenly, she turned back to the officer. ''Wait a minute. What about my car? How will I get it?''

''Call Bryson's Towing in Orlando. That's who we'll use.''

''So, I'll have to pay, even though I didn't hit anybody?'' Essence asked, but the policeman was already calling out to another group of people.

''We need you to clear the area if you don't need medical assistance.''

''Man,'' Essence steamed under her breath. She looked at Titan, who simply turned and started walking again. When they reached a white, convertible Sebring, Titan used a remote and unlocked it.

Essence slid into the car and closed the door. She looked around. It was immaculate. Seconds later, Titan settled in beside her. "So, like the policeman said, let's go." He cranked the ignition.

Essence hadn't expected to meet up with Titan Valentine so soon. As a matter of fact, she had counted on never seeing him again. She didn't know what was stronger, her resentment or her embarrassment. She had to say something, or she feared she might burst. "Now that you've so nobly offered to take me home, I think you've overlooked something."

"Like what?" His silky eyebrow rose.

"You don't know where I live." Then she turned and looked at him. "Or do you?"

Titan lowered his gaze. "Not exactly."

Essence leaned toward the radio. "Do you mind?"

"Be my guest." Titan edged his way into the slow-moving traffic.

She pressed the button and played with the tuner until she found the station. The recorded voice was tinny. "It's eighty-four degrees. Driving conditions: Hazardous. Three brush fires burning in the vicinity of I-4. Major accident near Exit 328 East. No thru traffic. I-4 closed between Orlando and Lakeland."

Essence sat back in her seat. "I just can't win for losing." She looked out of the window.

"So, I guess that affects you." Titan continued to look straight ahead.

"You guessed right," she snapped.

"Look, I know you've been through quite an ordeal here," Titan replied. "But why don't you try to calm down? I'm just trying to help."

Essence's hands flailed. "Yeah, and where does that fit in? Between investigating me and screwing me?"

Titan didn't respond. It was clear she knew about the investigation. He wondered how. Regardless, it was an uncomfortable situation, especially considering last night. Titan hadn't been able to classify what they'd done, but Essence sure had.

"That's what I thought," Essence retorted.

"Who said I was investigating you?"

"Are you going to deny it?"

"No." A part of Titan wished he could.

"Then why ask?" She looked out the window, then looked back. "Is this part of the job? Or are you so accustomed to doing this kind of . . . shit that you can't help yourself?" Essence couldn't believe she had cussed at him.

"I must admit the situation with you is a little complicated."

"Just a little, huh?" *I have allowed him to send me over the edge.* She tried to calm down. *This is not me.* "When we get to an exit where there is a hotel, you can drop me off."

"Whatever you say," Titan replied.

They drove in silence. For Essence, every mile they passed, every mile that Titan didn't give some kind of explanation, was excruciating. It didn't anger her. The truth was, Essence felt diminished by his silence—belittled. To her, it meant she wasn't worth an explanation. Essence was more than glad to see the Kissimmee exit not far away. She was certain she could find a hotel there. "You can get off at the next exit."

Titan did as he was told. Once he was off the highway, he followed the signs to the center of town. "That will do fine," Essence said, pointing at the first decent hotel they came to.

Titan stopped in front of the Innkeeper's Express.

Essence had no intention of saying thank you. She wanted to leave so bad she could taste it. Essence reached for her purse, but it wasn't there. She looked on the floor, then on the car seat, before she realized the truth.

"Your purse." Titan broke the silence.

With closed eyes, Essence leaned her head back against the headrest. "I left it in my car."

More silence stretched between them.

Finally, Essence quietly said, "I don't want to ask you to lend me any money. I don't want to ask you for anything. You or my . . . Cedric." She kept her eyes closed and waited. She heard Titan start the car, and her eyes opened. "Where are you going?"

"I'm going to my *grandmère's*," Titan replied as he drove off. "My grandmother's."

Essence looked at him as if he had lost his mind.

"And I didn't tell you I was investigating you because that's not how it's done. As far as the other part is concerned," Titan continued, "I've never . . . gotten involved with someone I'm investigating. It's new territory for me. I don't know the ropes."

"The ropes? Is that what it's called?" She shook her head. "There are none. It's life. We make it up as we go along." Essence turned toward the window and rested her face against the car seat. At least he was talking now, and Essence was strangely comforted knowing she was the only one with whom Titan had crossed the line. That had to mean something.

Chapter Fourteen

Essence couldn't believe she had fallen asleep. She looked over at Titan and sat up.

"Seems like you needed that," Titan said.

"I guess so," Essence replied. She noticed they were driving on a remote road. Farmhouses that sat a comfortable distance apart were nestled off to the sides. "How much farther is it?"

"Another five minutes or so," Titan replied.

If I didn't believe in fate, I would definitely believe something's up. What else could this be? The irony was not lost on Essence. She pulled down the visor and looked in the mirror. Her hair had a mind of its own. Dried traces of blood marked the side of her face.

"Look in the glove compartment," Titan said. "Some leftover towelettes from Tony Roma's are in there."

Essence pressed the latch and the door eased down. A couple of towelette packages had been tossed inside. She took one of them. "Thanks." Essence cleaned her face and smoothed her eyebrows. She tried to arrange her hair, which had turned into a headful of tight corkscrews. It was a hopeless situation.

"Your hair looks good that way," Titan remarked.

Essence couldn't hold back. "Careful, you've already gotten in bed with the enemy. There's no need to overdo it."

"There was no bed," Titan softly replied as he pulled off the road.

Essence flushed.

They stopped in front of a small, tricolored house. Several flower gardens grew out front. The house and the gardens were surrounded by a picket fence. Essence could see three porches. A wooden chime hung from the ceiling of the front porch, and an iron umbrella stand sat in the corner.

Titan got out of the car. Essence followed.

"This is it," Titan said.

"It sure is." A small woman rose out of the flowers. *"Pouchant,"* she said, smiling. "You're here!" She dusted herself off and adjusted a small straw hat with frayed edges, which sat comfortably on top of a larger sunbonnet.

"Grandni," Titan said.

Essence thought Titan's smile warmed his entire face. She watched the two of them come together. Titan bent over and gingerly hugged his grandmother.

"What kind of hug is that?" she chastised. "You better hug me. I won't break."

Titan threw his head back and laughed. When he hugged her again, he lifted her off the ground and swung her around.

"Now you're showing off," she wailed. When her feet touched the ground again, she grabbed Titan's face between her hands and gave him a noisy kiss.

Essence watched, amazed. There was no doubt in her mind that Titan and his grandmother had a special relationship. She didn't see the suave, handsome man she'd met in the hall, nor the tricky detective. This was simply a man who loved his grandmother, and she, in return, adored him.

"And who is this, Titan?" She placed her hands comfortably on her hips and stepped toward Essence. "You didn't tell me you were bringing someone with you."

"I didn't know it at the time. This is Essence Stuart." His

voice seemed to lower. "Essence, this is my grandmother, Cecilia-Marie Balan."

"Hello, Mrs. Balan." Essence extended her hand.

"Hello, Ms. Stuart." Cecilia-Marie returned the gesture. She looked at them. "My, my, my. So much can happen in such a short time."

Essence lowered her eyes.

"And what do you mean by that, *Grandni?*"

"I mean, I spoke to you this morning and you did not mention Ms. Stuart, and now here you both are."

"She was involved in a car pileup about forty-five minutes from here. She left her purse in her car, so I brought her with me."

"It's all soo simple." Cecilia-Marie smiled but said no more. "Come. Come in, both of you. I have been waiting for you, Titan. And now I know, I have been waiting for Ms. Stuart as well." She climbed the stairs and entered the house. "I was doing some gardening. Which I love," Cecilia-Marie continued. "But I don't know how much it loves me these days." She grimaced and pressed the small of her back. "And even though I didn't know you were coming, Ms. Stuart, I've got plenty of room."

"Please, call me Essence."

"Essence." Cecilia-Marie stopped and looked at her. "What a beautiful name."

Essence smiled.

"No. I mean it." Cecilia touched Essence's hand. "People say that kind of thing all of the time, but you can believe when I say something like that, I really mean it."

"Well, thank you," Essence replied.

"And of course, you must call me Cecilia-Marie."

"I will," Essence assured her.

"Like I was saying, Essence, I've got plenty of room for you, too. Titan can sleep on the sofa bed in the den."

Essence realized what Cecilia-Marie was thinking. "I don't think that will be necessary," she interrupted. "I won't be spending the night."

"You won't?" Cecilia-Marie said.

"I can't think of imposing like that." Essence glanced at Titan. His expression gave no indication of where he stood.

"How you will be imposing, my dear, is by having my Titan take you away from here anytime before I'm ready for him to leave tonight. You will be taking time away from his visit with me. And that won't do. So, you will spend the night, at least tonight," Cecilia-Marie informed her. "And we will see how it goes tomorrow. If you and I don't get along, I will quietly let him take you wherever you need to go. But I warn you, if I like you, you're in trouble. The only place you will find peace from me talking your head off is out in the barn. We've fixed it up beautifully." She made a face. "But I'm allergic to something out there. I have a sneezing fit every time I step my feet in there."

"Well, if you put it that way . . ." Essence didn't know what else to say.

"I do." Cecilia-Marie looked straight in Essence's eyes. "So, it is settled. Now come with me." She showed Essence her room. A quaint space decorated in white, except for the very colorful paintings on the walls. "Now for you." She turned to Titan. "I've got something special."

"Let me guess." Titan put his arm around her. "You fixed my favorite."

"You know your *titi*, don't you?" Cecilia-Marie's smile broadened.

"I know you cooked them because I can smell them all the way out here," Titan replied.

They stepped into the kitchen. Cecilia-Marie pointed to a pile of golden copper cakes on the stove.

"Have you ever seen cakes like this?" she asked Essence.

"No, I haven't." Essence sniffed the air. "But they smell like sweet potato pie."

"The sweet potato is right. The pie is not," Cecilia-Marie told her. "This is *pain patate*. Sweet potato cake. A big difference between this and sweet potato pie is, they are my *pouchant's* favorite"—she smiled at Titan—"and, they have bananas in them."

"Oh my," Essence imagined the taste of sweet potatoes and bananas combined.

"Here." Cecilia-Marie picked up a couple of napkins and *pain patates*. "You both must have one."

Hungry, Essence wasted no time. She took a bite. Her eyes closed naturally. "It's delicious," she replied, unaware of Titan's unwavering stare.

"It is, isn't it?" Cecilia-Marie beamed.

Essence took another bite. "Gosh, this is great. You know, I like to piddle around in the kitchen. Maybe you can give me the recipe before I leave. That is, if it's not some family secret or something."

"Secret. No-o." Cecilia-Marie shook her head.

"It's Haitian," Titan cut in. Essence couldn't read his body language or his tone, but there was something there Essence was certain she hadn't seen or heard before.

"You're Haitian?" Essence looked at Titan.

"He is Haitian." Cecilia-Marie took over. "His mother is my daughter, Babette-Michelle. He is American, too," she added. "But his Haitian roots will not be forgotten."

"Not if you have anything to do with it," Titan replied.

"And I do," she confirmed. "What about you? Where are your people from?"

"My mother—her name is Sadie—was born in Alabama. She was raised by her sister." Then Essence said softly, "She didn't know much about her mother."

"And she's not with you anymore," Cecilia-Marie said.

"No." Essence looked surprised. "At least not in body. It hasn't been a week since I buried her."

"My goodness. That's far too fresh." Cecilia-Marie looked concerned. "What are you doing down here without your family?"

Essence paused. "I was trying to do some connecting, but it, uhh . . ." She glanced at Titan. "It didn't quite work out."

"This is with your mother's side, or your father?" Cecilia-Marie asked.

"Father," Essence said, quickly. "Although I don't know much about him."

"Ohh," Cecilia-Marie said. "That can be an interesting place to be. Yes?"

Essence nodded. "Quite."

Cecilia-Marie pointed toward the ceiling. "But not insurmountable. These kinds of things can make you stronger, if they don't break you."

"It hasn't broken me yet," Essence replied, but she could feel her insides shivering.

"And you are what?" Cecilia-Marie looked her up and down. "Twenty-four? Twenty-five?"

"Twenty-nine," Essence said.

"Then you are beyond being broken," Cecilia Marie announced. "And you are right at the point where you can start building your strength with understanding."

"I was working on it." Essence's discouragement was obvious.

Cecilia-Marie placed her face close to Essence's. "Continue your work, for your sake if for nobody else's, huh?" She waited for a response.

Essence nodded. Her eyes brightened from the pressure of tears.

"And with that, shall we sit on the side porch?" Cecilia-Marie motioned. "There's a table out there, and we can enjoy our *pain patate* and some ginger tea?"

"I'd like that." Essence smiled. She decided she liked Cecilia-Marie Balan, too. "May I help you?" She picked up the plate of sweet potato cakes.

"Why, thank you. Grab the tea glasses, Titan," Cecilia-Marie instructed. "Then open the door for Essence. I'll be out in a moment."

With her hands full, Essence went and stood by the door.

"And by the way," Cecilia remarked, "I already know the answer to my question about you, Essence. So remember, if you need to get away from me, the barn is a wonderful place to do it."

Their gazes held, and Essence felt a tightening around

her heart. At that moment, it didn't matter that Cedric Johnson didn't accept her. Cecilia-Marie did, and for some reason
that meant a lot. "The feeling is mutual," she replied.

Cecilia-Marie smiled, then turned away.

Essence felt lighter before Titan walked over. The look
in his eyes diminished some of that. It was a look of distrust.
Then it hit her. *He thinks I am trying to manipulate Cecilia-
Marie!* She could feel her anger. *Well, you go on thinking
just that.* She fumed. *And I'll see how I can help. Just to
drive you crazy.*

Essence let her glance slide toward Titan's grandmother
before she looked at Titan. "The door, please," she said,
never batting an eye.

Chapter Fifteen

Titan watched Essence and his grandmother laugh. It seemed in a matter of minutes, in a fashion only women can, they had become fast friends. At least that's what his grandmother thought. Titan wasn't so sure about Essence.

"Titan, how can you sit there so straight-faced?" Cecilia-Marie mocked him. "When Essence and I can barely control ourselves."

Titan didn't get a chance to answer, because Essence broke out in another gale of laughter. "Cecilia-Marie, you looked just like him when you did that."

"I know. That's because he looks like me." She stuck out her chin.

Essence looked at Titan, then back at his grandmother. "Welll?"

"No, really," Cecilia Marie insisted. "You want to see proof?"

Essence giggled. She could tell Titan didn't like it. He had been eyeing them for the past ten minutes, but she was having such a good time. Essence didn't want it to end. "Sure," she replied.

"Wait right here." Cecilia-Marie rose from the table. "I'll be right back."

Essence's smile remained as she watched Cecilia-Marie disappear into the house. She was actually grateful for the reprieve. The stitch in her side had become nearly unbearable thanks to her unrestrained laughter, and with Cecilia-Marie gone, if only for a short time, Essence believed she might have an opportunity to recover.

She looked at Titan. He was sitting back watching her. Essence turned away. She preferred looking at the blanket of flowers that surrounded the house. They were colorful and joyful, just like Cecilia-Marie.

"Seems like you're enjoying yourself," Titan commented.

She glanced at him. "I am."

Titan laced his fingers. "My grandmother is a wonderful woman."

"Exceptional," Essence replied.

He looked around. "She's lived here for as long as I can remember. And I've spent many a night in this house. It was built in 1901."

Essence looked at the porch. "It's a hundred and one years old? It's in great shape." She looked through the screen door into the house. "It's beautiful."

"It's like my grandmother's pride and joy," Titan replied, wondering why he had brought Essence there. "I understand this was nothing but a little shack when my grandparents got ahold of it. *Grandni* and my grandfather, Jean-Paul, practically built it with their own hands." Essence's eyes widened, and Titan noted how velvety they appeared. "My grandfather's family, the Dieuris, were pretty well off in Haiti. So my grandparents had some money when they came here. Still, when they arrived, they had to do whatever it took to get things off the ground. *Grand-père* Jean-Paul used to make furniture. That's why they built the shop in the back of the barn."

"Wow," Essence said, almost to herself. "They must have had a real bond coming from a different country, and working together like that toward the same dream. It must have been hard for her when he died." She glanced inside the house.

"Yes, it was hard," Titan said. "But she refused to move. She's stayed out here alone, creating her own world. Believing no harm will come to her here. Trusting everyone."

Their eyes locked.

Essence couldn't let the insinuation pass. "If you think I'm going to hurt your grandmother, why did you bring me here?"

"It was a spur-of-the-moment decision. I hope it was the right one."

"But you're not so sure, are you?"

Essence had never known anyone that she *knew* did not trust her. She realized how much Titan's distrust hurt.

"I've got it." Cecilia-Marie burst onto the porch carrying a cloth photo album. "I bet you recognize this, don't you, Titan?"

"Of course I do, *Grandni*. But I don't think Essence is interested in those old photographs."

Essence threw Titan an angry look.

Cecilia-Marie stopped. Her disappointment was immediate. "He's right. I didn't think to ask if you wanted to see a whole book of—"

"No," Essence said directly to Titan. "He's not right. He has no clue." She turned to Cecilia-Marie. "I'd love to see them."

"Really?" Her eyes were soft, unsure, the vulnerable eyes of old age. "You're not just humoring me?"

Essence warmed to her. "I wouldn't do that."

"I believe you wouldn't." Cecilia-Maria bounced back. "So don't worry, *mon petit*," Cecilia-Marie winked at Titan before she opened the album, "I've found a friend in this one."

Titan didn't look so sure as he crossed his arms.

Cecilia-Marie continued, "Now, this is a picture of me when I was younger. It was taken fifty-two, fifty-three years ago. So I was about your age, Essence. Do you see the resemblance?'' She motioned toward the picture, then pointed at Titan.

Essence looked at the photograph. "You were beautiful."

"I was, wasn't I?" Cecilia-Marie cocked her head.

"You still are." Titan touched his grandmother's hand.

Essence couldn't help but appreciate the gesture. She looked at Titan and said, "He's your grandson, all right."

Their eyes met, and Essence knew everything she was thinking and feeling was there.

"Yes, he is. And he's a handsome one."

Essence's mouth went dry. "He gets a lot of it from you." She placed the focus back on Cecilia-Marie.

"Thank you," Cecilia-Marie said. "Thank both of you. A woman never gets to be too old to hear that."

"This is a picture of Titan's parents before he was born," she continued. "And this is a picture of Titan. He's only two months old here."

"He looks so precious." The soft words tumbled out.

"He was," Cecilia-Marie said. "Titan was a special baby."

"*Grandni*, please." A silky brow wavered curiously.

"There's no need to be shy about it," Cecilia-Marie said. "You were a special baby. You were pulling yourself around the floor at five months, and you started talking at eleven months."

"I don't feel," Titan said, hurriedly, "I don't think anybody wants their baby pictures shown to the world."

"It's not the world I'm showing them to. It's only Essence." Cecilia-Marie leaned toward him. "And don't tell me you're not feeling shy. Your eyebrow did that little weird thing it's always done when you're feeling uncomfortable."

Essence sat back. She saw how Titan's eyebrow quivered. Could it be he was really feeling shy? Essence couldn't imagine that. But Cecilia-Marie appeared quite certain of it.

Cecilia-Marie turned the page. A photograph popped out and fell to the porch floor. Essence picked it up. It was a picture of Titan and a girl. They were teenagers. It appeared the photograph had been taken at some kind of dance. Essence placed it in front of Cecilia-Marie.

"Ohh, this one." Cecilia-Marie gave the picture a closer examination. "Titan, I think this is the only photograph you took at one of those dances."

"I think you're right." Titan ran his hand over his hair. "That's right."

Cecilia-Marie turned the photo over. "Janice Wren. That was her name. Now she"—she tapped the picture—"was your first love."

The corners of Titan's lips turned up. "When I look back on it, that's probably true."

"She was." Titan's grandmother nodded her head continuously.

"Why are *you* so sure, Cecilia-Marie?" Essence had to know.

"I know my grandson. And I can tell when someone has touched his heart." She cocked her head in a meaningful fashion and looked directly into Essence's eyes. "Plus my daughter told me, when these two parted ways, Titan was very unhappy for a while."

"Somehow I can't imagine that," Essence replied.

"And why not?" Titan butted in.

Essence simply looked at him.

"She was special," Titan said.

"What was so special about her?" Essence took the bait while Cecilia-Marie watched, quietly.

Titan paused, then replied, "She was pretty in a unique way."

"Pretty?" Essence made a face. "Being pretty or handsome doesn't make someone special. Doesn't make someone truly worth caring for. You can always find someone prettier or more handsome," Essence retorted.

"That's true. But back then I wasn't thinking so deeply." Titan licked his lips. "But it wasn't just the way she looked. Janice was one of the sincerest people I'd ever met. That's true to this day. She was a sweet, naive girl. Thought everyone was good, they just needed to be given a chance."

Jealousy spoke for Essence. "Well, if she was so perfect"—Essence couldn't contain herself—"why didn't you stay with her?"

"I was young. I didn't know the ways of women, back then." He searched Essence's eyes. "And an older, slicker guy got to her, and she ended up pregnant. I didn't see her much after that."

"Oh." Essence looked down. She imagined how much that would have hurt a young man being in love for the first time. Essence also empathized with the teenage girl whose life had been forever changed. "People make mistakes," she said softly. "Sometimes they get swept away by a wave of uncontrollable feelings, and for that moment you forget your hurts . . . your pain. But once it's over . . . the aftermath can be a killer." By the look on his face, Essence knew Titan understood.

Cecelia-Marie's telephone rang.

Chapter Sixteen

"Would you get that for me, Titan?" Cecilia-Marie asked. "I can feel my legs stiffening up from all that gardening."

Titan went inside. Moments later, he reappeared at the screen door. "It's Mr. Pete, *Grand-père's* friend. He said he's going to choke you, *Grandni*, for not telling him I was coming down."

Cecilia-Marie rose from her chair. "Mr. Pete, that old fibber. He knew you were coming. I told him so." Titan opened the door for her. "He's coming here for supper to see you." She walked past him. " I guess we're done out here. Would you two bring everything in?

"Sure," Essence said. She grabbed the used napkins and the plate of leftover *pain patate*. Titan picked up the glasses and the pitcher.

"You're a strange woman, Essence," Titan said, standing inches away.

"Janice Wren was special, and I'm strange. Do you always categorize women?"

"Don't know if I do." He seemed to think about it. "Probably not. Most women are pretty clear-cut. It's only when they're different that I bother to wonder."

Their eyes met. The flutter in her stomach from the night before returned as they continued to stare.

"When they're not quite what they appear to be," Titan continued.

Essence opened the door. "Seeing that you're a private detective, you should be able to figure these things out quickly." She let go of the knob just as Titan was walking through.

"Mr. Pete is coming just like we planned," Cecilia-Marie announced. "One of his nieces and her new husband are going to bring him over."

"Will I have time to take a dip in the creek?" Titan asked.

"Sure, if there's enough water in it," Cecilia-Marie replied. "This drought has been going on forever."

"I thought that water came from underground," Titan said.

"It does, and it's probably okay. But I haven't been down there for a while. I kind of stick close to the house," Cecilia-Marie said. "Why don't you go with him, Essence?"

"I don't think so," Essence replied a bit too quickly. She tried to cover up her uneasiness about being alone with Titan. "I didn't bring a swimsuit."

"That never stopped Titan before," Cecilia-Marie replied.

"And it won't stop me today." His eyes brightened.

"You haven't changed a bit." Cecilia-Marie closed her eyes and turned her head. "I'm going to lie down for a minute, Essence. Make yourself at home. The television is in there, and I've got some old records that you might find interesting. There's a record player in the corner."

"Thanks," Essence said. "I'll look through them."

Cecilia-Marie left the kitchen.

"You sure you don't want to . . . swim?" Titan asked.

"Positive." Essence walked over to the album rack and began to riffle through the covers. The next thing she heard was the front screen door closing. She turned around. Essence watched Titan take off his shirt by the door. He laid it across the rail next to a bath towel, then he removed his shoes. She couldn't help but admire the way he moved. Essence could tell Titan was comfortable with his body, and there was no reason he shouldn't be. Titan was magnificent . . . more than any man had a right to be. Essence watched him pick up the towel and start down the stairs.

The albums couldn't hold Essence's attention. Titan's nude torso interrupted her thoughts repeatedly, and visions of him swimming nude in a crystal-clear creek abounded. She turned on the television. Soon she was lost in an old Billy Dee Williams—Diana Ross movie, *Mahogany*. Billy and Diana were deep into a love scene when the screen door slammed shut.

"So, you like old movies," Titan said as he entered the room. Essence turned to acknowledge him. He was wearing the towel. She involuntarily traced with her eyes the hair on his chest and stomach to the place where it disappeared beneath the fluffy material. Essence quickly looked at the television screen again. "Yeah, I like them."

"Have you ever seen *Carmen Jones* with Dorothy Dandridge?"

Surprised, Essence turned back toward him. "You like old movies?"

Titan nodded. "That and *The River of No Return*, with Robert Mitchum and Marilyn Monroe. I know it doesn't have any Bloods in it, but I like it anyway."

"So do I," Essence confessed. "But I've got to say, that's not the kind of movie I'd expect a man to remember. What do you like about it, besides Marilyn?"

"The way Robert Mitchum saw beyond what Marilyn had been before he met her. She was a good woman, and Mitchum was able to act on that."

Essence exhaled. "Is that supposed to be a hint?" She played it up. "Do you think I can be reformed?"

"Do you need to be?" Titan returned.

"You seem to know everything. I would think you'd have the answer to that."

"Not everything. Just preliminary answers," Titan replied.

"Oh. Preliminary answers," Essence fumed. "And what did the prestigious Cedric Johnson tell you? No, let me guess." She got wild. "I'm a call girl who puts on exotic wigs and clothes and I take a man totally away from reality before I take his money."

Titan raised a knowing eyebrow.

Essence's face fell. "You've got to be kidding. My fa— Cedric told you that I was a . . . he did, didn't he?"

"Not really," Titan replied.

"So, you jumped to that conclusion all by yourself?"

He walked over to her. "Look . . . I don't know your whole story. The truth is, maybe Cedric doesn't, either. He's hired me to find out."

"But I told him the truth. Now I'm telling you the same thing. On her deathbed, my mother told me Cedric Johnson is my father."

Titan knelt down and searched her eyes.

"Why is it so hard for you to believe that? Do people usually lie when they know they're dying?" Essence tried to control a wave of tremors.

Titan didn't speak because he didn't trust his own eyes. During his career they had seen so much—melodramatic to comical acts, even realistic ones, but acts just the same. But this time he wanted so much to believe.

Essence looked at him. She knew he was going to kiss her. Essence wanted him to, and she watched his mouth drift slowly toward hers. It was a way to erase the divide between.

When the kiss ended, Titan said, "My father has known Cedric for a long time. And Cedric has hired me to do a job. What I might want to believe shouldn't come into this."

"A lot of things shouldn't be," Essence replied. "I shouldn't be here at your grandmother's house. I shouldn't have just kissed you. And what we did last night shouldn't come into it, either, but it did."

"And like you said, that was a mistake."

"I did say that, didn't I?" She sat back. "And now you have thoroughly convinced me that I was right."

A horn honked outside. Titan looked through the screen door. "I better get dressed. I think Mr. Pete has arrived."

"Please do," Essence said. "We professional girls have to be extra careful, you know. Some guys pay to be in a room with us wearing just a raincoat or a towel." Her eyes narrowed. "Who knows? If you stayed any longer, I might have to charge you."

She turned off the television as Titan left the room. *This man thinks I'm a hooker! He says Cedric didn't tell him that, but he must have said something along that line.* Then it really hit Essence. *Does my father really believe that about me? Oh, Mama.* She called on the only one who she thought might understand her pain.

"Did I hear a car horn?" Cecilia-Marie entered the room yawning.

"Yes, you did." Essence held it together. "I guess Mr. Pete is here."

Cecilia-Marie looked at her. "Is everything all right?"

"Not everything." Essence looked away. "But nobody ever promised that it would be."

"No, a perfect life isn't promised to us," Cecilia-Marie said. Essence could hear her sigh. "What's that grandson of mine done now?"

Essence shrugged her shoulders. She couldn't deny Titan was a part of the problem.

"Yes, I know there's something going on between you two. I knew it from the moment he pulled up to this house with you in the car. Titan has never brought a woman to my house. Not in the thirty-plus years he's been on this earth."

Chapter Seventeen

"Helloo in there." The greeting drifted into the house. "Are you just going to leave an old man standing on the porch?"

"I should leave you," Cecilia-Marie replied, "for telling Titan I never told you he was coming."

Essence watched her open the door for Mr. Pete. A middle-aged woman and man entered the house behind him.

"Got to keep some kind of excitement in your life, CeCe." Mr. Pete stopped near Cecilia-Marie and opened his arms.

She remained standing with her arms folded, as if she were trying to make up her mind if she wanted to hug him or not. Finally, Cecilia-Marie gave in. "I'll accept that excuse for your being a busybody this time."

"Hold on there, Mr. Pete," Titan said when he walked in. "My grandmother doesn't need you to bring that kind of excitement to her life."

"Oh, boy." Cecilia-Marie brushed him off.

But Titan continued. "I'm protector of this treasure now that *Grand-père* is gone."

"Titan!" A huge smile lit Mr. Pete's wizened face. He stuck out his hand. Titan shook it vigorously as Mr. Pete patted his arm. Eventually Mr. Pete's hand landed on Titan's shoulder.

"My God, boy, you pretty strong there, aren't you? You must be pumping iron, as the young people say. And just as good-looking as they come."

"Great to see you, too, Mr. Pete. And you're dressed as sharp as ever."

Mr. Pete touched his white hat. "It's in my blood, Titan. It's in my blood." He stretched out his arm. "Let me introduce my family, here. This is my niece Veronica, and her husband, Charles Moore. They've been married all of two weeks now."

Hellos and congratulations were exchanged.

"And we've got a guest, too," Cecilia-Marie said. "Essence came down with Titan." She motioned for Essence to join them.

"Hello, everybody," Essence said, feeling awkward.

The cycle of greetings repeated.

"So, you came here with Titan." Mr. Pete made a show of rubbing his chin. "Do I smell something brewing?"

"I don't know," Titan replied. "Do you?"

They both laughed.

"But seriously now, son. How old are you? Twenty-six? Twenty-seven?"

"No, Mr. Pete. I'm thirty-three years old."

"Thirty-three?" Mr. Pete leaned back. "And way past time for your getting serious."

Essence glanced at Titan. He looked at her, then looked at Mr. Pete.

"Unck, you don't know their business," Veronica jumped in. "You've hooked them up all tight and you don't know what's going on between them."

"I know well enough," Mr. Pete said. "Nobody's told me, but when one part of you fails, another part kicks in. And I can sense something serious from a mile away. I knew about y'all long before you knew, didn't I?"

Charles grinned. "He sure did."

"I forgot about that." Veronica's eyes shone with love as she pecked her husband on the lips.

Cecilia-Marie took Mr. Pete's arm. "You come in here before you start something you can't finish."

"All right." He walked beside her. "I don't know why everybody's feeling nervous about what I said. I'll try to behave, but just like dressing sharp, is part of me. So is speaking the truth."

Essence wondered what Mr. Pete meant by "when one part of you fails, another part kicks in." Then she knew as she watched Cecilia-Marie guide Mr. Pete into the kitchen area. Mr. Pete was blind.

"Mr. Pete, I didn't realize—" Titan began, but stopped when his grandmother placed her finger up to her lips.

"What's going on?" Mr. Pete asked abruptly. "I can't see, but I know you well, Cecilia-Marie Balan. So you stop that. Y'all be trying to protect me, and I don't need no protecting. The boy didn't know I was blind because you didn't tell him. Didn't you think he'd find out soon enough?"

Cecilia-Marie looked embarrassed. "Of course I knew."

"Well, now I've said it, and now everybody here knows, and we can move on. I remember how folks used to do poor Mrs. Weaver. Me included. We acted like she was deaf and dumb because she was blind. Now, I know for sure blind doesn't mean deaf and dumb. And I tell you what, like Helen Keller said, 'Everything has its wonders, even darkness and silence, and I learn, whatever state I may be in, therein to be content.' Is everybody in this room as content with life as I am?"

"Very." Veronica snuggled up to Charles.

"You two don't count," Mr. Pete replied. "Newly married folks live in a whole different reality than everybody else."

"What about you, CeCe?" Mr. Pete lowered himself into the chair.

"I'm fine. Just getting old and wishing my body was as content as it used to be."

"You've spoken some truth there," Mr. Pete said. "Titan and . . . what was your name? Atta?"

"Essence."

"Titan and Essence can't use that excuse. Youth is with them and, as usual, wasted on the young. Are you two pretty content?"

"It's been better," Essence replied. "But of course it could be worse."

"Oh, my goodness." Mr. Pete shook his head. "Titan, I don't know what you've done to this woman to have her talking this way. She don't know if she's going or coming. You got to be clearer, boy."

Blind or not, it was uncanny how right Mr. Pete was. Essence walked over to the screen door and looked out. She couldn't stand everybody's eyes on her.

"Leave it to you, Mr. Pete, to be in here no more than five minutes and stirring up enough stuff for a lifetime," Cecilia-Marie said.

"I'd rather be a catalyst than be forgotten," Mr. Pete replied.

"Catalyst, my eye," Cecilia-Marie replied. "What about a bomb?"

Everybody laughed except for Cecilia-Marie. She chuckled softly.

"Let me ask you something," Charles's country voice cut in. "Do you live in Orlando?"

Essence turned. He was speaking to her. "No, I don't."

"Seems like I've seen you in Orlando," Charles continued.

"I go there from time to time," Essence replied.

"What you doing asking about Orlando?" Veronica flipped her hand onto her hip. "I hope you haven't been there recently. I told you to stay from up there. You end up going down to Paramoor."

"I ain't been up there recently, baby." Charles tried to kiss her cheek, but Veronica turned her head.

"You better not. Or the candy counter is going to be closed. Make me mad and I'll close the whole store."

"Goodness," Mr. Pete said. "She done threatened the man with closing the candy store."

"Baby, I told you I haven't been down there, so don't start talking crazy."

"What's Paramoor?" Titan asked.

Veronica gave Essence the eye. "An old neighborhood where you can buy whatever you want, including women."

Essence's eyes widened. She looked at Titan. She could see a muscle in his jaw going to town.

"I've never been to Paramoor," Essence said. "I've never heard of it."

Veronica pulled Charles's earlobe.

"Oww. Go on, baby. Stop messin' around."

"You live down here?" Mr. Pete asked.

"I live in Tampa, but I was born in Birmingham," Essence replied. "Sometimes I go to Orlando to shop." She included the information for Titan's benefit.

"I used to go to Birmingham quite I bit," Mr. Pete replied. "I'm a truck driver. Birmingham is where I heard of Titan's grandfather, Jean-Paul. Another man, who had a route that included central Florida, told me about this furniture he had made. He was so pleased with it all, that I decided to check it out. It was good stuff. I still have mine to this day. The rest is history." Mr. Pete stroked his hairline. "Came down here and saw this place, and I ended up buying me some land and building a house. I got relatives in Birmingham, too." Mr. Pete paused. "That's where your parents are, aren't they, Titan?"

"Yes." Titan looked at Essence. "They're in Birmingham."

"You still live there?" Mr. Pete tilted his head and waited for the answer.

"No, I live in Memphis."

"Ohh. Is that where you two met?" Mr. Pete trudged on.

"No," Titan replied. "Actually, we met in Orlando." His steely gaze rested on Essence.

"Come to think about it, I kind of like that place," Mr. Pete said. "Not Orlando, Birmingham. In fact, a cousin of mine is a principal at one of the schools there. Samuel is his name. Boy, and if you think I talk a lot, you ain't met Samuel.'' He chuckled. ''Ye-es. Samuel had plans of getting involved with the school board, heading that up, and moving on deeper into politics. He was really into that kind of stuff.''

''Do you know if he ever did?'' Essence asked. ''From the limited experience I've had with politicians, you have to have a certain kind of stomach for that business.'' She hoped Titan caught her inference.

''You know, I don't know if he did.'' Mr. Pete looked puzzled. ''I would think some of my folks would have told me if he'd really done well. But I agree with you; politics can be a rotten business. I don't know if it's the business that turns the politicians bad or if politics attracts bad people.''

''I would think there's some good politicians, too, it's just not the easiest business in the world,'' Cecilia-Marie said. ''Titan, isn't the guy we talked about earlier, uhh ... Cedric Johnson, in politics now?''

''Yes, he is. He's a city councilman,'' Titan said. ''He's going to be running for state representative.''

''Is this a black man you're talking about?'' Mr. Pete asked.

''Yes, he's black,'' Cecilia-Marie replied. ''He's a friend of my son-in-law, Titan's father.''

''You know, I believe I met him some years ago. He was one of the first black councilmen in that city, wasn't he?''

''That's what I understand,'' Titan said.

''Sure, I've heard of him,'' Mr. Pete continued. ''Actually, I ate at a fund-raiser held for him. That's where I met him. He was a really nice man. Seemed sincere. Had a pretty wife, too. Boy, she cooked some dangerous catfish in this huge black kettle they had stoked up for the event.''

''Vivian cooked catfish?'' Essence was surprised.

''I forgot her name,'' Mr. Pete said. ''But they seemed to be a good couple. He was a hard worker. She appeared to be, and from the buzz around him, he was doing quite a bit in that community. People really appreciated it.''

Essence crossed her arms. Against her better judgment,

she felt a strange sense of pride. "So, you think he was one of the exceptions? You think he was a good politician?"

Mr. Pete thought for a moment. "I think people thought so. But power can be a strange disease. You don't know you're eaten up with it until you look at your life, and see your main motivation is to keep the power, no matter the cost."

Chapter Eighteen

"All this talk of power and politics." Cecilia-Marie sighed. "It's enough to make a person tired."

"And hungry," Mr. Pete added.

"But you're the one who's doing all the talking. If you're so hungry, I'd think you'd say so," Cecilia-Marie said.

Mr. Pete chuckled. "I just did."

"And he wonders why I don't invite him over more often." Cecilia-Marie got up. "If I did, my blood pressure would be sky-high. Sky-high, do you hear me?"

"Ohh, stop complainin', CeCe. You're always trying to get me over here to eat some of your foreign food."

Cecilia-Marie shook her finger. "You keep telling those fibs and you're not going to get anything to eat," she warned. "You know if you could drive you'd be over here every day sitting at my table." She peered inside one of the pots.

Mr. Pete looked sheepish. "I think I better hush or she might not feed me."

"Thank God he's smarter than he looks," Cecilia-Marie remarked.

"Something smells real good," Charles said. He leaned over and kissed Veronica's shoulder. Veronica looked displeased, but Essence could tell she was already coming around. Titan got up and joined his grandmother at the stove.

"It sure does smell good. What are we having?"

"*Aubergine au crabe.*"

"Crabs and eggplant," Titan translated.

"*Griot.*"

"Mm,mm,mm. That sounds too strange. I don't know if I want any," Mr. Pete teased.

"He's just saying that because it's his favorite and he doesn't want nobody else to eat any," Cecilia-Marie said.

"What is *griot?*" Charles looked reluctant.

"Fried pork." Cecilia-Marie uncovered another dish.

"And in this one we have *riz et pois coles,*" Titan continued to translate. "Rice with red beans."

Essence liked the way Titan spoke French. As he stood there in his shorts and black T-shirt, Essence realized there were many things she liked about Titan Valentine. But she resented his need to see her in a bad light.

"And last but not least," Cecilia-Marie announced, "fried plantains."

"A feast for a king." Mr. Pete rubbed his hands. "So let's get started."

Essence helped set the table. On several occasions she tried to make eye contact with Titan, but he avoided it. When they settled in, Charles and Veronica sat on one side of the table, Essence and Titan on the other. Cecilia-Marie and Mr. Pete sat on the ends.

"Would you like for me to fix your plate, Mr. Pete?" Essence offered.

"I'd appreciate that," he replied.

"Do you want some of everything or—"

"I don't want an empty spot on my plate," Mr. Pete instructed.

Essence couldn't help but smile. She spooned up a large portion of *griot,* then reached for the plantains. Accidentally, her hand touched Titan's. Their eyes met. Essence was surprised to see so much anger. *What's he angry about?* Then she knew. *He thinks Charles has seen me in Orlando. In what was it called? Paramoor?* Essence finished Mr. Pete's plate just as Veronica completed her own. Charles was just sitting there.

"Are you going to eat?" Veronica asked.

"Yeah, I guess so," Charles replied. His gaze roamed from one dish to another.

She elbowed him. "Don't be like that. We got all this food here. You got to eat something." Veronica picked up his plate and looked around the table. "All Charles eats is hamburgers."

"If that's what I like, that's what I like," Charles retorted.

"Well, what you come here for? We could have dropped you off at Burger King." Veronica rolled her eyes. "Don't embarrass me, Charles Moore."

"I ain't trying to embarrass you, baby. I don't know about this stuff."

"Why don't you try the fried pork and rice and beans?" Cecilia-Marie suggested amiably. "That's pretty simple."

"Okay." Charles turned his big eyes on Cecilia-Marie. "I don't mean to disrespect you, Mrs. Balan."

"There's no problem, Charles. I understand," Cecilia-Marie replied.

"How long you going to be here, Titan?" Mr. Pete piped up.

"Until tomorrow."

"Will Essence's car be ready by then?" Cecilia-Marie inquired.

Essence wondered the same thing. Titan's tone had been so final, as if he couldn't wait to get rid of her.

"Did your car break down?" Mr. Pete asked.

"No," Essence said. "I was involved in a car pileup on I-4. My car didn't get hit, but it got drenched in gasoline from a truck that was really smashed up. Titan gave me a ride. They had blocked off the highway, so we couldn't drive through to Tampa."

"So you two met on the highway," Veronica replied.

"I met Titan in Orlando as he said." Essence tried to

hold on to her patience. It was obvious Veronica hadn't gotten past the earlier conversation.

"So, you've known each other for a long time?" Veronica chewed slowly.

"Long enough," Essence replied, very aware of Titan's silence.

"Stop grilling her, Veronica. That husband of yours ain't going nowhere no time soon," Mr. Pete told her. "He can't keep his hands off of you long enough."

"I done told her, I haven't been down to Paramoor, pretty much since I met her," Charles defended himself.

"Pretty much?" Veronica nearly dropped her fork in her plate.

"Don't break CeCe's china now. She's been nice today, but you don't know her like I do," Mr. Pete warned. "Don't make her show that other side."

"Mr. Pete, I don't know what I'm going to do with you," Cecilia-Marie said.

He lifted his plate. "Hopefully, give me some more plantains . . . please."

Essence was glad the conversation had shifted once again, but now Titan and Veronica weren't the only two at the table feeling angry. *He just sat there quietly while that woman practically interrogated me. Thanks a lot.* She tried not to roll her eyes. *So, you don't have anything to say? I'll see about that.*

Chapter Nineteen

"Anybody for dessert?" Cecilia-Marie asked.

"I couldn't if you paid me." Mr. Pete sat back.

Essence shook her head. "It was wonderful, but I don't have room for anything else."

"What kind of dessert is it?" Charles seemed to prepare himself for the worst.

"Chocolate cake," Cecilia-Marie replied. But the set of her jaw revealed her patience was wearing thin. "Something everybody knows."

"Want to share some cake with me, Boo?" Charles was oblivious to his hostess's annoyance.

Veronica batted her eyes. "I guess so."

"How about you, Titan?" Cecilia-Marie asked. "You want some of your *titi*'s cake?"

"Not now, *Grandni*. But I'm sure I'll be back in here later on. The food shouldn't have been so good," Titan praised her. "Then I wouldn't have eaten so much."

Essence listened as the conversation drifted from favorite desserts to favorite movies. The more everyone talked, the more Essence talked herself into giving Titan, and therefore her *father* what they deserved. *They want to believe the worst . . . then they deserve to have it. Titan will have more than enough to tell them when I'm done. That is, if he has the nerve. And hopefully they'll both realize people's lives aren't to be examined like flies under a microscope.*

Essence watched Titan charm his grandmother and everyone else at the table. He was smooth and gorgeous doing it. She tried not to think how big of an influence her own hormones had on her scheme. Sitting so close to Titan, smelling his cologne, feeling him, made her strongly aware of her own needs . . . needs that had taken a backseat during her mother's illness and death. Titan could probably bring any woman's desires forcefully to the surface, Essence thought, just as he had everyone at the table hanging on his every word. When you were a man like Titan, people admired you and wanted to please you. And he gave them what they wanted. He gave them all what they wanted, except for her. *For me there's only anger.* She couldn't appreciate it. *I'm going to leave a lasting impression on Titan and my biological father if it kills me. And it will be the biggest impact I've had on Cedric Johnson since I've been on this planet.*

Essence and Cecilia-Marie began to clear the table. Titan took Mr. Pete on the side porch. From the corner of her eye Essence watched Veronica suck the last vestiges of chocolate from her fingers. Charles watched as well. No, Essence thought, watched was not the proper word. From his breathing and the glint in his eye, it was clear Charles experienced Veronica's actions on some other level.

"Why don't you go wash your hands?" He leaned in closer. "I'll come and help."

Veronica looked smug. "I don't know if I want your help."

"Come on now, Boo." He tried to whisper. "You done got Willie all excited."

Veronica almost giggled. She stopped when Essence returned to get more dishes. Before Essence walked away, she heard Veronica say, "Willie's going to be waiting for a long, long time if I find out you've been lying to me."

"Baby, I ain't been lying to you." Charles almost got loud. "I've been bringing it all home. You know that."

Essence was fascinated with the way Veronica toyed with Charles. Veronica knew what she was doing, but Charles was clueless. Or else his desire for her simply overpowered everything else. Not that Essence thought Charles was the brightest bulb in the pack, but Veronica's manipulation of him was nothing less than artful. Begrudgingly, Essence knew she could learn a lot from a woman like Veronica.

"Come on," Charles urged. "Let's go to the bathroom."

Veronica looked him in the eyes. "Do you need any help, Mrs. Balan?"

Essence thought Charles would burst until Cecilia-Marie replied, "No, I think Essence and I have everything under control."

"All right. Where's your bathroom? I want to wash some of this chocolate off my hands."

Cecilia-Marie turned around. "Go straight to the back. It'll be on your right."

"I think I'll go with you, baby, I need to wash my hands, too," Charles said, springing out of his seat.

After Essence witnessed Charles give Veronica's butt a big squeeze, she joined Cecilia-Marie at the sink.

"I'm glad they finally went in there," Cecilia-Marie said. "I didn't want to have to put them out of my dining area."

Essence was embarrassed. "You could hear them?"

"Not all of it. But all you had to do was take one look at Charles and you knew he would have laid in the middle of the plates on the table, if Veronica had agreed to join him."

"How does a woman get such control over a man?" Essence really wondered.

"Using what comes naturally." Cecilia-Marie massaged her lower back. "And a little drama never hurts."

Essence realized Cecilia-Marie was in pain. "Why don't you go out there and join Titan and Mr. Pete? I can wash and dry the rest of these dishes. I'll leave them here on the counter since I don't know where to put them."

Cecilia-Marie nodded. "I think I will sit down. These muscle spasms hurt like the devil."

"Well, you go ahead. It won't take me but a minute," Essence assured her.

Cecilia-Marie went outside. Moments later, Titan walked in. He joined Essence at the sink.

"My grandmother thinks you could use some help."

Essence made a point of not turning around. "I guess you can put the dishes away. I assume you know where they go."

"I can do that," Titan replied. "But I need to wash my hands first."

Essence started to warn him about the Moores, but she changed her mind. What would she say? How would she say it? Sex was the most natural thing in the world, but not the easiest to talk about—at least not with Titan. Maybe it was because he'd seen her at her weakest moment . . . had her there.

She looked down the hall where Titan and the Moores had disappeared. The thought of Titan standing outside the bathroom door listening made Essence's sexual center contract. If Charles's and Veronica's actions at the dining table were any indication of their exuberance, Essence was sure there was only a certain amount of keeping it down they could do. Quickly, she turned back to the sink when she heard Titan coming.

"Perhaps I should use this sink."

It's either now or never, girl, Essence thought. She turned telltale eyes on him. "What happened? Three would have been a crowd?"

Titan squinted. "You could say that."

Essence washed another plate. "Sometimes more is better, you know."

"Really? So, are you telling me you know all about that?"

Essence rubbed the suds off of her hands in a stroking fashion. "Come on, don't we all?"

Titan stared at her. "This is quite a change. What happened to the Essence who was trying to convince me of her innocence?''

She sighed. ''I got tired.'' Essence gave him her sexiest half smile. ''And who says a threesome can't be innocent? It's according to what role you're playing. Now, how about putting up some of these dishes?''

Titan stood there for a moment, as if he were putting it all together. Finally, he dried a few plates and put them away. He came back to the sink. ''Well, well. So, the real Essence Stuart has just stood up.''

''In the flesh,'' Essence replied. She reached for another glass. Her body intimately brushed Titan's. Essence could feel him stiffen.

''And when you make a change, you just jump right on in there, don't you?''

Essence looked at him with sultry eyes. She removed the drying towel from his hand. ''Change? You'll know it when I really change.'' She ran her index finger up and down the zipper of his pants. ''You won't have to ask me.'' Essence turned back to the sink.

''Don't play with fire, Essence, you might get burned,'' Titan said from behind her. She could hear him breathe.

Essence dunked another glass into the suds. ''Maybe. But I've sampled that fire already, and believe me, I could turn it up a few degrees. It just takes the right set of circumstances.''

Titan moved closer. ''Meaning what? Money?'' His body was inches away.

Essence looked over her shoulder at him, into his face. A part of her wanted to say, *Is this really what you think of me?* It would have been comical if it wasn't so ridiculous. It was too bad Titan had bought into her father's ploy. At another time, another place, Essence could have liked him, liked him a lot. She feared when she was done there would be no room for that. *I guess I am a little like my old man. I can't just lie down. I've got to be able to say I had some say in this. Some power.*

Essence truly believed Cedric Johnson's motivation was power. He wanted to keep it. He shunned her mother out of fear of losing it, and he would destroy Essence's reputation for the same reason. "Not so fast, big boy. I never discuss business at the kitchen sink."

Titan just stood there. "I see."

Once again, Essence knew Titan was angry. She saw it in his eyes. She also saw desire and her chance to get really even. "But that doesn't matter, because I have no intention of doing business with you. Last night was just a freebie." She paused meaningfully. "But now that I know the truth, I don't want anything to do with you. And my father won't get off easily, either. So you tell him for me, if he doesn't treat me nice, I'll go straight to the media with my story. And I mean all of it."

"I could use something to drink," Charles said from somewhere behind them.

Titan nor Essence moved. The energy between them was like mortar. Finally, Titan picked up another dish and moved away. Essence felt woozy.

"Is there anything to drink around here?" Charles pressed.

"There's more fruit punch," Essence replied. "And I think I saw a couple of cans of soda in the refrigerator." Her voice quivered, just a little.

"I think Charles was looking for something stronger than that. No doubt you can relate." Titan gave her a steely look as Veronica walked in.

"Now, what do you want, baby?" Veronica patted Charles's face.

Essence glanced at her. Veronica wore her sexual escapade just like her lipstick and powder, fresh and right up front.

Charles grinned like a satisfied kid. "Boo, you know me. I'm ready for something to drink now, baby. Titan, man, you read me right."

"But I got bad news for you," Titan replied, looking at Essence. "I don't think you're going to find anything like that around here."

"He sure won't," Cecilia-Marie called from the porch.

Titan and Essence looked at each other. They wondered the same thing. If Cecilia-Marie heard that, how much of their conversation had she heard?

"I guess we're going to have to make a trip to the liquor store," Charles said as a cell phone melody played.

"What in the world is that?" Cecilia-Marie asked.

"Nothing but my cell phone, *Maman,*" Titan said.

Chapter Twenty

It was a bad time for the telephone to ring. Titan hoped it wasn't a business call. He hadn't recovered from what had gone down with Essence. His heart was still pumping. But when Titan thought about it, what she'd said didn't seem right. It didn't seem right at all. *I know people. My business is to study them. Watch them. And unless she's got some kind of multiple personality . . . it was too perfect. Like she was playing a role.* He stuck his hand in his pocket and pulled out his cell phone. He flipped it open. "Hello."

"Hello, Titan."

"What's up, Dad?" Titan looked down. "How's it going?"

"Pretty good," James replied. "How about with you?"

"Doing okay." It wasn't true. Titan felt like things had taken a turn for the worse. He should have been pleased that Essence had verified his suspicions. Instead it messed with him . . . messed with him real bad. *Just when I was beginning to believe her. Doubted that Cedric was right. That's why I got angry with the whole Orlando thing and Paramoor. I wanted Cedric to be wrong.*

"Cedric called me."

An important message from the ARABESQUE Editor

Dear Arabesque Reader,

Because you've chosen to read one of our Arabesque romance novels, we'd like to say "thank you"! And, as a special way to thank you, we've selected four more of the books you love so well to send you for FREE!

Please enjoy them with our compliments, and thank you for continuing to enjoy Arabesque...the soul of romance.

Karen Thomas
Senior Editor,
Arabesque Romance Novels

Check out our website at
www.arabesquebooks.com

3 QUICK STEPS
TO RECEIVE YOUR "THANK YOU" GIFT
FROM THE EDITOR

Send this card back and you'll receive 4 FREE Arabesque
novels! The introductory shipment of 4 Arabesque novels – a
$23.96 value – is yours absolutely FREE!

There's no catch. You're under no obligation to buy anything.
You'll receive your introductory shipment of 4 Arabesque
novels absolutely FREE (plus $1.99 to offset the costs of
shipping & handling). And you don't have to make any
minimum number of purchases—not even one!

We hope that after receiving your books you'll want to
remain an Arabesque subscriber. But the choice is yours to
continue or cancel, anytime at all! So why not take us up on
our invitation to receive 4 Arabesque Romance Novels, with
no risk of any kind. You'll be glad you did!

Call us
TOLL-FREE
at 1-800-770-1963

THE EDITOR'S "THANK YOU" GIFT INCLUDES:

- 4 books absolutely FREE (plus $1.99 for shipping and handling)
- A FREE newsletter, *Arabesque Romance News*, filled with author interviews, book previews, special offers, and more!
- No risks or obligations. You're free to cancel whenever you wish... with no questions asked.

BOOK CERTIFICATE

Yes! Please send me 4 FREE Arabesque novels (plus $1.99 for shipping & handling). I understand I am under no obligation to purchase any books, as explained on the back of this card.

Name _____

Address _____ Apt. _____

City _____ State _____ Zip _____

Telephone ( ) _____

Signature _____

Offer limited to one per household and not valid to current subscribers. All orders subject to approval. Terms, offer, & price subject to change. Offer valid only in the U.S.

Thank you!

AN092A

Accepting the four introductory books for FREE (plus $1.99 to offset the cost of shipping & handling) places you under no obligation to buy anything. You may kee the books and return the shipping statement marked "cancelled". If you do not cancel, about a month later we will send 4 additional Arabesque novels, and you will be billed the preferred subscriber's price of just $4.00 per title. That's $16.00 for all 4 books for a savings of 33% off the cover price (Plus $1.99 for shipping and handling). You may cancel at any time, but if you choose to continue, every month we'll send you 4 more books, which you may either purchase at the preferred discount price. . . or return to us and cancel your subscription.

THE ARABESQUE ROMANCE CLUB: HERE'S HOW IT WORKS

ll...l.lll....lll.l.l.l.l.l.l.l.l.l.l.l.l.l.l.l..l.l

ARABESQUE ROMANCE BOOK CLUB

P.O. Box 5214

Clifton NJ 07015-5214

PLACE
STAMP
HERE

"He did?" Titan glanced at Essence.

"He told me that woman showed up at the family reunion."

"Yeah, she did." Titan wandered toward the door. He could feel Essence's eyes on him. He stepped out onto the porch with Cecilia-Marie and Mr. Pete.

"She's got some nerve," James railed. "I'm surprised Cedric didn't lose it."

"He was surprised, all right. But you know Cedric, he knows how to keep up appearances."

James paused. "Yes, he does." He paused again. "But for this woman to come there and try to wreak havoc with his family, that's real low. I'm sure you'll be able to find plenty on her."

"Actually, Essen—she handled herself well." Titan walked down the stairs and out into the yard.

"Really? Cedric said she tried to cause a scene at the pool."

"She approached him at the pool," Titan replied. "Cedric was talking to me, so I heard the whole thing. She told him she didn't want to cause any problems with his family, and when Cedric got a little upset, Essence calmed him down. She didn't cower from him, but she wasn't for a scene, either."

"Cedric told me you had gotten a little close to her for business purposes, but . . . uh . . . I'm almost ready to ask you whose side you're on," James replied.

Titan closed his eyes. "I didn't realize I was picking a side. I'm simply telling you what happened."

"But of course you've picked a side. Our side." James's forceful personality reared up. "That woman is trying to wreck Cedric's family, which could ultimately wreck his career. We're not playing with beans here. This is real money and human life."

Right, Pops. I can always count on you to mention money. "That's right. I couldn't agree with you more when it comes to the human life aspect. From what *Grandni* told me, it's possible that Cedric was the kind of man that ran around.

Which means it's possible that he could have had a child by another woman.''

"What's Mama Cecilia got to do with this?" James's anger bubbled.

"We talked a little, that's all. She remembers the time Cedric came down here with you to drop me off. She told me what she felt about him."

"Now, wait a minute. Who are you investigating? Cedric? Or this woman who's parading around pretending she's his daughter?" James snapped.

"Dad, you know who I have been hired to investigate."

"Well, it doesn't sound like you know it. Maybe this woman has been able to get to you and you don't know it."

Titan looked out over the flowers. "I'm not a child. I know when I've been gotten to." *And I have.*

James paused again. "You know, although I love her, Mama Cecilia and I haven't always seen eye to eye. But sometimes your grandmother can get into the middle of stuff that doesn't have anything to do with her. How long you going to be there?"

"We'll probably get out of here sometime tomorrow," Titan replied.

"We? Oh, you took somebody down there with you?"

"I ended up bringing somebody." Titan hadn't looked forward to this moment.

"Who?"

"Essence Stuart. She was involved in a car pileup—"

"You've got that woman down there?"

"Didn't I just say that?" Titan's patience disappeared.

"What the hell are you doing, son?"

"Look, she was stranded on the highway. What was I supposed to do? Leave her there?"

"You could have," James retorted. "And how do you know she didn't set you up for that?"

Titan gave a short laugh. "What? So, I guess on top of having a crystal ball and knowing that I was coming that way, she staged the multiple car pileup, too. This is getting ridiculous, Pops."

"I'll say it is. A man who is my lifelong friend, and practically your uncle, has called on you for help, and you end up getting in bed with the enemy. And if it hasn't literally happened, I bet she'll have you in there soon enough. She's a whore, Titan. That's what whores do."

Titan could feel his teeth grinding. *In my business, I've probably known more whores and prostitutes than you've ever known.* "Look, Dad, I don't need to hear this."

"This woman could bring Cedric's entire political machine down with her lies. That means that's money out of his pocket and out of mine."

"And that's what this is really all about, isn't it? You and Cedric losing money."

"That's what it comes down to, son."

"Yeah, for you I guess there is no other answer. I thought it was also about the truth. About Cedric protecting his name, his reputation, his family." Titan's anger at feeling second to money in his father's life flared. "But I guess over the years he's become more like you."

"And what's that supposed to mean?"

"Money comes first. Money and power come first with you, Dad. It always has."

"Look, son." James sounded reconciliatory. "I know how women can be. God gave them something that can turn a man's mind, and when they really realize what they have, there's nothing more dangerous. But business is business, and this is important to Cedric, and to me, and therefore to you." He paused. "Because when your mother and I are gone, what we have will go to you, Michelle-Jeanne, and Wilhemina." James's voice turned hard. "I want you to get what we need on that woman. Maybe her being down there with you is a good thing. You might have some firsthand experiences. I say, whatever it takes. But I want you to help bring this woman down. Nothing else. I've got to go now. Good-bye." He hung up.

"I'm sure you do," Titan said to the dead line. He closed his phone. Titan knew his father was angry. But it was rare that he was the object of that anger. Over the years he'd tried to ensure he wasn't. Titan wanted his father's respect, his love. And sometimes he buckled down because of that, when his very nature cried out against it. That's why the conversation troubled him. Titan looked back at the house. He had spoken up for Essence, although he wasn't sure she deserved it. Either way, she didn't deserve to be a pawn in someone else's game. He saw enough of that in his work, and it wasn't pretty. Titan climbed onto the porch. He touched his grandmother's shoulder.

"Is everything all right?" Cecilia-Marie patted his hand.

"It's going to be," Titan said. He reentered the house.

"What was that all about?" Mr. Pete leaned in close to Cecilia-Marie.

"Something that's made Titan plenty hot. And it sounds like it involves that son-in-law of mine and his friends." Realization crossed her face. "Meaning that politician we were talking about earlier, Cedric Johnson. Seems like they've cooked up something that involves Essence."

"That's what it sounds like to me, too. Titan's in it, but he doesn't seem to be too happy about it."

"No, he doesn't." Cecilia-Marie frowned. "And I know you said people thought very highly of Cedric Johnson, but from what I remember, he was something else."

"What you mean?" Mr. Pete asked.

"With the women." Cecilia-Marie didn't bite her tongue.

"Oh, yeah," Mr. Pete replied. "He had a reputation for that, too."

Cecilia-Marie looked dissatisfied. "I heard Titan say James had managed to rub off on Cedric, and I think some of Cedric rubbed off on James, too. Babette never told me the whole story, but at one time she and Cedric's wife got close for a short while. I guess it was a pretty rough time for Cedric Johnson's wife. And Babette ended up asking me for some help." She looked down. "I gave her what she wanted."

"Children. It don't matter how old they get, they can always use some help. Meaning money," Mr. Pete replied.

"No, she didn't need any money."

"She didn't? What was it then?"

"You know I—"

"Aw, shoot. You and them dagnabbit herbs."

"They've helped your butt more than once."

"Well." Mr. Pete looked contrite. "I didn't say they didn't work. It's just that folks call all that stuff voodoo. Roots."

"Knowing about herbs, yes, is using roots, All plants have roots," Cecilia-Marie replied. "But it isn't voodoo and I should know."

"That's what I'm talking about," Mr. Pete replied. "Your being from Haiti and all . . . there's been some talk through the years—"

"And did you defend me? Or did you just sit back and let them walk all over me?"

"I spoke up for you as best I could," Mr. Pete said. "But folks just don't see it the same way you do."

Cecilia-Marie crossed her arms. "And I bet those same people's grandmothers and great grandmothers know as much about the plants as I do. Did they say they used voodoo?"

Mr. Pete shrugged. "Maybe."

"Then how ignorant of them." Cecilia-Marie got madder. "Folks all over this earth in all kinds of cultures—black, white, Hispanic, Asian—all know about using herbs for the body. Where do they think the bases for their medicines come from? A plastic bottle? No, they come from plants," she answered her own question.

"That's true. That's true. I—" Mr. Pete tried to get a word in and couldn't.

"And as far as *vodou* goes, and that's the proper pronunciation, it is a part of my people, but it doesn't mean every Haitian practices it. But even if a person does, they believe in one God who works through an army of *loa*, spirits. Does that sound familiar? God having his angels, God having his—"

Mr. Pete threw up his hands. "You don't have to convince me."

"Okay then, don't get me started." Cecilia-Marie sat back in her chair, but continued to talk under her breath. "People can get on my nerves."

"So, how about it, man?" Charles asked.

"How about what?" Titan was thinking about his father.

"Driving to the liquor store with me."

"At the moment that doesn't sound like too bad of an idea," Titan replied. "I could use a drink."

"You don't have to go to the liquor store right now," Veronica interjected. "Aren't we going to the club this evening?"

"Yeah, we're going," Charles replied. "But I thought Titan and I could run off and pick up a little something."

"We can't leave my uncle here. He'll be ready to go in a little while," Veronica protested.

"Naaw. I thought you'd stay here with them, and Titan and I would be right back."

Veronica gave him a look that said it all, and Charles replied with a sheepish expression. He seemed relieved when the screen door open and Veronica's attention shifted to Mr. Pete led by Cecilia-Marie.

"Y'all 'bout ready to go?" Mr. Pete asked.

"Sure," Veronica said. Charles nodded as if Mr. Pete could see him.

"It sure was good to spend some time with you, Titan." Mr. Pete reached out.

Titan took the old man's arm. "Same here." They started for the front door.

"Next time you come, you have to make sure your grandmother tells me. You know how she can be."

"Okay," Titan said with a halfhearted smile.

Mr. Pete continued, "Maybe you can take me fishing like I used to take you."

"Boy." Titan shook his head as he remembered those days. Yeah."

"The worm sure does turn, doesn't it?" Mr. Pete commented. "Uh,uh,uh. Never know what life's gonna throw at you. That's why you got to make your own decisions. That way you'll be better able to accept the consequences, because they'll be your consequences."

They got to the front door.

"Thanks for supper, Mrs. Balan," Veronica said.

"Yes, the food was good. As usual," Mr. Pete added.

"Sure was," Charles replied.

Veronica crossed the threshold. "Nice meeting you, Titan." She looked at Essence, and finally said, "You too, Essence."

Essence returned the good-bye.

"Too bad we weren't able to get that drink together, dawg," Charles said.

"Maybe another time," Titan replied.

"Yeah, too bad." Charles nodded. "I was looking forward to kickin' it with you a little bit. Hey! But what about tonight? You want to go to the club?"

"What club?" Titan's mind drifted to the telephone conversation with his father.

"It's a private club. We're having something tonight. I know you ain't got nothing else to do out here. You should come. Both of y'all."

"I think it's a good idea," Cecilia-Marie said. "I'm going to use some of my herbs and go to bed early. My back is killing me."

"See there," Charles replied. "Now you really don't have a reason not to come. We'll come back and pick you up."

Veronica looked at Essence, then turned so no one else could see her face.

"You don't have to do that," Titan said. "Why don't you give me the address and we'll find our way."

"So, you gon' come?" Charles insisted. "I'ma be looking for you now."

Titan thought about how badly he could use a drink. He looked at Essence. "How about it?"

She looked at him and lifted her chin. "Why not?"

Their eyes locked for a moment, his uncertain, hers defiant.

Chapter Twenty-one

Essence heard the screen door shut. She could feel Titan's eyes on her. Cecilia-Marie walked slowly ahead, rubbing and pressing her lower back. Essence was almost certain Titan was discussing her during his phone call, and it felt awful. *How in the world did I think acting like that was the right thing to do? I can only imagine what Titan said. Here I was trying to set him up for a big letdown and embarrass him so much he'd never tell a soul.* She held her lower lip between her teeth. *But I didn't think he'd talk to someone before I was done.*

"I've got to take something," Cecilia-Marie said. "Or my back will drive me crazy."

Crazy . . . that's how I feel right now. Essence watched Cecilia-Marie grab her back again and the therapist in her jumped in. "If it's that bad, could I give you a massage?"

"Oh, no." Cecilia-Marie looked back. "I'll do what I can for right now. Although sometimes my doctor sends me to this woman, and that's what she does for a living. She's a massage therapist."

"So am I," Essence replied. "I'm licensed. Been doing it for a while now."

Cecilia-Marie stopped. "Oh, really?" Her eyes brightened. "I didn't know that." She grimaced again. "In that case, would you mind?"

"Not at all," Essence replied. "I'd be glad to do it."

"I hope you don't mind, Titan," Cecilia-Marie said. "I know she came here with you, but I've been dominating a lot of her time. That's why it'll be good for you two to go out tonight. I'll feel better if you do."

Titan looked at Essence, then back at his grandmother.

"Is something wrong?" Cecilia-Marie asked.

After an extended pause, Essence said, "I don't think Titan has much confidence in my work." She gave him a stare. "But that's because he really doesn't know anything about it."

"I've got my ideas." Titan paused deliberately. "And this is my grandmother we're talking about." He turned real serious. "She's had some real problems. So when it comes to her physical needs—"

"Wait a minute," Cecilia-Marie barged in. "Stop discussing me like I'm not here. I can make my own decisions." She looked at Essence. "You say this is what you do for a living?"

"Yes, ma'am." She met Cecilia-Marie's gaze. "I wouldn't put you in jeopardy like that, Mrs. Balan."

"Well, that's all I need to hear." Cecilia-Marie continued toward the kitchen. She raised her hand. "Don't worry, *mon petit,* I'll be in good hands."

Essence turned away, too, but not before she saw deep uncertainty on Titan's face.

"I've got some stuff back here you can use," Cecilia-Marie said. "I make it up myself." She opened a cabinet door. There were shelves of dried plants in canning jars, and some smaller bottles of liquid.

"Where do you get all your herbs?" Essence asked.

"I grow them. I've got a nice herb patch right in the back of the house. It does pretty well."

"I would say so." Essence got closer to read the labels. Most were in patois, but she recognized the ones that weren't.

"We can make a kind of salve out of the valerian root and rub it on your back. And if you've got some passionflower, that would be great to mix in there." She continued to peruse the labels.

"What do you know about herbs?" Cecilia-Marie questioned with a smile.

Essence laughed. "Not much, I'm sure, in comparison to you. But I know what to do if I get a headache, or if I'm coming down with a cold. I've got a few things in my cabinet."

Cecilia-Marie called over her shoulder to Titan. "You've got a winner here. Don't let anybody tell you any different."

Essence appreciated Cecilia-Marie's support although Titan responded with a questionable look.

Cecilia-Marie reached for one of the bottles. "I made this liniment just for rubbing myself down. Like you said, it's got valerian root in it, but it's got kava kava root, wild lettuce, and"—she smiled at Essence again—"passionflower." She gave Essence the bottle. "Oo-oh." Cecilia-Marie grimaced. "I think I'll go in the room now and get ready. I'll call you when it's time to come in."

"All right," Essence replied.

Cecilia-Marie walked toward the bedroom.

Essence turned to Titan. "Look, just take my word for it, I know what I'm doing."

"You sound like it," Titan replied. "But you've sounded like a lot of things within the past hour or so."

Essence faced him straight on. "I'm aware of that, and that's all I got to say." She refused to defend herself any further. She had reacted out of hurt and anger. Deception wasn't her thing, and Essence hated that she had tried to play a game about which she knew nothing.

Titan came and stood in front of her. "This is not the time for pretending, Essence. This is serious business."

"Really? Like I didn't know that." Essence paused. "Well, let's see how serious I can be. I find out my biological father is having me investigated because he wants to pretend he's not my father. Or what about, I buried my mother

Sunday. This is Saturday. It'll be a week tomorrow. She was the closest person to me in this world. In this world. Do you hear me? Nobody was closer. When I was sad, full of joy, angry, sick ... so sick that even as a grown woman she bent over and bathed me in a tub like a baby." Essence wiped away a tear. "Do you hear me? Is that serious enough for you, Titan?"

"Essence." He reached for her.

She stepped back.

"I'm ready," Cecilia-Marie called.

"Coming." Essence turned and walked toward the bedroom. Titan just stood there. Before she closed the bedroom door, she heard him say, "What in the world have I gotten myself into?"

Not half as much as I have, Essence thought as she entered the bedroom. Her gaze wandered to a lamp with a reddish pink flower on the globe glowing in the corner.

"I didn't know what to take off," Cecilia-Marie said, lying facedown on the bed with a sheet over her. "Didn't know how intimately you wanted to get to know Titan's grandmother."

"I'm comfortable with whatever makes you feel comfortable." Essence made sure her eyes were dry.

"Well, I'm down to my undies."

"That's fine," Essence replied. "You got a bath towel we can use?"

"Sure. There's some in that closet right outside the bathroom. Use any one you want."

Essence went and got a towel and returned to the bedroom. She pulled the sheet down to the bottom of Cecilia-Marie's lower back, and placed the towel over her upper body.

"Comfortable?"

"That feels good," Cecilia-Marie replied. "The liniment's over on the dresser."

"I see it." Essence picked up the bottle and opened it.

"I've never had anybody I know rub me down," Cecilia-Marie said.

Essence poured some of the liquid in her hand. "Not even your husband?"

Cecilia-Marie chuckled. "He started off giving me a massage a couple of times, but he never got very far. It always ended up with something else before my aches were addressed. That even happened after I turned old and wrinkled like you see me now."

"My-y." Essence rubbed her hands together, warming the herbs and oil before she placed them on Cecilia-Marie's back. "Do you mind if I ask you something?"

"No. Go right ahead," Cecilia-Marie said.

"When did he die?"

"Jean-Paul died three years ago last month."

Essence warmed and stretched Cecilia-Marie's muscles. "Does it get any easier with time? His being gone, I mean?"

"I think it does. But there's a void you feel. It's always there. Sometimes I'll be out in the flower garden and I'll see something that I know he'd like to see. I'll get up"— Cecilia-Marie paused—"and start for the house to tell Jean-Paul to come look. One time I got all the way up on the porch and then I remembered."

"Is this too much pressure?" Essence asked.

"No. I'm fine," Cecilia-Marie replied.

"If it gets too deep, let me know," Essence said. She worked Cecilia-Marie's lower back muscles; Essence's mind was just as busy as her hands. "I've heard people say that sometimes it feels as if the person who passed away is right there with them. That they feel like they're watching them."

"I've definitely experienced that with Jean-Paul, and believe in that kind of thing. A lot of other people do, too." Cecilia-Marie laid her other cheek against the bed. "There's a show that comes on television called *Crossing Over*, where this guy serves as a medium for an audience of folks. Some of them are there because they believe, others come because somebody forced them to. But I think a lot of people believe it's possible to communicate with those on the other side. They may not want to talk about it, but they believe it."

The room remained quiet as Essence worked methodically but conscientiously.

Cecilia-Marie's voice broke the silence. "You know it's not good to concentrate on death."

"I know but with my mother dying, it seems like I can't help it."

"Was she sick?"

"She was." Essence pressed and pulled Cecilia's small frame. "So I knew that it was going to happen, but when it did, I felt like someone had turned the lights out in my life. I remember sitting in this chair that I would sit in, and feeling like I'd never move again. Then I thought about something my mother told me, how she believed I was this person who would definitely go on, and that's the only reason I moved. Because she believed in me."

"Bless your heart," Cecilia-Marie said. "So, was Titan there for you during that time?"

Essence hesitated, but for some reason she felt close enough to Cecilia-Marie to tell her the truth. "I didn't know Titan then."

"So, you two just met?"

"Yes."

"Mmm. You got to give yourself time to grieve, Essence."

"I know, only there was some unfinished business that involved my mother. And I jumped on that with everything I had. I realize that I believed fighting for her—for us—in this situation, would make her death less painful." Essence paused. "And her life more meaningful."

"But it's not that simple, is it?"

"No." Essence reached for more liniment. "I can't believe some of the things that I've done. Some of the things that have happened."

The room filled with silence.

"Now can I ask *you* something?" Cecilia-Marie inquired.

"Sure," Essence replied, although she felt a little uncomfortable.

"What is really going on between you and my grandson?"

Essence gave a laugh that wasn't a laugh. "That's a good question. It's not what you think it is. I'm certain of that."

"And what do I think it is?" Cecilia-Marie countered.

"I'm sorry." Essence exhaled. "I guess that does sound pretty presumptuous. I may not have a clue about what you think."

"I think you do," Cecilia-Marie replied, "but I'd like to hear it anyway."

Essence cupped Cecilia-Marie's side with her hands and began to lift it, rapidly.

"You think, or maybe I should say you thought up until now, that we were a couple. Happily together. So happy that Titan decided to bring me here to meet you."

Cecilia-Marie nodded her head against the sheet. "I thought you were a couple of sorts. But I could tell whatever your relationship had developed into had taken Titan by surprise."

Something inside Essence sparked. "How could you tell?"

"He didn't say anything about you this morning when I talked to him on the telephone, and then there you were."

"Titan didn't expect to find me stranded after a car pileup," Essence replied.

"I can accept that," Cecilia-Marie said, "but just because you were, didn't mean he had to bring you here. If Titan had wanted to, he would have found a way around it."

"Yes, Titan is very resourceful, isn't he?" Essence sighed. "It's all a part of being a private investigator."

"Are you working with Titan on something?"

"Hah!" Essence almost laughed. "It's more like Titan's working on me."

Cecilia-Marie rose up and looked back. "Titan's investigating you?"

Essence felt she might have said too much.

Cecilia-Marie lay down again. "This is getting better all the time." The room went silent. "Why?" she finally asked.

Essence was feeling more uncomfortable then ever.

Cecilia-Marie was Titan's grandmother. "The unfinished business involving my mother?"

"Yes."

"That's what it's about."

Essence could feel Cecilia-Marie exhale.

"Come on, Essence, this is no time for being vague."

"Cecilia-Marie, I like you and all but . . . you are Titan's grandmother."

"And? Now tell me something I didn't know."

Essence thought for a moment. "I never knew who my father was until my mother told me when she knew she was dying. My mother asked me not to do anything about it while she was still alive. She said she had lived with dignity and she wanted to die that way. What I did after she was gone would be my business. I buried her, and called him that very day. When he refused to accept the truth, I decided to confront him."

"And it got pretty messy," Cecilia-Marie said.

"It was messy long before that. He knew about me, but he never helped us in any way. It would have been different if he couldn't help, if he didn't have any money or was perpetually down on his luck. But my father was too busy keeping face. Making everybody think he was the best thing since sliced bread."

"And he hired Titan to . . . ohh." Cecilia-Marie sounded as if she had come to some kind of realization. "I see. I see."

"And so, here we are," Essence said.

"Yes. So, here you are, thrown together, and finding yourselves in a love-hate situation."

"I don't know if I would go that far." Essence put the top back on the liniment.

"Have you ever heard of the Haitian spirit Ezili?" Cecilia-Marie asked.

"Ezili? No."

"She's an interesting *loa* . . . spirit. Some believe she is uniquely Haitian, and say Ezili did not come from the Daho-

mey or the Yoruba. Did not come from Africa. They say
she was born in my homeland, Haiti.''

Essence waited for Cecilia-Marie to continue.

"Ezili possesses a duality within her. She can be
extremely protective, beautiful and desirable, but Ezili can
also be cruel, violent, grotesque, even.''

"Wow,'' Essence remarked. "It can be difficult when
two things like that exist together. I think it would tear an
ordinary human being apart.''

"But that's just it,'' Cecilia-Marie said. "If one of God's
helpers can be so changeable, so much a chameleon, we
can't expect more from ourselves. Can we? It's all in the
way that we handle it.''

"You overheard my conversation with Titan while we
were doing the dishes, didn't you?'' Essence removed the
towel and pulled the sheet up over Cecilia-Marie.

"I've heard a lot of things today. My hearing is real
good.'' She clasped the yellow cloth to her body and turned
around. "Boy, do I feel worked over.''

Essence noticed how Cecilia-Marie never answered her
question. "Was it too much?''

"No. It was wonderful,'' Cecilia-Marie replied. Then she
cocked her head. "You should approach life, Essence, just
like you approach your work. You know, sometimes you
just have to get in there and work out the kinks, if you think
it's worth it.''

Essence returned the liniment bottle to the dresser. "If I
think it's worth it.''

Their eyes held.

Chapter Twenty-two

Essence tried to separate some of her curls. The lighting in the bathroom was bright, and it was hot in the small space. It was obvious looking at the shower curtain, soaps, and towels that Cecilia-Marie loved roses, the way they looked and the way they smelled. A rose room freshener validated that.

Essence dug into the pile of makeup samples Cecilia-Marie had received from a Mary Kay representative. She freshened her eyebrows and her powder, put on a little mascara and a bright fuchsia lipstick. Her performance at the kitchen sink popped into her mind and she wiped off the fuchsia. She replaced it with a burnt bronze. ''I've kept going, Mama, but I don't think I'm doing too well,'' she said to her own reflection. A popping sound came from the direction of the rose room freshener inserted in a socket. Essence turned and looked. She thought about how her mother had been partial to the scent of roses, too.

Essence stepped out of the bathroom. Titan was standing outside his grandmother's bedroom door. Suddenly, she felt a little shy.

"You ready?" he asked as she approached.

"Yes," Essence replied. She stopped a comfortable distance away from him.

"Good. Now I can say good-bye, because I'm so sleepy," Cecilia-Marie said from inside the bedroom.

Essence stepped closer. "Some sleep would be good for you. I stirred up a lot of toxins. But you'll need to drink a couple of glasses of water at least. The more the merrier," Essence instructed.

"I had Titan bring me a glass while you were in the bathroom. I know the routine," Cecilia-Marie replied. "So you two go ahead. I'm going to snuggle down into these covers and close my eyes. Titan, you know where I put the extra key, don't you?"

"Yes. I remember." He entered the bedroom and kissed his grandmother on the cheek. "Good night, *Titi*."

"Good night," Cecilia-Marie replied. "Have a good time."

"Good night," Essence said, and left the doorway.

Titan and Essence walked out to the car and climbed inside. He turned to her, placing both hands on the steering wheel. "I feel like we need to set some ground rules."

Essence locked her seat belt, then looked at him.

"This hasn't been the easiest day. It started with a bad accident, and all kinds of things have been added since then." Titan hesitated. "I'm truly sorry about you losing your mother."

Their eyes met. Essence could see Titan's sincerity. She felt he recognized the depth of her loss.

"I don't know about you," Titan continued, "but I need a break. I don't want to work this evening. I don't want to think about it. I just want to chill out."

Essence sighed. "You won't find any resistance here."

Titan nodded and started the car. "My grandmother enjoyed the massage. Thank you."

Essence looked at her hands. "I enjoy my work. I enjoy helping people. She should definitely feel better in the morning."

Titan looked as if he was about to say something else, but changed his mind. He drove down the winding road until he took another one void of lights.

"I guess you have to know where you're going down here," Essence commented. "Even with your high beams, they only light up so much."

"Yeah, it's pretty rural," Titan replied. "But I've got a good idea where the club is. From the way Charles described it, I think it's almost sitting out in a field."

"In a field?" Essence repeated, surprised.

"Ye-ep." Titan's lips curved up a bit. "We're going to a real sophisticated party."

Essence gave a small laugh. "Sounds like it."

"Well, when you think about it, you got to create something to do out here. You either drive all the way in town to try and find something, or you make something happen nearer to home. But I suspect even if a brother thought about putting a club downtown, he probably couldn't afford the rent. So, they come up with their own thing. Like converting a barn into a private club."

"Wow. This is going to be interesting," Essence replied.

"Hey, we'll feel it out, and if you're not comfortable, we can leave."

Essence glanced at Titan. "Thanks."

"Surprised again?" Titan kept his eyes on the road.

"A little."

"Don't be. It's who I really am." Titan looked at her. "Most people think I'm a pretty nice guy, when I allow them to get to know me."

"So, you make a conscious choice to let people get to know you?"

"Yes, I do. It's safer that way," Titan replied. "There are all kinds of folks out here, and believe me, I've run across them."

"I don't know how that would affect me," Essence replied. "If that was a daily part of my life, having to be on guard like that. As a healer, most of the people who come to me come with the highest hopes. They're in pain, but they're hoping to find relief, to get better, and they put their hopes in me. But I always tell them, I believe their healing is really up to them.''

"How's that?'' Titan glanced at Essence. His gaze lingered on her profile before he looked back at the road.

"A person really has to be ready to be healed. They have to really want it, and give themselves permission. Then the sky's the limit. Who knows? Then God might work through me and miracles might occur.''

"So, you believe in miracles,'' Titan said.

"Absolutely. And I don't have to be a part of the picture. Miraculous cures can happen for them without me.''

"Miracles.'' Titan repeated the word and his head seemed to shake involuntarily.

"What? You don't believe in miracles?''

"I don't know. It's not something that I've thought about. There's too much reality staring me in the face.''

"Too much reality. Mm-mm.'' Essence pretended to study the concept. "Sounds like that could turn a person into a really skeptical, cynical human being.''

Titan shrugged. "Like I said, I haven't thought about it.'' But his eyebrows furrowed just the same.

"So, in your mind there's no hope at all for mankind?'' Essence challenged him.

"What?''

"If you don't believe in miracles, then there's no hope for us.''

"I would think if what you've been claiming about Cedric is true, you'd be the last person talking about having hope for mankind,'' Titan replied.

"Can't let one rotten apple spoil the entire barrel, can we? Doesn't mean it isn't rotten. Maybe it doesn't know it's rotten.'' Essence shrugged. "You just can't let it spoil your whole life.'' She looked out the window. "At least that's what I'm trying to tell myself.''

"I think that's the club over there.'' Titan pointed to a lone, well-lit building with several vehicles parked out front. Tall tiki lamps served as guideposts and lighting.

Essence looked around. There wasn't another light in sight. "It's got to be."

Titan pulled off the road and they bumped along until they reached the other cars. A man smoking a cigarette stood outside the front door, which was open.

"That looks like Charles's car," Titan said.

"It does?" Essence looked at the vehicle. "I don't know how you can tell. It looks like any other black Camry to me."

"It's the rims. Charles had Giovannis. I don't think there are going to be two black Camrys with Giovannis down here."

"Ohh. I guess I'm not into rims," Essence said, stepping out of the car into ankle-high grass. "The truth is, I don't know much about them."

"They are a sure mark if you want to follow somebody," Titan replied.

A slow tune oozed out of the front door as they approached. Essence could see a couple holding each other but barely moving. "Well, if that music doesn't put you in the mood, nothing will."

"Are you looking to be put in the mood?" Titan asked as they climbed the wooden stairs.

"Just commenting on the music," Essence replied.

"And I was just asking," Titan said.

The man had stopped smoking and was listening to their exchange. Essence felt as if his interest in her peaked as a result of it.

"Whatzzup?" Titan said.

"Whatzzup?" he replied, then gave Essence another sweeping look before nodding.

Essence returned the greeting before she focused on the interior of the club. It had a curious bluish-black tint. When they stepped into the room, the reason was obvious. Three bare blue lightbulbs glowed from the ceiling on a crowd of maybe twenty to twenty-five people. There appeared to be more men than women.

"Hey, dawg! You made it!" came from a dark corner to

the left of them. It was Charles. He came out and exchanged a handshake with Titan. Charles gave Essence a hug. Veronica emerged at that moment, as if to break it up. Essence noticed Veronica had on a skirt that was shorter than the one she'd worn earlier, if that was possible.

"I told you we would," Titan replied.

Charles grabbed Veronica. "Baby, look who's here."

"How y'all doin'?"

"Just fine," Essence said.

"You want something to drink?" Veronica turned hostess.

"Definitely," Titan replied.

"Why don't you come on over here to the bar? I'll get you taken care of."

"Yeah. Veronica can set you straight," Charles added. "This is her cousin Ronnie's place."

"Really?" Titan said as they walked over to the bar. "How long has he had it?"

"I'd say a little over two years." Veronica slid onto one of the stools and motioned for Titan and Essence to have a seat. "Hey, Roach," she called.

The bartender looked up from passing another customer a beer.

"How long has Ronnie been open?"

" 'Bout two years."

"Yeah. That's what I thought," Veronica replied.

"Can I get y'all something?" the bartender inquired.

"Got any scotch?" Titan asked.

"Yep. You want that on the rocks?"

"That'll work," Titan replied.

"How about you, young lady?" Roach looked at Essence.

"I'd like some white wine," Essence said. She could feel Veronica cutting her eyes at her.

"We out of wine. We've got beer, rum, scot—"

"I'll take a rum and coke," Essence replied.

"We can do that," the bartender said before walking away.

Essence turned and looked around the club. One other

couple had joined the lone pair on the dance floor who remained perpetually locked together. The other people sitting and standing around the ten tables were laughing, talking, and drinking.

"You like craps?" Charles asked.

"It's okay," Titan replied. "I've played a few games in my life."

"Well, I got to show you the back room." Charles's eyes brightened. "From what I understand, there's a pretty hot game going on tonight."

"Charles, you're not going to start that, are you?" Veronica asked.

"Start what?" Charles looked stricken. "Now, look, we out here to have a good time. Titan has come here and the man likes craps. Why can't I show him the game?"

"Because you'll end up spending all our money back there."

"No, I won't. I ain't never spent all our money on no gamblin'." Charles glanced at a guy who was sitting within hearing distance.

"Almost," Veronica replied as the bartender brought the drinks.

"Almost ain't all," Charles retorted. "And, baby, you got to lighten up on me." He made a sound of frustration. "Damn! I got one mama, I don't need another." Charles looked down. His head weaved from side to side. "What is this? You been on me all day long. I tried to work with you at Mrs. Balan's house, but now you gone bring it down here to the club. That ain't right. That just ain't right, baby. A man need some love sometime."

Veronica turned her head.

Essence felt uncomfortable, and she felt sorry for Charles. "Where are you from, Charles?"

"I'm from Haines City, Florida. It's a little farther south."

"I know where it is. I've seen the signs when I drive I-4."

"Yep, I'm just a country boy." Charles looked at Veronica. "Can't help what I am. Sometimes some folks act like it ain't good enough."

There was a prolonged pause. Veronica kept her head averted.

"There's nothing wrong with being from the South," Essence replied. "I think most of us either came from down South or have folks who grew up on a farm."

Charles looked as if he was about to say something to Veronica, but he turned to Titan instead. "You want to check out the crap game?"

Veronica looked halfway over her shoulder. Titan looked at Essence.

"Go ahead," Essence said. "I'll just sit here and finish my drink."

"Don't worry, I won't keep him long." Once again Charles looked as if he wanted to say something to Veronica, but changed his mind.

Essence took a sip and watched Titan and Charles disappear behind a black curtain. Thirty seconds hadn't passed before Veronica turned her full wrath on Essence.

Chapter Twenty-three

"Do you always make it a habit to come between a husband and his wife?"

"I don't think that's what I did. I simply asked Charles where he was from," Essence replied.

"And you don't call that butting in?"

Essence looked at Veronica. She could see she'd be the kind of woman who would take her shoe off and start whaling away. Essence wasn't up for that. "That wasn't my intention."

"Yeah, I bet it wasn't." Veronica got up and walked away.

Essence turned and watched the crowd again. The DJ was playing "Candy," and more people were on the dance floor. She found herself bobbing to the music, although she wished Veronica hadn't left her alone. Essence watched Veronica talk to a man wearing a matching pants-and-vest set over a colorful shirt.

"You want to dance?" A heavyset fellow smelling of Old Spice stood beside her picking his teeth.

"No. Not right now," Essence replied.

"You're not from 'round here, are you?"

"No, I'm not." Essence looked at him. "I live in Tampa."

"I didn't think so. I would have copped you before now."

"T-Roe, what you talkin' about?" the man who had been talking to Veronica said. "You're a little out of your league, aren't you? A woman like this wouldn't be interested in you."

The Old Spice man squinted. "Dawg. Why you play me like that? I come in here all the time and I don't deserve this."

"You know we down, bro." He stuck out his hand in a gesture of reconciliation. "But I just saw the lady myself and thought I'd come and holler at her."

"I don't even want to hear it." The Old Spice man shook his head and walked away.

"You get around, don't you? I just saw you talking to Veronica," Essence said.

"Yeah. Vee's my cousin. Let me introduce myself. I'm Ronnie. This is my place."

Essence could tell he said that to gain brownie points. It wasn't working. "Yeah. Your cousin told me."

Ronnie smiled in a way that made Essence think he had been looking at too many gangster movies. "Yeah, Vee's my number one cuz. She told me you and me should get along well. That we could have a good time together tonight." He touched Essence's cheek.

Essence moved away. "What?" She looked for Veronica but didn't see her. "You don't know me and she doesn't, either."

"If I have my way you gon' get to know me."

He was leaning on Essence's last nerve. "Maybe I don't want to," she replied. "Maybe I'm not interested."

There was a glimpse of hardness before Ronnie put on a sweet smile.

"Let me freshen this up for you on the house." He took her glass. "Then we'll talk about it." Ronnie headed around the bar.

Essence looked at the black curtain. She wished Titan and Charles would come back. There was no sign of Veronica.

"Here you go, baby." Ronnie passed Essence the drink. "Now, what was you sayin'?" He leaned on the bar top. "I don't know why you're tryin' so hard to reject me."

"Yeah, well." Essence looked away.

"Where you from?" Ronnie persisted.

"Tampa." Essence took a swallow and kept looking around. The rum and coke was stronger than before. "I think you've put too much rum in this," Essence complained.

"Just tryin' to give you your money's worth," Ronnie said. "Stir it up. The rum is probably all on top." He waited until Essence did what he suggested. "I hear you're a big-city girl. Is that what's up with you? You think that you can't deal with a man like me?"

She didn't look at him. "You said it. I didn't."

Ronnie lowered his eyes in a fashion with which Essence was all too familiar. "So, all you got to give me is a smart mouth."

"Look," Essence said, "I just met you, and you came on so strong you rubbed me the wrong way. I don't know how else to say it."

"All right, Miss Thang. I'ma leave you alone . . . for now."

Essence took another drink. She hadn't wanted rum and coke in the first place, and the way this one tasted, she was certain she didn't want another. She scanned the dance floor again. Titan and Charles had been gone no more than ten minutes, but Essence was ready to go get Titan herself. She could see Ronnie out of the corner of her eye; he was talking to another customer. At least she had gotten rid of him.

"Brick House" blared from the speakers, and Essence watched a woman who seemed to think she was the epitome of that dance. Essence had never seen so much moving and squirming. The little man who was the woman's partner was trying to keep up with her, but like a person sitting down to a meal that was too big for him to eat, his eyes were definitely bigger than his stomach.

Essence noticed the speakers were going in and out, but no one appeared to care. The crowd kept dancing, and she wondered how they did it when the music was so chaotic. Some of the folks started doing strange things to go along with it, like putting on Halloween masks; then their dancing became so sexual, she thought at any moment it would turn into a live pornography show. It was unbelievable. Essence leaned forward to make sure she was seeing correctly, and the club started to spin. The room spun, but she didn't feel dizzy.

"How you comin' down here?" The question sounded as if it came out of a tube.

Essence turned her head slowly, because she couldn't move any faster. She started to speak, but neither her mouth nor her voice box worked.

"I can see you're doing just fine," Ronnie answered for her. "As a matter of fact, I'm going to come on around there and we're going to take a walk outside. You'd like that, wouldn't ya?"

Essence heard him, but responding was impossible. She watched Ronnie circumvent the bar in slow motion. There were wavy colors all around him, mostly red and some black. Once again she tried to speak. There was no way.

"Come on, baby, let's go outside for some fresh air." Ronnie put his arm around her and literally removed Essence from the stool. "I told you I was going to get to know you better."

Essence's legs worked, but she didn't feel as if she was in control of them. Ronnie's strong arm forced her to move toward the door. She could feel his wiry body through their clothes, and his hand around her waist felt like a clamp. When the night air hit Essence's face, it was warm, but void of the grassy, country smell it had had earlier. She could barely see the cars in front of her, and the night sky, which had been so full of stars, was totally black.

"You didn't think I was good enough for you. Dealin' with me would be comin' down a notch for you," Ronnie taunted. "Well, I'ma show you just what you woulda been missin'." He moved them down the stairs. "I got my van over here. It's got a VCR in it, and seats that let down and everythang.''

Essence heard Ronnie, but what he was saying didn't really register. She looked up at the sky again. This time there were lots of stars forming concentric circles that turned in opposite directions.

"Yeah, we gon' have a good time tonight." Ronnie stuck the key in the van door with one hand and held onto Essence with the other. "Veronica told me all about you. But I never met a ho that was so snotty befo.' You probably was waitin' for me to talk money, but I don't pay for no tail. It's either free or I take what I want."

Titan parted the black curtains and saw the empty stool. He looked on the dance floor for Essence, but he didn't see her. He stepped farther into the room. No sight of her at the tables, either. Titan looked at Charles when he came up beside him. Charles smiled as he stuffed a ten-dollar bill in his pocket.

"Veronica gon' have to be nice to me now. I done won some money and ain't lost a damn thang." He, too, scanned the room. "Where they at?"

"I don't know." Titan continued to look until he spotted Veronica. She was walking toward them, slowly.

Charles grabbed her around the waist. "Hey, Boo. Who you think was on the winning side of that crap game?"

She gave him a big kiss. "You won me some money?"

"You know I did." Charles tried for another kiss, but Veronica was looking at Titan. "You looking for Essence?"

"Yes." Titan looked around the room again.

"I don't know where she went. One minute she was sitting on the stool"—she motioned—"then I saw this dude come up and talk to her, and the next thing I knew she was gone. Maybe they left together. You can't tell about women like that," she said condescendingly.

Charles looked at Titan. "She's probably still in here, dawg. I bet she's in the bathroom."

"So, you just turned around and she had disappeared?" Titan questioned.

"Actually, I just came from the bathroom," Veronica explained. "And as you can see, she's not here."

Titan tilted his head. He looked Veronica in the eyes. Veronica tried to hold contact, but she looked down. Titan walked over to the bar. Charles pulled Veronica along after him. The bartender was engaged in a lively conversation with a man reeking of Old Spice.

"Naw, dawg, I'ma stop comin' in here, cuz Ronnie ain't right. He thinks every woman that comes in here is for him. Damn, what the customers s'pose to do?"

"Keep it down, man," the bartender cautioned.

"Forget keepin' it down. He saw I was talkin' to that woman. And I'm hip to his game. Everybody around here is. Don't too many women want to drink nothin' up in here, cuz they afraid what's gon' be in it. He might as well put Special K on the menu."

"What did you say?" Titan demanded.

The customer looked Titan up and down. "You talkin' to me?"

"Yeah. You're the one who said something about Special K. So I'm talkin' to you." Titan's expression was past serious. "Did you see a woman sitting on this stool?"

"What if I did?"

Titan got up, trying to control himself. "Dawg, don't play with me right now. Did you see a woman sitting on this stool a few minutes ago?"

"Is she yo' woman?" the Old Spice wearer asked.

"Yeah, that's right," Titan replied.

The man snorted. "Well, you better go get her. I saw Ronnie takin' her out of here. That man's bad news. I ain't comin' back up in here givin' him my money."

Titan didn't hear the rest of his gripe. He was already to the door.

Chapter Twenty-four

There wasn't a soul in sight outside the club. Titan wondered how many minutes had passed since Veronica's cousin had taken Essence. He could feel his heart beating. His feelings pressed him to respond erratically. But Titan forced those feelings down. They wouldn't serve him now. He had to be able to think clearly.

He could see Charles and Veronica approach out of the corner of his eye. They joined him at the top of the stairs.

"I don't know what that man's talkin' about," Veronica claimed. "He just don't like my cousin. He's probably jealous because my cousin owns a business like this."

"Veronica, you need to be quiet," Charles said. "I done heard tales about Ronnie and women, and I know you have, too."

"Tales like what?" She placed her hand on her hip.

Titan heard them, but his mind was on Essence. He couldn't help thinking about the conversation they'd had on their way to the club. Despite everything that had happened to her, she had such a bright outlook on life—something Titan felt he could use a little more of. *Hope for mankind. She was talking about hope for mankind, and look at this.*

He fished his car keys out of his pocket. He had to do something. But what? Titan wasn't sure. A little voice in his head kept saying, *This isn't happening. This isn't happening.* But Titan knew this kind of thing happened all the time. Date-rape drugs like Ecstasy and the liquid Special K were used far too often. But they had never been used on someone he cared about. Yes, Titan admitted to himself, he definitely did care. "Veronica, I need you to show me where your cousin lives."

"Ronnie's married. He wouldn't take no woman up in hi—"

Her voice faded when Titan noticed a dim light coming from a vehicle parked near the side of the building. "Whose van is that?" he asked, but his senses already knew.

"That's Ronnie's van," Charles said. "And there's a light on in there."

Titan ran across the yard. He didn't know what he would find, but if Ronnie was in the midst of raping her, Titan feared nothing would stop him from killing him.

He got to the van and flung open the side door. Ronnie's bare behind was the first thing he saw. His shocked face looking back was the next.

"What the fu—"

With one angry yank, Titan pulled Ronnie out of the van and onto the ground. He looked at Essence, who was obviously out of it. Her dress was up around her waist, her underwear pulled slightly askew.

Ronnie got up. He tried to pull up his underwear and his pants. "Who the hell are you?"

Titan hit him. "You no-good son of a bitch. You're going to think twice before you do this to another woman."

Ronnie fell hard on his side. He tried again to pull up his pants and BVDs, which were below his knees. Charles and Veronica stood by watching as the Old Spice wearer yelled from the door, "Hey, come on out here and take a look at your boss."

Titan looked at Veronica and commanded, "Get over to that van and see about her."

Veronica jumped and started toward the van.

Titan turned his attention back to Ronnie. "Why you want them up now? You were so eager to pull your pants down." He kicked Ronnie on his exposed butt cheek. "Noo, you're not going to pull them up. You're going to take them off, and I mean take them off right now."

"Forget you." Ronnie tried to avoid the grass that was filling his mouth. "You must be out of your mind."

"I'm not out of my mind," Titan said as a group of clubgoers drew nearer to get a better look. "I'm just mad as hell, so don't make me take your ass to jail." Titan pulled out his badge and flashed it. "Because if I take you to jail, I won't stop until I find the other women you've done this to."

"Yeah, like my sister," a woman yelled.

Ronnie looked scared. The fire of the tiki lamp turned his face into a comical mask.

"Ronnie don't do this kind of thing all the time," Veronica defended her cousin.

"Yeah! What's the big deal?" Ronnie asked. "Vee told me that woman ain't nothin' but a ho."

Titan's eyes turned to slits. "Whore or not, no woman deserves this. Now take off your pants."

A crowd had gathered, and Titan could tell Ronnie was weighing the situation. He hoped he wouldn't call his bluff. It wasn't a police badge. It was a badge he flashed sometimes during his private detective work.

"Man, I didn't get to do nothin'. Hell, she ain't hurt."

"She's lying over there, she can't talk, she can't even move or anything . . . and you say she's not hurt." Titan flashed his gun and holster. "I see I'm going to have to take you on in."

"Naw, man. Naw," Ronnie pleaded. "I got some warrants out on me already."

"Come on. Let's go." Titan took a step toward him.

Ronnie kicked off one shoe using his foot. Then he removed the other. "All right. All right." He pulled one leg then the other out of his clothes.

"Now, stand up," Titan ordered.

"Ma-an. Damn," Ronnie cried.

Titan gave him a threatening look.

Ronnie got up slowly. He kept his butt to the crowd.

Titan made a circle with his hand. "Turn around."

Ronnie huffed, but he did as he was told. Defiantly, he looked at the giggling, laughing crowd.

"We see why you have to drug women," a buxom woman shouted. "My six-year-old nephew could take care of business better than you."

Ronnie winced. "You shut up talkin' to me."

A few more guffaws burst through the night air.

"What you lookin' at?" Ronnie demanded.

"Nothin' much," a female voice replied. A few people turned back toward the building, some started for their cars.

"Y'all ain't never seen a man befo'?" Ronnie kept his attitude going.

"We're surely not seeing one now," someone said.

More people headed for their cars.

"I hate to break up your vest and pants set, but I'm going to keep these." Titan picked up Ronnie's pants and heard keys rattling. He reached inside one of the pockets and pulled out the keys to the van. "I don't want you getting any bright ideas about following me, so I'm going to hold on to these, too."

"You can't keep my keys to my van," Ronnie yelled.

Titan ignored him and stepped over to the vehicle. Essence was still lying down. Veronica stood guiltily to the side.

Gently, Titan maneuvered until he had Essence firmly in his arms. He stood outside the van and looked at Veronica. "You better get ahold of your jealousy, or one day it's going to really get you in trouble."

Veronica sucked her teeth, then looked at Charles.

"Charles, I can't tell you what to do," Titan began, "but you need to get a grip on your woman. You don't want her doing something that could get her hurt in the end."

Real concern flickered across Charles's face. "Yeah, dawg. I'ma do somethin' about that."

"I don't know what you gon' do," Veronica mumbled.

Titan looked at Ronnie, who was looking around as if he were trying to come up with something. "You better be cool," Titan warned. "If you ever want your keys back, you better stand there until I pull away from here."

Ronnie glared at him.

But Titan didn't care. He unlocked his car and laid Essence on the backseat, then got in behind the wheel and rolled down the window. "Thanks for the invite, Charles. If you ever come to Memphis, look me up. I'll take you to the mother of all crap games."

"I'ma take you up on that," Charles shouted as Titan tossed Ronnie's keys into the high grass.

Titan could hear, "Aww, shit. I ain't never gon' find those keys tonight," as he drove away, followed by, "I'll help you find them, Ronnie."

"No, you won't," Charles said. "We goin' home. Right now."

Chapter Twenty-five

Titan drove in silence, repeatedly glancing over his shoulder at Essence, who had begun to move on the back seat of the car.

"Whooa," Essence wailed when Titan's car hit a pothole.

"How you comin' back there?" He looked at her.

"I don't know." Her answer had a singsong quality.

"Just take it easy," Titan said. "We're on our way back to the house."

"He-ey," Essence sounded. "You're like one of those sixties hippies. You've got flowers painted in the top of your car."

Titan glanced up, then focused on the road again. "That's the ketamine hydrochloride talking."

"The what?"

"The Special K. It's a date rape-drug. It appears Ronnie used it quite a bit in women's cocktails."

"I thought my rum and coke tasted funny," Essence replied. "So he tried to—"

"*Tried* is the operative word, but I found you two in time."

"Titan to the rescue." Essence made it sound like a movie title.

They rode in silence.

"I didn't like him from the beginning," Essence piped up again. "He was too—" The car hit another rough spot. "Take it easy," she said. "I can feel every pebble in this road."

"It'll wear off soon," Titan said, then he asked, "Can you move your arms and your legs now?"

But there was no reply.

"Essence?"

Nothing.

"Essence." Titan looked over the seat. She was staring up at the ceiling, smiling.

"The color is draining out of the flowers. It's spilling all over me. It's warm and it feels so good."

"I'm sure it does," Titan replied. "The Special K is definitely wearing off. The hallucinogenic effects usually come near the end. You're lucky. From what I've heard, sometimes it can be real bad."

"That's because," Essence started to sing, "It was Titan to the rescue."

"Yeah, that's right. Titan to the rescue."

He turned in at the house and brought the car to a stop. Next, Titan got out and opened the back door. "Let's see if you can you move your legs."

"Sure I can." Essence moved her arms, but her legs stayed stationary.

"Not your arms, your legs," Titan repeated.

"Didn't I move my legs?"

Titan shook his head. "I'll be right back. I'm going to unlock the door. I'll come back for you once I've opened it."

He mounted the steps and looked under the flowerpot where his grandmother kept the extra key. It wasn't there. Confused, he checked under the umbrella stand. There was nothing. "Damn. Where is it?" Titan started to knock on the door, but decided against it. He didn't want to wake his grandmother. Titan looked back at the car, then over at the barn. "Maybe it's over there."

He cut across the grass. A porcupine boot cleaner sat outside the barn door. He lifted it up. A key was beneath it. Titan took a chance and stuck it in the lock, and the barn door opened.

"He-ey. He-ey. What about me?" Essence called, laughing.

Titan listened. She sounded like a child. He was so grateful he'd gotten to Essence and Ronnie. So grateful, he thought as he went back to the car. "It looks like we'll be camping out in the barn tonight." Titan reached inside the car and took hold of Essence. "Le-et's go." He pulled her into his arms.

"The barn? I'm not a cow or a pig. Are you?" she asked with her eyes closed.

"Moo-oo," Titan sounded.

"You're a cow." Essence laughed again, and her head dropped forward. Her face landed against Titan's pecs. "Your chest is so hard. It feels like a rock. How is a woman supposed to use a man's chest for a pillow, when it feels like a rock?"

"So, you prefer a soft chest, huh?" Titan looked down into her shining eyes.

"I prefer a hard chest that feels like a marshmallow."

Titan had to laugh. "Well, good luck finding that."

"I am lucky, you know." Essence kicked her legs. "See there. I told you I could move my legs." She kicked again. "What's wrong with you, Titan? Did somebody put Grape-Nuts in your drink?"

"It's not Grape-Nuts. It's Special K. And you better stop that or I'll drop you right here," Titan admonished her, but he actually was enjoying the feel of Essence in his arms.

Titan pushed the barn door open with his foot. He wondered how much ketamine hydrochloride Essence had ingested. "Did you drink the entire rum and coke?" he asked, but he doubted she had.

"Nope. It was nasty," Essence replied.

"Hooray for nasty," Titan said. "I'm going to put you on this old sofa bed," He told Essence as he lowered her onto the couch. "Now, let's put some light on the situation." Titan looked around.

"We don't need any. It's pretty like this." Essence stared off into the darkness.

"Pretty to you. Dark to me." Titan turned on a lamp, with a large yellowed shade. The room contained the sofa bed, a cocktail table, a chair, a couple of lamps, and an old radio. Titan glanced at an adjoining door. He knew, back there, he would find his grandfather's woodshop equipment.

Titan noted how things had changed a lot since his grandfather had passed. Still, the barn was a place full of memories, and he knew tonight would be added to the list. "This is going to be a long night," Titan murmured.

"Why is it going to be longer than others?" Essence asked.

Titan studied her wild, cottony spirals of hair. Each one seemed to have its own mind. Some hung near Essence's eyes. He liked the way she looked. There were many things Titan liked about Essence. "It just is." He walked over and turned on the radio. A sultry male voice declared, "Stay with us through the Quiet Storm." Several bars of sensuous music played. "I'll guarantee if you're not with the one you love, when we're done, you'll want to love the one you're with."

Titan turned the dial. *That's all I need, to be out here with her all night long, listening to the Quiet Storm. This is already complicated enough.*

"Why did you turn away?" Essence protested. "I love that music. Couldn't you feel it?"

The radio crackled between stations as Titan looked at her. "Feel what?" But he already knew.

"His voice. That music." Essence raised her arms to the ceiling. "It was like the Pied Piper, calling to everyone who hears. It said, stay and listen."

"I'm not in the mood for that kind of music," he replied. But all the time Titan was thinking, *I can't take but so much.*

"Not in the mood?" Essence's voice was wispy. "Have you ever heard the Quiet Storm stations at night?"

"Yeah, I've heard them." Titan watched her turn on her side.

She closed her eyes. "So beautiful. Soo beautiful." She looked at him.

At that moment, to Titan, Essence was more beautiful than anyone he had ever seen. He tore his eyes away from her and concentrated on the radio, turning back to the Quiet Storm.

Titan walked around the room. He felt restless. What was he going to do? He really cared about this woman. For how long had he wanted truly to care about someone? Titan looked at Essence. But he would end up caring for a woman who was most likely the bastard daughter of his father's best friend . . . a woman they wanted him to help bring down.

"Titan!" Essence called, abruptly.

"What is it?"

"Titan! Something's happening." Essence closed her eyes.

He went and knelt down beside her. "What is it, Essence?"

"I don't know. I feel like I'm being drawn into a tunnel."

"The drug is just surging. You'll be all right." Titan raised his hand to stroke her hair. He drew back before he touched her.

"But I'm afraid," Essence replied.

"Don't be." His brow furrowed. "Are you in pain?"

"No. It's not painful. It's just . . . strange."

This time Titan did stroke Essence's hair. He arranged the cottony cloud away from her face. "You'll be all right. I'm right here. And I'm not going anywhere."

"Please don't leave me, Titan, Don't ever leave me."

Titan touched Essence's hand. He didn't know what to say.

Essence's expression changed. "I see a light. Now I see

a light." She inhaled. "It feels wonderful. Peaceful even. I don't know how a light can feel peaceful, but this one does."

Titan studied her changing expressions. "That's good. Because it's all going to be fine in the end. Just a little while longer and you'll be your old self again."

"This feels like nothing I've ever known before. I wish you could feel it, Titan. The light is getting bigger and bigger as I move toward it. And I can see someone in the middle of it. I don't know who it is but . . . it's my mother! It's my mother!" Essence rose up.

"Sh-sh-sh." Titan got on the couch with her. He drew her into his arms. Titan had heard that ketamine could create all kinds of strange experiences, but this was his first time witnessing it. "Your mother? That should make you happy."

"I can't believe it." Tears streamed down Essence's face. "I can't believe it. Mama," she called.

Suddenly, Essence went quiet. Titan watched her face soften, and immense joy appeared. "I love you, too, Mama."

The way Essence looked when she told her mother she loved her touched Titan deeply.

"He is?" Essence continued to speak. "But he denied he was my father. And it hurt, Mama. I tried not to show it, but it hurt so bad." Essence appeared to be listening, and Titan realized he had been holding his breath. "I will try to remember," Essence finally said. "I will try my best to remember."

Titan continued to hold Essence. He knew Essence believed she was having a conversation with her mother. A conversation about Cedric, and the look of pain on her face was so real. Titan would never forget it. If nothing else, he knew Essence believed Cedric was her father. There was no doubt in Titan's mind.

Chapter Twenty-six

Essence opened her eyes, and Titan's face was the first thing she saw. She was surprised to feel tears running down her cheeks.

"Hello," he said.

"Hello."

"How you feelin'?"

Essence held her forehead. "Groggy."

"And you will probably feel that way for a little while," Titan replied.

Essence nodded. She looked around the room. "How long have we been here?"

"In the barn? Or on the couch?" Titan replied.

"Both."

"We've been in the barn about fifteen minutes. On the couch . . . about five."

"So we left the club a while ago."

"Yep. You don't remember?"

"Not really." A trembling breath escaped. "It's almost like a puzzle. There are a few pieces that I recall, but I don't know if they're real." Essence looked Titan straight in the eye. "Ronnie put something in my drink, didn't he?"

"Right again." Titan nodded. "A lot of folks call it Special K. It's a kind of animal tranquilizer."

"That son of a . . ." Essence clenched her teeth and closed her eyes.

"But I got to the two of you before he did what he had in mind." She focused on Titan again. "And I don't think he'll try that on another woman anytime soon."

"Thank you." Essence felt her stomach contract. She felt awkward, although Titan's arms felt wonderful around her. "I think I'll be okay now." She slowly sat back on the sofa. "Titan?"

"Yes."

"Did I say anything?"

"You said lots of things," he replied.

Their eyes locked.

"Anything significant?" She looked away. "I don't know. I feel like I went away somewhere."

"You've been with me for the last forty minutes."

"Physically I've been with you." She looked at him with searching eyes. "But that doesn't mean I was totally here."

"Well," Titan replied, "the ketamine hydrochloride can have all kinds of effects."

Essence took several deep breaths. "I felt like I-I . . . did I say anything about my mother?"

Titan nodded.

"I did?"

He nodded again.

"Because I felt like I visited with her." Essence looked up. "It was wonderful. She didn't look sick. As a matter of fact, I know she wasn't."

"I guess that was comforting," Titan said softly.

"Yes, it was, because she was sick for so long, and to see her well, totally back to her old self . . . filled me with joy."

"I could tell you were experiencing something good nearer to the end."

"But I wasn't before that?"

Titan shook his head. He seemed to hesitate before he continued. "And you said something about your father."

Their eyes locked again.

"Yes," Essence spoke slowly. "I told my mother Cedric denied he was my father. Instead of her condemning him, she told me he was having a difficult time."

"With the denial?" Titan questioned.

"With lots of things. My being his daughter . . . his denying it, and what's going to happen as a result of all of this. And his life in general, right now." Essence looked confused. "I don't know why she told me that. It wasn't my intention to hurt anyone. It's just that I . . ."

"You said his denial hurt you." Titan placed his hand on top of Essence's.

She looked down. "It did."

"Well, I got to tell you, you put up a great front. Nobody would have known."

"Really?"

"Excellent," Titan replied.

Essence sighed. "I didn't want anyone to know. It was too much for me to get my arms around. Shiri, Brenda, and I have been friends for years, and to think their uncle that they love so much is the father that abandoned me. I couldn't tell them." She looked into Titan's eyes. "And those who did know didn't believe me anyway."

"That's right. Didn't," Titan said. "As in the past."

Essence's lips trembled. "You do now?"

Titan kissed her gently. "I do now."

Essence could feel tears forming. She gave a short laugh and kissed him again. "I'm glad. Although I'm not happy it took my being drugged to convince you."

"I was already weakening," Titan replied.

"Were you really?"

It was Titan's turn to laugh. "Couldn't you tell?

Essence thought about it. "No."

"Well, I was." He put his arm around her. "But I've got to ask you something." Titan put on a quizzical look. "What was that act at the kitchen sink?"

Essence covered her face. "I knew you were going to ask me that."

Titan attempted to pry her hands away. "What was that?"

Finally, she removed them. Essence shook her head. "You have to admit I had you going for a minute. You can't say I didn't." She laughed.

"Yeah, you did. And you made me angry. All I could think was, I would end up liking a woman like this."

Essence stopped laughing. "So you like me?"

Titan searched her eyes. "A hell of a lot."

They studied each other.

Finally, Essence touched Titan's face. "You're beautiful," she whispered.

"I'm anything you want me to be, Essence," Titan replied. "Anything."

His eyes were so serious. His voice so rich. "Oh, God." Essence could feel the threat of tears again.

"What?" Titan said softly.

"I'm so emotional these days," she said, embarrassed.

"That should be expected."

"I know." Essence managed to keep the tears at bay. "Right then I was thinking, my mother has been taken away, but maybe you're here to give my heart something else to do."

Titan pulled Essence to him and they sat in silence.

"I wish I was like you, Essence," Titan spoke over her head. "You are able to find hope in the middle of sorrow. That's a gift. We all could use more of that."

"But it's something we all have," Essence replied. "We only have two choices in this life. Hope or despair. So, for the life of me, when I think about it, I don't understand why someone would choose despair if they can have hope. It doesn't make sense."

"But so many people do. As a private detective I've seen it over and over again. Life beats them down when they try it your way. Finally they give up." Titan took a deep breath. "The truth is, I understand why."

Essence looked at him. "But as long as we are alive, and

there's a sky above us, and our feet can touch the earth, there is another way. And the more you have hope, the easier it becomes. It's a way of life. That's how my heart feels right now, Titan. Hopeful. Filled to the brink with hope.''

"Hopeful. I haven't felt like that since I was a little boy. Since I started understanding how complicated life can be.'' Then he added quietly, "I'd give anything to feel that way again.''

"You can,'' Essence said.

Titan gave a half smile, but it didn't erase the heaviness in his eyes.

"I want you to do something for me,'' Essence said.

"What?''

She moved back a little farther. "Raise your arms over your head.''

Titan squinted.

"Come on. Hold them up.''

Titan lifted his arms.

With her eyes remaining on his, Essence pulled Titan's shirt over his head. His eyes darkened.

"What are you doing?'' he asked softly.

"You'll see.'' Slowly, she reached down and pulled her dress over her head. "I want you to feel my heart. Feel it beating inside me.'' In her black lingerie, she snuggled close to him. "All the hope that I have. I want to share it with you.''

She could see the desire mounting in his eyes as Titan's arms went around her. "Slowly. Slowly,'' Essence whispered. "Try to feel my heart. Feel what it's saying.''

Essence felt Titan's arms tremble as he controlled his natural impulses. They sat as still as statues, feeling one another—each heartbeat, each breath, until their heartbeats and breathing were in sync.

"I can't believe you've got me doing this,'' Titan said, his voice raspy. "Woman, you're something else.''

"I am when I'm with you,'' Essence replied. "Because I want you to know me, Titan. I want you to know who I really am.'' She looked down. "How I think. What I believe." Essence looked into his eyes again. "Because it's my belief that allows me to have hope." She paused. "I want you to have hope, too."

Titan's arms tightened about her again. "Hope for us?"

"If that's meant to be," Essence replied softly. But her inner voice cried yes, and so did her eyes.

Essence started to look away, but Titan steadied her chin and kept her focused on him. That nudge, that insistence that Titan wanted to see her, really see her, made all the difference. They had taken another step. What she saw in Titan's eyes was the door.

"Essence," Titan said as he examined her face. "Essence means the very nature of a thing." He pressed his lips against hers in a slow kiss. "Something that's indispensable. The most important qualities. Your mother was a smart woman. She named you well."

Suddenly, Essence felt high. For a moment she wondered if it was the Special K surging again. But Essence knew it wasn't. She was sure of that. This was different. Her body, her mind, and her heart were beaming, as if a light had been shown on all of them. Nothing had been taken away from her. It was as if everything had been given.

Titan kissed Essence again, and she had never been more aware of another human being. It was a delicious feeling of being consumed by something wonderful, but at the same time being the consummate consumer. Titan's lips were firm, yet they slid across Essence's like warm butter. Sweet, warm butter. *This is what being with a man is all about. When all of you is here, and nothing is being held back. I don't want to hold anything back.* Essence willed herself to feel the entire moment. *I've been living in a constant state of pause ever since Mama died. She believed I'd go on, and here is Titan to help me do it in a way I've never done before.* She drowned in another kiss as her mind echoed, *There are no accidents. There are no accidents. None.*

Essence touched Titan's lips with the tip of her tongue, and he boldly answered the invitation. They flirted with one another until their tongues become deeply acquainted, parting with several smaller kisses, punctuated by deep eye contact.

"What are we doing, Titan?" Essence was clear about her motives, but the way she felt . . . nothing had come close to it. She needed to know where Titan stood.

"We're getting to know each other." He moved his face against her cheek.

Essence felt a spark of disappointment. "That's part of it," she replied. "But it's not all." Essence touched his brow, then his hair. "I've known other men before . . . and it never started like this. Never felt like this," she confessed.

Titan's eyes bore into her before he nodded slowly.

"For you, too?" Essence's eyes held a tinge of apprehension at her own boldness.

"For me, too."

The words amplified that special something they had been feeling, and Titan held on to Essence as she lowered herself onto the couch. Their lips couldn't wait to touch again, and the kiss was intoxicating. It was followed by several more.

Essence didn't know how long they kissed and stroked. But it was long enough for them to end up nude and wanting. Titan and Essence had found something precious, and there was no such thing as enough.

"I want to make love to you," Titan whispered, then kissed Essence again.

Her body shuddered and trembled, moving in waves that matched her breaths. "Thank God," Essence replied softly. "I'd go out of my mind if you didn't."

Titan moaned and placed both hands beneath her bottom. "I want you more than I ever knew was possible." He molded her to him. "If having you is anything like wanting you, it should be illegal."

Essence's mouth almost turned into a smile, but desire made her mouth pouty and soft. "Then show me." She fondled his muscular, bare butt cheeks.

Titan rose a little, and Essence looked down. What she saw made her stomach quiver. Titan was well equipped to satisfy, and Essence was ready for that satisfaction. But he nibbled and suckled her lips first and trailed kisses to her ears while he put on protection. Titan said things that on the street would have brought heat to Essence's face, but at that moment they made her wet with welcome.

This time it was Essence who tightened her hold, and attempted to draw Titan into her. But there was no need. Titan had the same goal in mind, and he entered her with a surety that made Essence groan. He found her mouth again, and with his kiss and powerful strokes changed Essence's groan to a whimper.

"Give it to me, Essence," he rasped. "I want all of you." Titan's body pumped until it worked up a sheen.

"Yes, yes." Essence rode his wave with vigor. "I'm yours. All yours." She held on to every word, every movement, encouraging him, not because Titan needed it, but because he deserved it. There was no part of her that she did not open to him, no twist or turn Essence did not meet. Essence made love to Titan until her body signaled release was on the way. "Are you almost there, Titan? Are you?" She moaned. "Because—because . . . ohh, Titan."

"Yes. Say my name," he replied, and buried his face between her breasts as his movements heightened.

"I'm going to . . . Titan!" She cried.

"God, woman! God!" Titan replied.

The pleasure was exquisite. It sent vibrations through Essence's body and ringing in her ears. She could not move. They could not move, so they remained frozen until Titan collapsed in her arms, and their mouths met in a luxurious, satiated kiss.

Chapter Twenty-seven

"Ohh, I'm tired." Lela Johnson grunted as she negotiated the last step from the chartered bus. "I told y'all I didn't want to go to no Disney World. All that doggone walking and standing." She complained to whomever might hear as she moved toward the hotel.

"Aww, Mama." Pamela got off behind her. "You must have had a good time. How many times did you ride Space Mountain?"

"Three," George Johnson answered for his wife. "Once I heard your mama in there screaming, 'Wee, this is fun'." He patted his small belly.

Lela waved her hand. "You didn't hear no such thing." She tugged on the sleeves of her burgundy-and-white pantsuit. "And when you've got as many grandchildren as we've got, and they all want you to ride, what else are you going to do?"

George winked at Pamela, Brenda, and Shiri, indicating Lela's bark was much worse than her bite. "Well, I had a wonderful time," he said. "Now I'm ready for my afternoon nap."

"Afternoon nap?" Lela replied. "And you know you don't need no nap. You snored all the way here on the bus."

"Bus rides don't count," George replied. "That's just a bonus." He smiled and patted Vivian on the back. "It's a shame Cedric didn't go with us. So, he was pretty sick this morning, huh, Vivian?"

"Yeah." She looked down at her hands. Her mouth formed a rigid line. "He couldn't get out of bed."

"I'ma have to have a talk with that boy, and you got to take better care of him." George looked at his daughter-in-law. "Cedric's going to be the patriarch of this family after I'm gone. He's supposed to be rallying the family on, but here he is sick. I hope he's better by tomorrow. We're going to Sea World. Ain't that right, Doris?"

"After we have breakfast, we sure are," Doris replied.

"I'm not going to nobody's Sea World," Lela retorted. "I'll be at the family dinner if I'm able to walk tomorrow. Here you are worried about Cedric." She grumbled. "You better be thinking about me. My neck and everything hurts."

"You want me to give you a massage?" George put on a crafty smile and wiggled his fingers like spider legs.

Lela tried not to smile. "You better behave yourself and go to that room."

"You see how she's trying to hurry up and get me in there, don't you?" George looked around.

There were a few giggles until Lela put the eye on everyone.

"You're just a dirty old man." Lela started down the hall. "Come on before you embarrass yourself . . . and me."

George leaned stiffly to the side. "Look at that woman. Don't she still got it? Hips swingin' side to side to side."

"Come on, George," Lela called without looking back.

"Daddy's so funny." Karen watched her father trail behind her mother. "I think they both had a good time."

"I know I did," Brenda replied. "I think everybody did, even Grandma, although she'll never admit. But I hate that Essence missed it."

"Me, too," Shiri said.

"And I think that Titan had something to do with it. Hey, Uncle Cedric," Shiri said as he entered the lobby. She put her arm through his. "You feeling better?"

Cedric looked at her and at the other expectant faces.

"I told them you weren't feeling well," Vivian said, her expression flat. "That's why you didn't go to Disney World with everybody else."

"Oh." Cedric attempted a smile. "I'm feeling okay." He saw several sets of eyes look at each other questioningly. "Has anybody seen Titan?" He tried a bigger smile.

"Titan?" Rosie put her hand on her hip. "You two attached at the hip or something? I'd think you'd ask about your mama and your papa first." She walked over to him and moved her lips so only he could see. "And you're not fooling me." She turned and walked away.

Cedric watched the small figure in the multicolored dress. He knew Aunt Rosie was right. But without the alcohol, there was too much on his mind and his heart to think about anything else. Cedric felt like he was walking though a field of land mines, and any step might be his last. His life and career would blow up right in his face. Everything would be lost. Everything. Guiltily, he focused on his family. "How are Mama and Papa?"

"They're fine, Uncle Cedric. You just missed them," Brenda replied. "They went back to their room. Granddaddy is going to try to catch up on his sleep."

"That's good. That's good." Cedric looked around.

"Titan and Essence didn't go to Disney World," Shiri added. "If you ask me, I think they decided our family reunion was too boring and they went to do some uniting of their own."

Brenda made a face. "You might be right."

"They didn't go to Disney World?" Cedric was shocked. It was one thing for Titan to get with Essence for business's sake, but totally another if he found he was really attracted to her. Still another voice said, *And why wouldn't he be? She's a pretty girl, just like her mama, and if she's anything like her, deserving of a man to care for her.*

Shiri drew back. "No, they didn't."

"Well, what makes you think they're together?" Cedric hoped he sounded more conversational.

"Anybody with eyes would guess that from last night," Karen replied. "Do you have some kind of problem with it or something?"

"What do you mean?" Cedric said.

"I don't know, but you and Essence had a few words at the pool yesterday, and now you're acting as if it's some big deal that Essence and Titan didn't go to Disney World." Karen examined her brother's face. "They're grown, and since they're not a part of this family, I can see why they might want to skip it, if you know what I mean."

Cedric shrugged. "Yeah, well." He looked at Vivian. "Have you eaten?"

"I ate something a little while ago." Vivian's face was as tight as the muscles in her neck.

"Well, I'm hungry. Let's go get something to eat."

Vivian just looked at him.

"We'll see you all tomorrow," Cedric said as he walked toward the automatic sliding door with Vivian walking slowly behind. Cedric knew he was acting strange, and he could tell the others thought so, too, but he couldn't help it. He could feel their eyes on him and Vivian as they made their way into the parking lot.

"What in the world is wrong with you?" Vivian demanded before they made it to the first car.

"There's nothing wrong with me." Cedric kept walking.

"Cedric Johnson, if you walk away from me right now you better keep walking."

Cedric turned. He could see his sisters and nieces still standing in the lobby. "What is it, Vivian?"

"Don't do that. Don't turn this into Vivian's-got-an-imaginary-problem, because I'm not up for it." She raised her palms.

"I didn't say you had a problem. I'm simply asking why you are asking me these questions."

"Why?" Vivian's eyes narrowed as she shook her head. "After all these—how long have we been married, Cedric?"

Cedric's head bobbed.

"Or do you know?" Vivian demanded.

"Of course I know," Cedric replied. "We got married in '68, so that means we've been married for . . . thirty-four years."

Vivian nodded. "You've always been a smart man . . . in some ways." She took a deep breath. "Yes, thirty-four years. My God, I was a baby when I married you, and so happy to be Cedric Johnson's wife that I would have done anything. And practically did. For years, whatever you asked me to do, I did it with no questions asked. I tried to be everything for you. Maybe that's why I'm so tired now." She stood as if she were waiting for Cedric to reply.

But he didn't say a word. *I've got enough on me right now, Vivian. I don't need to hear this.*

"I thought we were done with this kind of thing, Cedric. You promised me." Vivian crossed her arms. "So, what is it with you and this girl?"

"Who?" Cedric's brows knitted.

"Essence Stuart."

Exasperated, Cedric looked away. "Vivian, look—"

"I am not crazy," she hurled. "I've lived with you long enough to know when you're trying to hide something. Are you going with that girl?"

"Going with her?" Cedric looked as if he had tasted something sour. The thought that he might lie down with his own daughter repulsed him.

"Yes. Having sex with her." Vivian's hands went to her hips. "She's young enough to be your daughter."

Cedric wanted to scream, *And she just might be.* But he locked his mouth. "I'm not even going to answer that."

Their eyes engaged in a standoff.

Finally, Vivian said, "Don't answer it then, Cedric. You don't ever have to answer anything else to me again." She stalked away.

Chapter Twenty-eight

Cedric would have called after Vivian, but Pamela, Karen, and Doris were still watching from the lobby. There was no place for his conversation with Vivian to go but downhill. If he told her the truth, it would be over, but holding back hadn't helped, either, because she knew something was wrong. *You can't be with a woman for as long as I've been with Vivian without her knowing you inside and out.*

Cedric went to the car and climbed inside. He stared sightlessly out the windshield before he laid his head back on the headrest. "Damn, what is going on? Everything is falling apart." Tears were so near the surface. The last time he cried, he was eight years old. It was Christmas and he had received a bicycle, his first. But his father had gone to put air in the tires, and had allowed Cedric's next-door neighbor, his archenemy, to ride the new bike before Cedric did. Afterward, the boy had teased him mercilessly. It had been such a blow. He had finally gotten something he'd wanted, they had finally had enough money, and the glory of the moment had been snatched away. Right then he'd decided he would not allow his moment to be snatched away again. Maybe that's when he'd started down the road of the taker, giving back only when he received more.

He thought of Sadie Stuart. She had given him everything she'd had and gotten nothing in return. Perhaps he had done that with too many people in his life, and it was time for the great payback. Cedric sat for a few moments longer before he dialed James on his cell phone.

"Hello."

"Hey, Babette. How you doin'?" Cedric rubbed his hand over his hair.

"Fine, Cedric. How are you?"

He couldn't stop the heavy sigh. "Doin' okay. I meant to dial James's cell phone."

"That's all right. James is sitting right here."

Cedric listened as Babette handed James the telephone. He thought he heard Babette say something about him sounding funny.

"Hey, Cedric. What's goin' on?"

"Are you still in the room with Babette?"

"Not anymore," James replied. "What's up? You sound pretty stressed."

"James, man . . . I don't know what's happening. I feel like I'm falling apart." Cedric's words were broken.

"Hold up, Cedric, man. Calm down."

"I'm trying to keep it together, but it looks like I'm destined to come down, dawg."

"What do you mean?"

"Vivian is acting crazy, and I just found out Titan and Essence might have spent the day together. To me that means there's more going on between them than what is in my best interest."

James paused. "That's not necessarily true, but yes, they did spend the day together."

Cedric stopped rubbing his forehead. "What are you talkin' about?"

"I talked to Titan. It seems the Stuart girl was involved in a car pileup on I-4. Titan took her with him to Mama Cecilia's house."

"What?" Cedric couldn't believe it.

"Yeah. I talked to him earlier today. Everything was okay."

"And you didn't call me?"

"Noo, I didn't see a need to put that on your mind. And from the way you sound seems like I was right."

"Right?" Cedric yelled. "Look, man, don't start thinking for me. You should have told me this right away."

"For what? So that you could be more upset than you are now?" James replied. "I know you, Cedric, you can get a little whacked when it comes to certain things."

Cedric cussed to himself. "Whacked! James . . . man . . . I've carried you with me my entire political career. If I was so easy to get *whacked,* as you call it, I wouldn't be where I am now."

"Politics is one thing. Personal is another," James replied, evenly.

"Oh, I see."

"I hope you do. And I hope you don't really believe you have carried me in any form or fashion."

"So, what? You've been carrying me?" Cedric challenged.

"You're the one that brought up carrying. I'm not even going to go there."

"Oh. You're not going to go there. You're the big man. The worldly one that's just holding up a not-so-blessed brother."

"Cedric, I think we need to end the conversation right here. Let's talk at another time when you're not so . . . stressed."

"I don't need you to tell me when I can talk. And you know what, James? I don't need this."

"You don't need what, Cedric?"

"I don't need you thinking for me. I don't need you telling me I can't handle my personal affairs because your son chose to get cozy with my—with Essence Stuart."

"You about said it right." James's voice cut. "And this

is the kind of mess I've been keeping at bay all these years.
And it hasn't been easy.''

"Oh, it hasn't?"

"No."

There was a pause.

"Well, since working with me is so damn hard, James,
you don't have to work with me. Let me ease your burden.''
Cedric hung up the phone and slammed it onto the car seat.
"I don't need him. I don't need nobody. They've all fed
off of me, and I'm sick of being everybody's poster boy.''

He cranked up the car and put it in gear.

James Valentine walked back into the living room.

"What was that all about?" Babette asked.

"Cedric's gone off on another tangent." He flopped down
into his favorite easy chair.

"Sounds like you were kind of going off yourself."

"Believe me, I was trying not to, but when you deal with
somebody who came up with nothing like Cedric did . . .''

"I don't believe you said that." Babette crossed her arms.
"You're never going to change."

"Well, I'm just telling the truth." He looked at his Rolex.

"No, you're not," Babette replied. "There aren't any
better people than Lela and George Johnson. Now, if you
are referring to the money they have, or had at the time
Cedric was growing up, that's a whole different thing. One,
I might add, that you haven't understood yet."

"Aww, Babette." James put up his hand. "You just stay
out of it."

"I'm not going to stay out of it. I wish to God, when you
said stuff like that when Titan was coming up, I had spoken
up more. Things that implied money determined the quality
of a man." Babette stretched out her hand. "Maybe Titan
would have known that at least one of us didn't worship
money as our God."

"You're talking crazy," James said.

"Huh." Babette tossed her head. "I'm making more sense

than you are. And I don't know who's worse off as a result of your pounding your money views into them—Titan or Cedric. Now, I'm not saying Cedric was no angel when you met him. But one thing I have personally witnessed is Cedric trying to be high and mighty because you put him down whenever he wasn't meeting your standards. And Titan? Titan grew up believing everybody could be bought. Everybody's motive is money, and now the boy doesn't trust anybody. Maybe me." Babette pointed at herself. "But he barely trusts you. There's some respect there, but trust . . . I don't think so."

"Aw, woman," James grumbled. "That's not how it is." But James recalled what Titan had said during their last phone conversation. "Well." He wrestled with his thoughts. "I didn't see either one of you complaining when you were spending all that godlike money."

"There's nothing wrong with money, James, in and of itself. It's the worship of money that will get you in trouble."

The room went quiet.

"Well." James felt somewhat deflated. "We don't have to worry about Cedric's money anymore."

"Not worry about Cedric's money?"

"Or his paying me," James replied. "He fired me."

"Lord have mercy. How many times is this?" Babette asked.

"Noo, I think he's serious this time," James said.

"Cedric has been serious every time. It's just this time you have taken it more seriously," Babette replied. "You better go on over there and talk to him before he does something stupid. Vivian's got enough on her hands already."

"It seems Vivian is part of the problem. Cedric won't have her to lean on this time."

Babette's brows went up. "Then I know you better go."

"I can't," James said.

"Why not?"

"He's in Orlando."

"That's right, at the family reunion." Babette shook her

head. "James, I think you need to go on down there. Cedric can be . . . well, you know him better than I do. He's a great politician, but if you ask me, he's got some self-worth issues going on that can be a little destructive."

James looked worried. Cedric had been his employer for over twenty years, but he was also his friend. "What am I supposed to do? Hop on a plane? That's going to be mighty expensive."

"Well, drive then," Babette said. "You were talking about putting the new Lexus on the road anyway."

He looked at her, his eyes seeking. "You going to ride with me?"

Babette let go a long breath. "Sure, I'll ride. It'll give us some time to repair whatever damage I just did to your ego." She gave him a tender smile.

Chapter Twenty-nine

The morning sun was bright as Essence stood beside Titan. She watched him knock on the front door of his grandmother's house. Essence's state of mind was as brilliant as the sunshine. She couldn't remember a time, since her mother's death, when she had slept so well. She'd slept soundly after hours of lovemaking, although Essence was certain the effervescent feeling had more to do with Titan than with sleep. He looked down at her and smiled.

"Who you smiling at?" Essence asked lightly, meeting his gaze.

"You." Titan made a loud kissing noise as he kissed her forehead.

"You better be careful, I might start believing you truly like me," Essence replied.

"Believe it." He kissed her and the front door opened.

"We-ell. Good morning." Cecilia-Marie looked at them, but she didn't open the screen door.

"Good morning, *Maman.*" Titan's lips twitched as if he were trying not to smile.

"Good morning, Cecilia-Marie," Essence replied, but she didn't find Cecilia-Marie's stance so amusing. "Titan couldn't find the spare key last night and he didn't want to wake you, so we spent the night in the barn,'' she explained.

Cecilia-Marie's expression changed. ''Ohh.'' She opened the screen door. ''How convenient.''

''Did she say 'how convenient'?'' Essence mouthed for Titan only.

He shrugged. ''What did you say, *Maman?*''

''I said, I was wondering what happened. I could tell Essence hadn't slept in her bed.'' Cecilia-Marie stepped outside and examined the drop. ''The key wasn't underneath the flowerpot?''

''Nope,'' Titan replied. ''I looked there and under the umbrella stand. Nothing. So I checked in front of the barn and found a key. But, of course, it fit the barn door.'' He appeared to be getting a kick out of Essence's discomfort.

''My, my, my,'' Cecilia-Marie sounded, as she came and stood in front of Titan. ''What in the world did I do with that key? That's one thing about getting old that I can't stand. My memory just isn't what it used to be.''

''You're as quick as a newborn babe.'' Titan hugged her. ''Old age is no match for you.''

''And how quick is that?'' Cecilia-Marie smacked his cheek playfully. ''You two hungry?''

''I am,'' Essence replied, glad the subject of her and Titan sleeping in the barn together was over.

''I could eat a horse,'' Titan said.

Cecilia-Marie proceeded into the kitchen. ''And what did you do to work up such an appetite? Or shouldn't I ask.''

''Ask Essence,'' Titan said. He secretly squeezed one of her butt cheeks.

Essence started. She looked at him. Titan challenged her with an expression of *now, fix that.*

She showed him her fist. ''Why should she ask me? You're the one who could eat a horse.''

''Titan, stop putting Essence on the spot.'' Cecilia-Marie walked over to the stove. ''And you two have a seat. But there's no sense in trying to hide what's been going on from me. Titan knows I have eyes in the back of my head, but even Mr. Pete could see the two of you. It's written all over you."

Essence's eyes widened as she sat down. She attempted eye contact with Titan, but he avoided it.

"So, what's written all over us, *Grandni?*" Titan sat at the table and stretched out his legs.

"There's sumpin'-sumpin' going on between you two, and lots of it," Cecilia-Marie said. "But from what I know about you, my dear grandson, and what I've discovered about you, Essence, the chemistry isn't all you've got going for you. I want you to know that." She paused. "You're two good people. Good people with the same kind of values, and that makes for grand possibilities." Cecilia-Marie turned her attention to the stove.

"Really?" Titan smiled. He looked at Essence, who was dead serious.

"Really," Cecilia-Marie replied. "Now, let's see here. I've got some sweet potato bread left over from yesterday, and I fried some bacon. I plan to put on some eggs if you want them."

"That sounds good to me," Essence replied, but she was thinking about what Cecilia-Marie had said.

"So, are you trying to marry me off, *Maman?*"

Essence couldn't believe her ears, although Titan's tone was playful.

"Now, it's no secret that I want grandbabies before I leave this earth, and in my opinion, you've taken more than enough time to come up with them."

"I don't have to be married to give you grandbabies," Titan teased.

Cecilia-Marie kept her back turned. "Boy, don't make me come over there and hit you upside the head with this spatula."

"Abuse. You hear that, Essence? That's what I grew up under," Titan replied.

"You have never been abused in your life. At least not by me," Cecilia-Marie said. She waited a split second. "Do you want children, Essence?"

Surprised again, Essence said, "Sure. Someday."

"*Maman*, I think you're pouring it on a little heavy, now," Titan warned. "You've got Essence ready to walk back to Tampa."

Essence thought Titan's eyes gleamed especially bright.

"Having babies is a much lighter subject than dying," Cecilia-Marie replied. "And I figure since Essence and I have talked about death, discussing new life would be a breeze."

"Let me do that." Essence sprang up as Cecilia-Marie's gnarled hand cracked the first egg.

"No. You sit right there," Cecilia-Marie said. "My back hasn't felt this good in weeks, so I want to show you my appreciation."

Essence lowered herself back into the chair.

"So, you two talked about death?" Titan directed the question to Essence.

"Yes." Sadie's passing took a hold of Essence again. "I thought I'd ask your grandmother how she was able to cope with your grandfather's passing." She looked down. "I thought it might help."

"Losing a loved one isn't easy," Cecilia-Marie concurred.

"No, it's not," Essence echoed. She could feel Titan's eyes on her. "Seems like I've been running around like a chicken with my head cut off ever since." Essence gave a half chuckle, half sigh. "My mother used to use that expression." The words trailed away.

"Her death is really fresh," Titan said, his eyes deep and feeling.

"Yes, it is." Tears welled up, and spilled instantly. "I'm sorry," Essence said as she tried to keep them from falling. The tears stopped as quickly as they'd begun.

"There's no need to apologize," Titan assured her. "What makes you feel you've been doing that?" he asked.

"Doing what?"

"Running around like a chicken with his head cut off."

"I've just gone from one thing to the next." She held

her hands in her lap. "Saying things and doing things that I wouldn't normally do." Essence reflected on her impetuous session with Titan in the hotel room.

"Like you're going through a phase." Titan's eyes turned hooded.

"Yes. Something like that," Essence replied. "As if tomorrow might never come for me. And it's not that I fear that I am going to die," she attempted to explain.

"I told Essence she's got to let herself grieve," Cecilia-Marie said. "She can't run away from it, and there's no need to be ashamed of how she or anybody else reacts when someone close to them dies. That's even if you've been expecting it." She turned the burner under the scrambled eggs off. "There's no book of rules about what's acceptable and what's not. I won't even tell you something I did after Jean-Paul died."

"What did you do, *Maman?*" Titan pressed.

She looked over her shoulder. "I'm not telling you because you might disown me as your *Grand-mère.*"

It was Titan's turn to look surprised.

"But what I'm trying to tell Essence is this . . . there are no perfect human beings. If we were perfect, we wouldn't be down here, we'd up there with the angels. So, what we've got to do is learn to forgive ourselves and to forgive others." Cecilia-Marie made her way to the table. "Dragging stuff around with you, thinking how things might have been better . . . could have been better. If I haven't learned anything else at eighty-two, I've learned it takes too much energy to hold something against somebody. You could be doing something else with all of that." She sat down. "The food's ready. You can serve yourselves."

Essence and Titan got up. Titan appeared to be taking what Cecilia-Marie had to say in stride, but Cedric was on Essence's mind. She was definitely holding something against him. He had abandoned her mother and denied she was his child. Forgive Cedric? That wouldn't be easy.

"But some things are difficult to accept." Essence picked up a plate.

"Life's difficult." Cecilia-Marie watched them dish up the breakfast food. "Trying to keep going, trying to progress and grow . . . if you've got issues against someone, it's like dragging a ball and chain around on your foot. Do yourself a favor. Let go."

Cecilia-Marie was still at it by the time Essence and Titan sat down with their food. "If the other person is wrong . . . go on and tell them you believe they're wrong. But after that, you must decide to leave them alone, or to keep loving them." She took another bite of sweet potato bread.

"You sure have a lot to say this morning." Titan forked up some eggs.

"I do, after being around you young people. I hear and am aware of more than you think I am. And I'm not just talking to Essence now, Titan."

Titan closed his eyes before he looked at his grandmother. "You're not?"

"No. You know what I'm talking about."

Titan didn't reply, but Essence detected a somberness in his expression. For a while they ate their breakfast in silence. Cecilia-Marie only ate *pain patate* and was the first to finish. She took her plate over to the counter. "I'm going outside to mess around in my flowers," she announced. "I'll leave the dishes to you two since you seem to be so handy at the sink."

Essence nearly choked on her bacon.

Cecilia-Marie tied the bow of her gardening hat under her chin. "You know, a father is an interesting thing. With girls . . . girls just want him to recognize them, and boys . . . the very thing they want is sometimes the very thing they fear, that they might be just like their father." She gave Titan a telltale look.

Chapter Thirty

"Your grandmother sure has a way with words, doesn't she?" Essence asked from across the table.

"Yeah. Titi is famous, or should I say infamous for her tongue."

"Has she always been that way?"

"For as long as I can remember," Titan replied. "But, of course, she was in her fifties when I was born."

"My mother would have been fifty next year." Essence's tone saddened. "She said she was forty years old before she felt like she was the master of her own life. Mama couldn't wait to turn fifty, because fifty legitimately gives a woman license to do and say anything she wants. She said that right is earned through years of heartbreak and joy, which, she said, equals wisdom." Essence looked away. "One more year and she would have been fifty. She was forty-nine," she added softly.

"You two were close?" Titan asked.

"Very. She was my world, and a wonderful woman." Essence smiled. "And you could have fooled me when it came to her not saying what was on her mind. I'm sure, when I was a teenager, a few of my old boyfriends would disagree with that.''

Titan tilted his head back. "You have any brothers or sisters?"

"No," Essence replied, then said, "Other than Cedric Jr."

There was a small silence.

"You have any brothers and sisters?" Essence asked.

"Two," Titan replied. "I'm the oldest. I've got two sisters, Michelle-Jeanne and Wilhemina."

"The only boy, huh? And the first one. I bet you were spoiled," Essence teased.

"Noo," Titan replied.

Essence leaned on the table. "Your mother didn't spoil you? I don't believe that."

Titan laughed, and a rarely sighted dimple emerged. "I don't think so."

"What about your father?"

"He didn't spoil me." The smile disappeared.

"But were you close?" Essence visualized Titan as a little boy on his father's shoulders. It was a place she wished she could have experienced being. "I mean, did he do all those things with you like play baseball, roll around in the grass, and tussle over a—"

"No," he cut her short. "It wasn't like that. My mother tried, but she's not very athletically inclined. My father was too busy taking care of us."

"Oh, I see." Essence sat back. "That could be a good thing."

"I suppose so," Titan said. "As long as those that are being taken care of know that you care for them." His cynicism was thick.

"So, you don't feel he . . . did you know that, Titan? Did you think your father loved you?"

He shrugged. "That was a long time ago." Titan intertwined his fingers. "Water under the bridge, as they say."

"You don't look as if it's water under the bridge,"

Essence said softly. "As your grandmother said, how you feel is written all over you."

Titan's face hardened. "You don't know me as well as my grandmother does. So don't start assuming things."

"Ouch," Essence replied.

Titan looked down before he got up from the table.

Essence watched him cross the room. "Believe me, I don't think I know you as well as your grandmother does."

"That's smart." Titan's tone held a note of superiority.

"Smart? What is this?" Essence retorted. "I don't need you to tell me I'm smart. Like you're congratulating a dog for fetching the right bone."

"Have it your way." Titan turned on the faucet.

She walked over and put her plate on the counter. "You know, you're really a piece of work. I just compared how you treated me with how you might treat a dog, and all you could say was, 'Have it your way.' "

"What do you mean, I'm a piece of work?" He added some detergent without looking at her.

"I mean, you can open up and talk when it's something that affects somebody else. When you're investigating somebody else. But when it's your stuff, when you have to look at your own issues, you're as closed as a person can get."

"My life's not an open book for anybody," Titan replied.

"But mine is, huh?"

"I didn't say that."

"You didn't have to say it. We know it is. Cedric Johnson . . . my father hired you to investigate me." Essence's gaze bore into his profile.

"I didn't know we were talking about you," Titan said coolly. "I thought this was about me, and my issues, which I don't have."

"Hello?" Essence said dramatically. "Didn't you hear your grandmother say there are no perfect people?"

"I didn't say I was perfect." He washed his plate. "I said I don't have any issues."

Essence took the dishcloth from him. "No issues. Perfect. It's the same thing." She rinsed her plate after he was done.

"So, outside of being a massage therapist, you're also a psychiatrist," Titan remarked.

"Ohh," Essence crooned. "You've finally accepted I'm a massage therapist." She clapped. "Ye-ey. How smart of you," she threw back. "But I don't have to be a psychiatrist to see you've got some kind of issue with your father. Your face tightened up and everything when I mentioned him."

Titan looked at her without an ounce of kindness. "I think you need to leave that alone. You don't know anything about me and my father."

Essence almost recoiled. "No, I don't know anything about *you.*"

Titan wrung out the dish towel, and Essence just stood there watching. She wanted to say something else . . . wanted to ask what had happened to what they'd created last night, how she'd been feeling when they'd walked into Cecilia-Marie's house no more than an hour before. But there didn't seem to be a space for that. Titan had closed it.

"I guess I'll call and find out if my car is ready."

"That sounds like a good idea," Titan said as he passed by her on his way to the living room. But he said nothing else.

Essence placed the call. She could not remember the specifics of the conversation, but she knew her car was ready. They said it could be picked up at the main Orlando police station. She wandered into the living room.

"So, what did you find out?"

"It's ready," she replied.

"What did you say?" Cecilia-Marie asked from the other side of the screen door.

"I was telling Titan that my car is ready. They say I can pick it up at any time."

"And are you two ready to leave me already?"

Essence looked at Titan.

"I think this is as good a time as any. I'm sure Essence wants to get her car."

"Absolutely." She tried to sound practical. "When you're still paying a car note and you've got a long way to go, you breathe a little easier when you can put your hands on that steering wheel."

"Of course, I know you'll be happy to pick up your car." Cecilia-Marie rubbed Essence's arm. "I'm just sad that that means you're leaving. At first I was concerned that your car troubles might cut my visit with Titan short. But now, I'm afraid I might never see you again unless there's another car pileup on I-4, and Titan just happens by."

Essence grabbed Cecilia-Marie's hand. "Don't worry, we'll see each other again."

"You promise?"

"I promise," Essence replied.

"You heard that, Titan?" Cecilia-Marie said.

"Yes, I heard it."

Cecilia-Marie looked up at him. "I'm not going to drag you into this, but you know I want to mighty bad."

Titan made a noncommittal expression, and Essence felt a pang in her chest.

"Well," Cecilia-Marie said to Essence, "I want to give you some of my homegrown herbs before you leave."

"I'd love that," Essence replied, but her heart wasn't in it.

Cecilia-Marie turned in the direction of the kitchen.

"I'll get my bags and put them in the car," Titan said.

"That's fine. It will only take us a few minutes."

Cecilia-Marie arrived in the kitchen and opened the cabinet door. "I want you to have a couple of tinctures and oils that I've made." She shuffled the bottles around. "Here. This lemongrass blend will be wonderful for your bath water." She handed the bottle to Essence. "And this is great for your hair. And, let's see, one more." Cecilia-Marie scanned the myriad bottles. "This one is a wonderful—"

"I don't think you meant to give me this, Cecilia-Marie," Essence said. *Pennyroyal, b—,* she read silently as if reading it out loud would tell what the blend was for.

"What is it?' Cecilia-Marie asked innocently.

"It's not for your hair, I can tell you that." Essence gave her the bottle.

"Ohh." She placed her index finger against her lips. "I remember putting this together. How did it get up front? It's so old. I blended this for Vivian." She looked at Essence with bright eyes. "Vivian Johnson . . . many years ago."

"Vivian Johnson wanted that?"

"Well, actually, I gave it to my daughter, Babette, for Vivian," Cecilia-Marie lightly replied, but Essence was certain she knew the combination of herbs was quite powerful. Cecilia-Marie placed it back in the cabinet. "This is the one for your hair. It contains jojoba oil."

"Thanks," Essence said. But she had drawn some dire conclusions. *Vivian used some of Cecilia-Marie's herbs to help her get rid of a child! But she had to be married to my father then.*

"Titan," Cecilia-Marie called.

There was no answer.

"I guess he's out at the car," she said.

Essence gazed at the herbs in her hands. But her mind was on the bottle Cecilia-Marie had put back in the cabinet.

"Do you want a little bag to put those in?" Cecilia-Marie carried on as usual.

"Yes, please," Essence replied.

"Good." She smiled. "I hope you enjoy them."

Essence put the herbs in the bag and followed Cecilia-Marie outside. Titan stood at the rear of the car. He closed the trunk door as they approached.

"It was good spending time with you, *Grandni.*" He bent low and hugged his grandmother.

"You know I can never get enough of you." She patted his face. "And it was wonderful having you in my home." Cecilia-Marie opened her arms to Essence.

"It was great being here." Essence hugged her. "And I thank you . . . for everything."

"You're very welcome." Cecilia-Marie's gaze bore into her. "Now, you two go ahead and get on the road. I guess I'll go in the house and relax a bit."

Titan opened the driver's door, as Essence sat down in the passenger's seat.

"I'll see you soon, Titi," he said.

"Bye, Cecilia-Marie."

"Good-bye. Good-bye." She waved.

They closed the doors and Titan started the car.

"Wait a minute," Cecilia-Marie called. She stepped over to Essence's window. "Your mother called me this morning, Titan. It seems she and your father are going to Orlando to check on Cedric Johnson. Must be some kind of emergency. They said they hope to see you there." Her eyes held an interesting gleam. "Just thought I'd let you know, in case you weren't planning on going back to the reunion."

"What kind of an emergency?" Essence asked, suddenly concerned for Cedric's welfare.

"She didn't say. But for them to drive all the way from Birmingham, I would think it has to be serious." Cecilia-Marie backed away from the car and waved.

Chapter Thirty-one

Titan pulled away from his grandmother's house. He looked over at Essence. Her brow was wrinkled, and before he could turn away, their eyes met.

"Your parents must be mighty close to Cedric to drive down here like that."

Titan scanned the road and pulled out. "They've been friends for years. Really it's Cedric and my father."

"I think Karen said something about that at the reception. That your father"—she swallowed—"and Cedric were close."

Titan nodded, but he wasn't talking.

"I wonder what could have happened," Essence continued. "Despite everything"—she paused—"I don't want anything to happen to . . . my father. Regardless of what he has said about me, I don't wish anything bad on him. I didn't really realize that until now." Slowly, Essence turned to Titan.

"What is it?"

"Didn't Karen say that your father and Cedric worked together?"

"I don't recall," Titan replied.

Essence nodded. "She did. She did say that."

"She might have," Titan said. "My father is Cedric's campaign chairman and PR person."

"Your father handles Cedric's public relations?"

"That's exactly what he does."

"So, wait a minute." Essence calculated with her finger in the air. "Did your father have anything to do with your being hired to investigate me?"

Titan nodded his head.

Essence strained at her seat belt. "That means I was discussed—you mean to tell me that all of you believe that I . . ." She held her breath. "Who thought of it?" came out on the exhale.

Titan's face turned masklike. "What difference does that make?"

Essence pointed at her chest. "It makes a difference to me. I want to know which one of you is the biggest asshole. You, your father, or my father."

Titan glanced at her with veiled eyes. "I don't know whose idea it was. All I know is I received a phone call."

"Unfortunately, that takes you out of the running." Essence continued to try and provoke him. "From the little I know about Cedric, it could easily be him. But from your attitude toward your father, he might deserve the title, too. Or do you dislike him just because?"

"I never said I disliked my father," Titan replied.

"You don't have to say it. I can see you're trying to avoid saying it at all costs. Unlike me . . . my saying it comes out as easily as the word asshole." Titan flinched. "But of course, I was abandoned. It's okay for me to say I don't like my father. But coming from the kind of environment I suspect you come from it would almost be like blasphemy to say something like that."

Titan looked at her. The muscles in his face were working overtime. "What are you trying to do? Make me angry?"

"Hell, yeah." Essence leaned in with the word. "Maybe I'll get something real out of you then. Ever since I asked questions about your precious family, you've turned off. It's like last night might as well not have happened.''

"But it did happen, Essence. I know it did.'' Titan looked ahead and breathed out slowly.

"Yes, it did.'' She looked out the window. "And even though you may want to . . . I don't want to forget it. Last night was one of the most beautiful times of my life. And I'm not going to be quiet about it, and I'm not going to be nice when the man I shared it with acts as if he wants to put it behind him.''

Titan closed his eyes for a moment before he looked back at the road. He wanted to respond to Essence, to openly address what she'd said, but he felt constricted. He didn't know if Essence knew how true her words were. Part of him wanted to distance himself from what had happened, what he was feeling for her, but he couldn't. It was an uncomfortable place to be.

Essence continued to look out of the window. "You don't think I'm good enough for you, do you? I don't measure up to the Valentine standards. To Cecilia-Marie's standard, yes. Maybe even your mother's.'' She looked down at her hands. "But I can just hear your father and my father talking, plotting how the so-called masseuse is nothing but a problem. You can't be the one to get involved with the masseuse. Can you, Titan?'' Essence accused. "You can't let yourself believe that something good happened between us last night.'' She shook her head. "For some reason you need to hold on to an uglier view of life. You can blame it on being a private detective, but I think it's because deep down inside, you feel you're better than me. Why? I don't know. But I believe that's the reason.''

"I need to sort some things out. That's all,'' Titan replied, but he could see his father's face, through the years, telling him the kind of woman he should have in his life, and Essence didn't fit the bill. She didn't come from money, and she wasn't on her way to acquiring a lot of it. His father would also question Essence's lifestyle, although Titan didn't believe Essence was any more of a prostitute than he was. But James would never be convinced. *Still, why does that matter. I've always been able to speak my mind to my father, but somehow this is different. Maybe because what I feel for her is different, and I don't want to make a mistake. Or maybe it's because deep down inside I am as money-hungry and as much of a snob as my old man.*

"Sort what out? There's nothing to sort out," Essence hammered.

"There's plenty," Titan replied.

"No, there's not. You either care for me or you don't. You either believe me or you don't."

Titan wrestled with his conscience. *Why am I backing away from her? I don't want to.* He tried to make amends. "I believe you believe Cedric is your father."

"So, my mother could have been lying? Is that what you're saying?"

"Mistaken, Essence. Not lying. Mistaken."

Titan could almost feel the heat coming from Essence's eyes as she squinted at him. "My mother never had one boyfriend the entire time I was growing up, and you're going to tell me that when it comes to the one association that she claims with a man, it was a mistake? I don't think so," Essence declared. "I think you need to look in another direction. At Cedric Johnson and at your father. That's where the mistake or lie lies. Take your pick." She crossed her arms. "Why is that so hard for you? You so easily believed the worst about me, but you won't even look at the possibilities there."

"That's not true," Titan replied.

"So, you considered that my father could be lying?"

"Of course I considered it."

Essence sat back. "Still, you're afraid to look at what that might mean. Not so much for Cedric, but what it says about your father. That they didn't care about ruining my life—an innocent person's life—if it suited their purpose."

Titan's jaw tightened. *The one constant feeling that I've had for my father is respect. If I can no longer have that . . . what will I have?*

Essence leaned her head against the headrest. "Remember what Cecilia-Marie said: There are no perfect human beings. If they've been wrong, tell them about it, but then it's up to you to decide if you're going to continue loving them or not."

Chapter Thirty-two

Vivian rapped on the hotel door. She heard a faint "Just a minute." A few seconds passed and she heard Lela Johnson say, "It's Vivian."

Lela opened the door. "Come on in. I just took off my clothes to rest a bit before dinner. I don't know how I let them talk me into going to Sea World after what I went through at Disney World yesterday." She closed the door.

Vivian glanced around the room. "Where's Papa George?"

"He's in the bathroom. He'll be out in a minute. Have a seat."

Vivian sat down and clasped her hands.

Lela sat on the bed. "Where's Cedric? Is he feeling any better?" She put her feet up and leaned against the headboard. "We didn't see you two at Sea World, but I just figured it wasn't Cedric's thing. He never did like zoos and stuff like that."

"I haven't seen Cedric, Mama Lela," Vivian said with her back straight. Her voice shook a bit.

"Say what?" Lela crooked her neck forward.

Vivian looked at George as he stepped out of the bathroom. "Hi, Papa George."

"Afternoon, daughter."

A strange, charged silence followed.

Vivian looked at Lela, then looked at the floor. "I haven't seen him."

"You haven't seen him?" Lela repeated.

"Not since last night." Vivian straightened her back again.

George stopped in the middle of the floor and looked at both their faces. "Who you talkin' about?"

"We're talking about Cedric," Lela was the first to answer.

"You haven't seen Cedric since last night!" Papa George looked surprised. "Did you call the police? Cedric's an important man. They'd get on this right away."

"And that's why I didn't call them," Vivian replied.

"Come again?" Papa George said above a knocking on the door. "I don't understand." He disappeared into the short corridor. "What in the world is goin' on here?"

Vivian's and Lela's eyes met.

"So, I take it this isn't the first time he's stayed away all night," she said calmly, but her eyes were far from serene.

Vivian sighed. "No. But it's been a while since he's done it."

"Hold up in there. I can't hear you." Papa George opened the door and Karen burst into the room.

"That damn Vivian!"

"Karen, hush! Don't cuss in here," Lela admonished.

But Karen continued. "I left a message on Cedric and Vivian's hotel phone yesterday evening telling Cedric to call me right away. I bet she didn't even tell him. I don't know why he even married that witch." Karen stepped out of the corridor.

"I tend to wonder why he married me, too," Vivian replied. "He wasn't ready to marry anybody."

Karen looked shocked, but she recovered in an instant.

"My brother is the best man any woman could have. If you're so unhappy, why are you still with him?"

"I'm beginning to wonder that myself." Vivian looked at Lela. "Before I stayed because of Cedric Jr. Now, I guess—"

"I don't believe that mess for one minute." Karen put her hands on her hips. "You're with him because he takes good care of your a—butt. What would you do without him, since you always have to have the best of everything?"

"Karen, I think you need to be quiet," Lela said.

"I don't care what Karen says, Mama Lela." Vivian waved her hand.

"What do you mean, you don't care? Don't get up on your high horse with me." Karen stood in front of Vivian.

Vivian could feel years of restrained anger rise inside of her. "Karen, if you don't get out of my face, I'm going to slap you into tomorrow."

"I'd like to see you—" Karen bent forward.

"Karen. Daughter. You get out of this hotel room if you can't obey your mama," Papa George boomed. "And I mean it."

"She's the one talking about hitting somebody."

"I don't care what she said. You're going to respect our room and your mama. Now, either sit down, or leave," Papa George commanded.

Karen flopped down on the edge of the bed.

"Now, what were you two saying before Karen came in here?" He looked at Vivian, then Lela.

Vivian glanced at Karen, who rolled her eyes and turned away. "I told Mama Lela it's been a while since he's done this, but it isn't the first time."

"Lord, God." Lela folded her hands, then pressed them against her lips.

"So, you don't think he's in trouble?" Papa George asked.

"I'm not sure," Vivian replied. "He's been . . . he's been drinking even more lately."

"What are you all talking about?" Karen looked around the room.

There was a pause. Finally, Lela said, "Vivian hasn't seen Cedric since yesterday evening."

"I wouldn't come back, either, after you two were arguing in the parking lot," Karen charged.

"We argued because I'm sick of hiding things for your brother and taking up for him."

"What do you mean? You have run Cedric off and now you're making him out to be the bad one."

"Karen, you're just jealous," Vivian replied.

Karen looked Vivian up and down. "I'm not jealous of you."

"Yes, you are. You've always been because I'm married—"

"I don't know what you're talking about."

"To your brother"—Vivian got louder—"and it looks like we got a little bit of notoriety and money."

"Notoriety?" Karen repeated. "Don't nobody know who you are. It's my brother who's responsible for anything and everything you've got."

They talked over each other.

"You're jealous, and nothing I do or say is going to satisfy you. I can't help that you see my life as this perfect life." Vivian wouldn't stop talking. "Well, I want you to know that it's not. Your brother has cheated on me. He drinks, and right now he's going through a midlife crisis that could end everything. He's not this perfect angel that your family has painted him to be."

Karen looked stunned, and so did George and Lela.

Finally Karen said, "You're lying."

"I wish to God I was," Vivian replied. "But your brother is just a man, and when you get down to the truth behind the glitter, a pretty low-down one. So, all these years that you've been waiting for a man to marry that could fill your brothers' shoes have been a waste. Because now you're old, and you'll never find anybody who will want you."

Karen blinked several times. "You can say what you want to say, Vivian"—she stood up—"but if anything has happened to my brother, I'm going to blame you. You have

never been a good wife for him, and I have never accepted
you as part of this family."

She stormed out.

"You didn't have to come down on her like that, Vivian,"
Lela said.

"Karen and I have been building up to this point for
years."

"I know that. We all know that. But regardless of what
Karen said, you are a part of this family, and your life has
been blessed when you compare it to others." Lela paused.
"So don't discount what the Lord has given you, even if
it's not perfect. Especially when there are others, like Karen,
who haven't even had that."

Vivian looked down. "I guess I just . . . I thought Cedric
and I had put these days behind us." She looked up, her
eyes desperate. "I don't know if I could live through them
again."

Chapter Thirty-three

"You called the police on me!" Cedric said to the hotel clerk as a police car pull up outside Nick's Motel.

"We had no choice," the paunchy man replied.

"Yes, you did." Cedric was more than a little aware of the other people standing in the lobby. "You and I could have settled this."

"Mr. Johnson." A man emerged from the back room. "You claim you've been robbed, and you can't pay the motel bill, so we're turning it over to the proper authorities."

"You think I'm trying to get over on you. And I don't appreciate it. I'm a . . ." He looked around the room. Cedric started to say he was a powerful man, a city councilman perched to become a state representative of Alabama. But how would he explain being in a place like Nick's Motel? If it ever got out, it could affect his campaign. *But maybe that would be a good thing. Maybe I'm not qualified to be a state rep. Maybe I don't want to be.* Those thoughts had come to him before, but he'd never voiced them to anyone. He had pushed them down, away from his own mind whenever they started to emerge. He had to run for state representative. Everyone was counting on him—his constituents, his family.

The motel manager leaned back as if Cedric's breath were offensive, then he looked at his rumpled shirt. "Would you step over there . . . please? We've got other people to take care of."

Cedric wanted to argue, but he didn't. Instead, he quickly walked to the motel door and stepped outside. He wanted to avoid the further embarrassment of having the police question him inside the motel. Cedric pulled his politician's stature together and approached the policemen. His head banged from an awful hangover. "Officers, you must be here on my behalf."

One of the officers tilted his head. "Are you Cedric Johnson?'

"Yes, I am," Cedric spoke quickly. "I was robbed. They took my wallet and therefore my money and credit cards, so I couldn't pay the motel bill. My cell phone is also gone."

"Who robbed you?' the other officer asked.

Cedric's eyes shifted. "A woman."

"Did you know her?"

Cedric hesitated. "We got acquainted last night."

The questioning officer nodded. The other looked back at the motel. "And are you married?" the policeman continued.

"Yes, I am," Cedric replied. He forced himself to keep eye contact with the officer.

"So, was this a working lady you picked up?"

"No—no. It wasn't anything like that."

"How can you be so sure, Mr. Johnson? This kind of thing happens all the time. You old men take these young women to cheesy motels, like this, and what do you expect?"

Cedric had to look away.

"She's out to take you any way she can, and this one did." The policeman wrote something on a pad. He gestured with an ink pen. "So, what do you plan to do about the bill here?"

"There's nothing I can do at the moment, Officer. Like I said, she took my wallet and my cell phone."

The other officer shifted his weight. "We understand, but we can't let you leave here without paying. We'll have to take you in."

"Damn." Cedric rubbed his forehead.

"Is there anybody you can call who'll pay the bill over the phone?" the main officer asked.

Cedric broke out in a sweat. In the past he would have called James, and James would have bailed him out. But James was no longer in the picture. Suddenly, Cedric felt sad. Not that he hadn't fired him before. It was just that . . . normally, they would patch things up pretty quickly. Cedric tried to ignore an overwhelming feeling of impending doom. "I can't think of anybody right offhand. It's not like I can call my wife or my family." He tried to laugh, but the officers didn't join in.

"So, you've got your car." Titan looked at Essence's red Toyota. "Seems like everything's okay." He walked around the vehicle.

Essence watched him. The farther away Titan walked, the more it reminded her of the emotional gap that was developing between them. "I'm sure it is," she replied. "I'll just have to deal with the smell of gasoline for a while."

"Yeah." Titan completed his inspection. "For a while." They stood in silence.

"Well, I better be going," Titan said.

"Sure." Essence stepped back as if to give him room. "I guess you're headed back to the Wyndham Resort."

"Yes."

Essence watched his teeth pull against his bottom lip.

"Since my parents are going to be there . . . and expecting to see me."

She searched Titan's eyes. She couldn't read a thing.

"Are you coming back to the reunion?" he asked.

"No." Essence shook her head quickly. "I've had enough

of that. I'm going home where I belong. I don't feel like throwing myself up against that brick wall anymore."

"I can understand that," Titan replied.

"Can you really?" Essence said, thinking he couldn't know how she felt. Titan had been hired to investigate her—hired by her father to prove he had no ties to her. How could he know how she felt? Essence felt a wry smile cross her lips. How it felt to realize the family she was closest to, the Johnsons, were really her family, but not being able to legitimately claim them. That if she told Brenda and Shiri that Cedric was her father, it could cost her their friendship. Perhaps if Cedric had handled it differently, had acknowledged her, it could have had a happier ending . . . at least for Essence.

Titan artfully ignored her question. "Hope to see you again, Essence."

"I don't know why you have to hope that," she replied. "If you wanted to see me, it wouldn't be a problem. You'd do it. So just tell the truth, Titan." Essence's eyes showed her frustration. "I'm sick of people lying. Say you don't want to see me." Her insides quivered, but Essence had to speak her truth. "Just say it."

"It's not that I don't want to see you, Essence." Titan looked into her eyes, but his feelings hid somewhere else. He leaned forward, as if to give Essence a light kiss.

She moved away. "No kiss for me," Essence said as her eyes smarted. She climbed into her car. Essence refused to look up at Titan, who remained in the same spot. Once she started the vehicle, it took everything Essence had not to acknowledge Titan before she drove away.

"God. What was that?" A tear ran down her cheek. She swiped it away angrily. "I don't want you to kiss me. I don't want you to do anything for me, but stay away, Titan Valentine. Just stay away. Since that's what you want." Essence stopped another tear before it fell. "You're a wimp," she berated him, as her mind conjured up images of their stay in his grandmother's barn.

Essence forced herself to focus on driving, but it was too

late. She drove past her exit. "Damn. I needed to get on the expressway right there." She watched the cars whizzing by where she wanted to be. "How do I get back over there?" Frustrated, she shook the steering wheel. Essence looked around. She was in a section of town cut off from everything by the highway. It was a somewhat neglected area with businesses that were badly kept.

"Damn," she cussed again as she drove past two police officers standing in front of a motel, talking to a man. "This is crazy." Essence continued to drive before she stared in the rearview mirror. "That looked like Cedric." She tried to see the man through the side mirror. "I think that is Cedric." Her tires squealed as she made a quick turn into a laundry parking lot, backed out, and went back up the street.

"That had to be him." She drove leaning forward. When the group came into view again, Essence saw it was Cedric. He appeared to be explaining something to the police. All Essence could think of was how Cecilia-Marie had implied Cedric could be in trouble. A red flag waved, telling her not to interfere, but it was against Essence's nature. Any human being deserved to be helped . . . even her father.

A red Toyota pulled up into the motel parking lot not far from the police car and a young woman got out. Cedric watched her along with the police officers. Then he realized who it was. Essence Stuart! A wash of disbelief, apprehension, and embarrassment went through him.

"Is everything okay?" she asked hesitantly.

Cedric looked down as if he didn't hear her. *What is she doing here?*

The police officers looked from Essence to Cedric, then back again.

"Do you two know each other?" the least talkative officer inquired.

Essence began to nod her head, but she stopped when Cedric looked at her.

"Do you know him?" the officer with the pad pressed.

Essence looked at the motel, then at Cedric. Her face showed surprise. Cedric was more aware than ever that he had slept in his clothes all night.

"Would you answer the question, ma'am?" the policeman demanded.

"We've met once before," Cedric replied.

"So, she can verify who you are?" The officer who'd spoken first appeared to be getting irritated.

"Yes." Cedric looked down.

"Would you come over here, ma'am?"

Out of the corner of his eye, Cedric could see Essence did as she was told.

"Can you verify that this man is Cedric Johnson?"

"Yes." Essence dipped her head forward.

"And how do you know him?"

Cedric looked into his daughter's eyes. They were surprised, confused even, but they were his eyes. He looked away, he felt so ashamed. Ashamed that he had denied this beautiful, young woman. Ashamed that she had found him outside a seedy hotel, a victim of his own actions. Ashamed that Essence would tell others. "Don't bring her into this," Cedric spoke with his eyes down. "She doesn't have anything to do with this."

"So, you're telling us this woman stopped for no reason at all."

Cedric looked at the officer. "That's right." *The quicker she leaves this place, the better.*

He could feel Essence's eyes on his face. Cedric wished he were clean shaven, and as intent to do good as he'd been when he'd met her mother. In the early days, he wouldn't have been caught dead in a motel like this. Things seemed to go downhill after his relationship with Sadie. Her claims that she was pregnant had haunted Cedric. He'd tried to turn to Vivian, to rekindle the bright loving trust that had always been in her eyes, but he couldn't. Something had extinguished it . . . for good. So he'd sought other women to comfort his bruised ego. But none of them had loved him like

Vivian or Sadie. Sadie had been an accident, an attraction he should never have moved on. The women that followed had been inconsequential.

The policeman adjusted his holster. "Maybe she could help you out if you let her speak up."

"No." Cedric looked down again. "I don't want her help."

The officer threw up his hands. "Well, I guess that's that. Sorry, ma'am. You can leave now. We can't make him cooperate. Soo . . ."

Cedric glanced at Essence. She was backing away. The stunned look on her face hurt his heart. Cedric could tell she thought he preferred to remain in trouble than accept her help. The thing was, Essence was right, but Cedric didn't believe she understood his reason. *I can't allow her to help me. I've never done anything for her. I hurt her mother deeply, and denied she was my daughter. I don't want her main memory to be that she helped me out of a jam with the police in front of a sleazy motel.*

"I've got insurance information in my car." Cedric looked at the policeman who appeared to be in charge. "I'm sure I can come up with a way to take care of the bill, if I can make a phone call or two."

He looked over at Essence when she closed her car door. Cedric didn't know when he'd see her again. But he wouldn't forget that despite how he had treated her, Essence was still willing to help him. *I can't investigate Sadie's girl. I've got to find another way to deal with the mess I've gotten myself into.*

"All right. Let's see your insurance papers," the officer said.

Cedric glanced at Essence's car one more time before he turned toward his vehicle.

Essence could hear Cedric say, "I've got insurance information in my car, and I'm sure—" as she got into her car. She shut the door. Her body trembled.

"This man really hates me." Essence's voice shook, too. "He'd rather be taken away by the police than allow me to help him." Her chin dropped to her chest. "What did I do except for be born, to make him hate me so?"

She started the car and drove away. But Essence felt something building inside of her that she had never known before. She began to shake. It got so bad she had to pull over. "Ohh, Mama," she called, "I said I was going to fight this battle for you, but I'm beginning to feel I can't win. All I wanted was for him to admit that you were a good woman. That he cared for you, and that he made a mistake." She choked on the word. "And that mistake was me." Essence refused to let the tears fall, even though they stung her eyes. "But now I know, I was also fighting for myself. I wanted Cedric Johnson to acknowledge me as his child. Would that have been so horrible?" She looked up. "I wanted to be a member of the Johnson family. Because with you gone, I don't have anybody else to claim as family." She blew air through a heavy sigh. "Yes, I have Shiri and Brenda, and I'm sure I'll always be welcomed at Mama Pam's and Mama Doris's . . . but it won't be the same. I'll always feel like I'm keeping a mighty secret from them. How can friendship last under that kind of deceit?"

The pressure of tears subsided. "I'm going to be okay though. I know this is a time of change for me, Mama. I just have to get through it." She thought of Titan standing outside her car as she pulled away. "And the only reason I believe I can keep going, is because you believe that I can."

Essence reached down to put the car in gear again, and she saw the green leather box sitting on the car seat.

Her heart fluttered. "How did that get there?"

She picked it up and opened it. Cedric's star sapphire cuff links winked at her.

"Oh, my God!" Essence's words were filled with breathy wonder as she looked around the car. "Mama? Did you do this? Are you here?"

Essence waited for a verbal answer, but received none.

Lovingly, she touched the cuff links. "Of course, you're here. How else would they have gotten there? You put them there as a sign for me to have hope. To believe in more than I can see and touch. And I will, Mama. And I will."

Essence closed the lid and put the jewelry box back in her purse. "I'm going to do exactly what Cecilia-Marie said. When a person has wronged you, you tell them about it. So I'm going to tell Cedric—my father—just that. Then I'm going to give him back his cuff links, because the way I'm going to go forward is to let him go. And I'm going to do it with dignity, and I'm going to do it with love. Because no matter if he never loves me, Mama, I know you do."

Essence started the car and pulled onto the road again. Her breaths came easily, and her focus was clear. She would return to the Wyndham. "I'll have to tell Brenda and Shiri the truth. If they're my friends, truly my friends, they won't turn their backs on me, and they'll find a way to accept the truth about their uncle." Essence's eyes closed for only a second. "But if they don't . . . I'll find a way to live with that, too."

She merged with the highway traffic. "And as for Titan, everything that happened with him is just a part of the test that I'm going through right now. But whatever they do to me, I'll be able to get through it, because there's more to life than these everyday human things. My mother has shown me that."

Chapter Thirty-four

"I've sat in this room as long as I can, and I can't take it anymore." Vivian opened the door and started down the hotel hall. "And I'm through lying to the public and everyone else for Cedric. I'm sick of it." Her hand sliced the air. "And I'm going to tell Cedric Jr. about his father when we get back to Birmingham." That brought the biggest pang to her heart. "I just can't bring myself to break it to him here. Although I'm sure Karen has blabbed and twisted what I said in Mama and Papa Johnson's room to everybody, poisoning their minds against me." She threw back her head. "So they can believe what they want, but nobody else is going to take advantage of me in this family." "I'm done being the whipping post for the Johnsons." She clutched her purse as a woman passed quickly through the hallway intersection. "Babette!"

Babette turned and looked.

Vivian walked toward her. "What are you doing here?"

Babette moved her mouth but nothing came out.

"You're here because of Cedric. You know where he is." Vivian squinted. "Cedric must have gotten himself in a helluva lot of trouble this time for you and James to come down here. James is here, isn't he?''

"Vivian . . . I—''

"Don't bullshit me, Babette. Did you and James come here because of Cedric?'' Vivian raised her voice.

"Yes. Yes.'' Babette patted down with her palms. "Don't get upset, Vivian.''

"Don't get upset,'' Vivian repeated. "You of all people know what my life has been like with this man.'' She probed Babette's gaze. "It's a miracle I'm not dead or crazy.'' Vivian flung her arm out. "Most of his family thinks the worst of me. That I wanted too much. That I pushed too hard for him to be in the limelight.'' Vivian grabbed her chest. "But you know that isn't true.''

Babette looked down and sighed.

"So where is he, Babette?''

Vivian watched Babette look up the hall, then back at her.

"Is he hiding out in your room?''

"He needed to get himself together, Vivian,'' Babette explained. "Cedric's going through something. You know that.''

Vivian was stunned. Cedric was still able to surprise her. She didn't expect Babette would answer in the affirmative. "He's in your room. Probably hiding from me.'' The corners of her eyes twitched. "And yes, I know he's going through something, but he's married to me. Don't I deserve to know where he is?'' Vivian waited for an answer, but Babette had none. "God, he could have been killed or something, but here I am not knowing if I should call the police because I'm afraid he just spent the night with some woman. This doesn't make any damn sense.'' She started marching up the hall. "Which room is it?''

Babette hurried behind her. "Now, Vivian, that's my hotel room, and James's hotel room. You don't have any right to—''

"Don't tell me about no goddamn rights. It's my right as a wife to know where my husband is. And any second now, I'm going to scream this hotel down if you don't tell me which room he's in."

"Vivian, there's no need to act like this." Babette's tone turned sharp.

"Goddamn it!" Vivian yelled, shaking her head like a madwoman.

"Okay!" Babette threw her hands up. "Okay. We're down here. Just be quiet." She walked past Vivian.

Vivian watched Babette shake her head over and over. "There's no need to shake your head about me. No need at all. You should save that for Cedric."

Babette stopped in front of a door. "I'm not just thinking about you, Vivian. I'm thinking about all of it. Sometimes it gets to be too much for me."

Vivian looked at Babette. "So, imagine how I feel."

Understanding flashed in Babette's eyes before she unlocked the door. She stepped in quickly. "James."

There was no answer.

Vivian could see James and Cedric standing on the patio outside the sliding glass door. She pulled Babette back. "You don't need to try and warn them, Babette, like I'm some crazy woman. You said sometimes this stuff gets to be too much for you. . . . I tell you, you don't know what too much is." Vivian stopped talking when she heard Cedric laugh. "See, he's okay. I'm the one left with the worries. With the memories." She paused. "But that's all right." Her expression toughened. "Babette, I want you to do exactly as I tell you."

"Don't ask me to do anything else, Vivian. This has gone too far as it is."

"You don't know how far this might go if you don't do what I tell you to do. Somebody's going to get hurt."

"Vivian." Babette stepped toward her.

"No, Babette." Vivian dug in her purse frantically. "I don't need you to comfort me."

"What are you looking for?"

Vivian removed a tiny handgun from her bag. "I need you to do exactly as I say."

"My God, Vivian!"

"I'm warning you, Babette." Vivian's tone was unstable.

"All right." Babette covered her mouth with her hands. "What do you want me to do?"

"Get James and Cedric back in here. Get them to talk about everything that has happened."

"Vivian—look—we can just call them in here and talk about it," Babette implored.

"No." She shook her head. "Cedric always lies to me. And I don't want him to be able to lie his way out of this one."

Babette looked at Cedric and James, then back at Vivian.

"I'm going to back into this closet." Vivian stepped backward. "And I want you to stand right there and get them to talk about it."

Babette swallowed hard. "James," she called.

Vivian listened, but the patio door didn't open.

"James," she called louder.

Still nothing.

"They can't hear me," Babette pleaded.

"Call them again." Vivian put the gun to her own head.

"James," Babette cried out in fear.

Vivian heard the sliding glass door open. "Did you call me?"

"Yes." Babette attempted a smile. "I was just wondering . . . what you two were talking about out there."

"Talking over some business."

Babette spoke quickly. "Didn't Cedric say he needed to be at a family dinner at six? It's almost six now."

"What time did you say that dinner was, man?" Vivian heard James ask. She couldn't hear the answer.

"It's about that time," James replied.

Vivian heard the sliding glass door close.

"I guess I should get ready to get out of here," Cedric said. "Vivian is probably furious with me by now."

"You're going to have to talk to her, Cedric," James replied.

"Yeah. But I'm sure it'll be okay. I can handle Vivian."

Vivian heard what sounded like two palms slapping together.

"I want to thank you again, man, for paying that motel bill. I tell you, it was hard calling you up after firing you."

"Don't worry about it, Cedric. But we don't need this kind of thing. We already got to deal with the Stuart girl. So, can you just lay low?"

"Sure. I just got to thinking and drinking." There was a pause. "Now I've got to cancel all those credit cards. Boy, it's going to be a mess. I can't believe that woman stole my wallet. God, Vivian's going to have a fit. I don't know what I'm going to tell her."

Vivian stepped out of the closet with the gun hidden behind her purse. "Tell me a lie, like you always do."

Chapter Thirty-five

"Cedric Johnson's room, please." Essence held the hotel house phone and waited to be connected. *I'll just tell him the truth. I've got his cuff links and I want to return them. After this, he won't have to worry about me trying to contact him or lay claims on him in any fashion. Giving Cedric the cuff links will be closure for me.* The phone rang over and over again. "Shoot." She hung up. "I wonder if he's back yet? He's had plenty of time, and I just checked the ballroom where the dinner is going to be held and he wasn't there."

Essence recalled the scene in the motel parking lot and how Cedric had preferred police custody to acknowledging their relationship. The hurt was still there. "I've got to get this over with."

She leaned against the opposite wall and picked up the phone again. "I'll ask for the Valentines. They know everything. They drove all the way down here for Cedric. They're bound to know where he is. But I don't know Titan's father's name." She hit zero. "Titan Valentine's room, please." Essence waited.

"I'm sorry," the operator said. "He checked out already."

"Oh, that's right. He moved in with his father." She grimaced.

"James Valentine?" the operator volunteered.

"Yes, that's him. Titan moved in with his father in Building Three."

"You mean Building Four," the attendant said.

"That's right." She made a face. "But I can't remember the room number."

"Well, I'm sorry, ma'am, for security reasons I can't give you that information."

"I know," Essence replied. *But I was hoping you would.*

"Do you want me to put you through to the room?"

"Sure," Essence said. She heard the phone ring and she hung up. "I can't do this over the phone. What am I going to say? Hello, I'm Essence Stuart, and I know you're having me investigated, but I'd like to know where my father is?" She stepped into the hall. *And what if Titan answered the telephone?*

She wandered the halls in Building Four. The leather box virtually appearing out of nowhere on the car seat replayed in her mind. *All I want to do is give Cedric his cuff links. And I don't want to do it at the dinner. That would cause a big scene, and I want to be able to tell Brenda and Shiri myself. Without all that drama. I'm sure there will be drama enough.*

Essence turned the corner and saw Titan knocking on one of the doors.

"What are you doing in here, Vivian?" Cedric looked stunned.

"I'm here because you've been lying to me all these years." Her eyes bore into him. "This marriage has been one big lie."

Someone knocked on the hotel door, but Cedric's eyes remained glued to Vivian. "That's not true," he replied.

The knock sounded again.

"Who is it?" Babette called, her voice strained.

"What do you mean, who is it? You too short to look through the peephole these days?" Titan's teasing forced its way through.

"Yes, it is true," Vivian shot back. "Then where were you last night?"

Cedric just stood there.

Titan knocked again.

Babette looked back at the door.

"Come on, Mama. What's going on in there? You're going to make me go get somebody in a minute."

"Open the door, Babette," James said. "Let him in. Titan knows all about this."

Babette hesitated. "James, I don't know."

Vivian turned to her. "Yes, Babette, open the door. It seems your whole family knows more about my husband than I do."

"Do it before Titan brings somebody from the hotel," James insisted.

"But James—" Babette resisted.

"Do it," James nearly yelled.

Reluctantly, Babette opened the door. She blocked Titan's entrance. "This isn't a good time, Titan."

"Mama, what's wrong with you?" Titan looked into his mother's frightened face.

"Let him in here, Babette," Vivian demanded. "Let's see what else your family is hiding for my husband."

Babette moved aside to allow Titan in.

"Vivian, this has gone far enough," Cedric warned. "You and I are going back to our room and talking this thing out."

Essence ran up the hall as Titan stepped inside the doorway. "Titan. Wait!"

"Essence," Titan said, surprised. "I thought you weren't coming back to the hotel."

She looked at him and at the woman who stood beside him. "I've got something to give to Ce—my father," she said confidently.

"Her what?" a female voice demanded. "Open that door, Babette."

Essence was stunned to see her father, Vivian, and another man standing inside.

"Did I hear her right?' Vivian's body trembled as she looked at Cedric. "What did she say?" Vivian turned around.

"Oh, God," he said.

She turned to Essence. "You're his daughter?"

Essence just stood there. She looked at Titan, then her father.

"That's what you just said." Vivian looked around wildly. "We all heard you. Are you Cedric's daughter?"

Essence didn't know if she could speak. "Yes." She squeezed the leather box in her hand.

Vivian looked at Cedric. "You have a daughter by somebody else? You no-good bastard. I knew I didn't want to have any more children by you. You were screwing around, bringing me every goddamn thing on the planet, and you had a child by another woman!" Vivian screamed. "That's why I got rid of your baby! Yes, our baby, Cedric. We didn't need another child. If I had known it was going to be this way, I would have aborted Cedric Jr., too."

"You did what?" Cedric said, stunned. "You got rid of our child, when you knew I wanted another baby? You knew I wanted a little girl."

"A little girl." Vivian started to cry. "It was a little girl. And yes, I got rid of her. What would she have been? Another ornament for you?" Vivian's smile was grotesque. "We would have been the perfect family for Mr. Cedric Johnson, the big politician. But it would have been nothing but a scam. A farce. Just like my marriage to you."

"I can't believe you did that, Vivian. You murdered our child?" Cedric accused.

Vivian stood still, but tears streamed down her face. "Yes, I did. And I wanted that baby. I wanted a little girl, too, but I wasn't going to have another child while you ran around on me."

"I'm not going to stand here and listen to any more of this." Cedric charged forward.

"Yes, you are going to listen." Vivian pulled out the gun. "You have turned me off and shut me out whenever you wanted to. But you're not going to do it today."

"My God, Vivian, what are you doing?" Cedric's eyes turned huge.

"I won't be left out this time, Cedric. I won't be the one not knowing where you are. I won't be the one who you leave in the background and use only when it's to your political advantage. And I won't be the one without a daughter." Vivian turned and aimed.

Essence froze. She had never had a gun pointed at her before. It was as if her body couldn't react to the things that had been said and the emotional charges that had gone with them. Essence just stood there looking at Vivian in disbelief.

"Vivian! What are you doing?" Cedric grabbed her by the waist.

"Let go of me! Let go of me!" Vivian's arm jerked with Cedric's impact and the gun went off.

The sound exploded in Essence's ears. It was like a movie. Babette ducked and covered her face, but Titan . . . Titan dove in front of her, then fell to the ground.

"Titan!" Essence dropped to the floor beside him.

"Titan!" Babette called in horror. "Titan!" his mother screamed as she crawled toward him.

Then the other man was on the floor beside them. He yelled, "Somebody call an ambulance! My son has been shot."

Chapter Thirty-six

Karen looked at the ballroom doors and crossed her arms. "Don't let me see Vivian again. I don't know what I might do to her."

"Look, you and Vivian have always had your differences. And Lord knows I don't see them ever ending. But this is supposed to be a family reunion, not some kind of catfight." Pamela tried to talk some sense into her sister. "So, come on into the ballroom with us. We're going to have a great dinner, and a good time. Just forget about Vivian for the time being."

"But you didn't hear her, Pam. She bad-mouthed Cedric in front of Mama and Papa." Karen shook her head. "They didn't need to hear all that. And it wasn't nothing but a pack of lies."

"Just come on in here," Doris insisted.

"Yeah, Aunt Karen." Brenda patted her back. "You better leave Aunt Vivian alone. You said she already threatened to hit you."

"And if she does, I'll have something for her, too."

Shiri tried not to laugh. "Brenda, you're just instigating now. Don't listen to her, Aunt Karen. She's not making the situation any better." Shiri eyeballed Brenda behind her aunt's shoulders as a hotel attendant talking on a walkie-talkie ran past. She met another hotel employee at the hall intersection.

"Where are they?" the man asked.

"Room four-o-six. Building Four. The ambulance is on the way."

"What happened?" He bent his head as if he didn't want anyone to hear.

The woman's answer faded as they hurried down the hall.

"An ambulance," Brenda said. "I hope it's not for anyone in the family."

"Well, I don't think it's Mama and Daddy," Karen spoke up. "Like I said, I left their room about twenty minutes ago. They were doing okay then."

Another group of Johnsons walked up to the ballroom door. Karen and Brenda stepped aside.

"What's your name?" Pamela asked the heavyset woman in a red glittery top. "We met each other a few years ago at Jessie and Cynthia's wedding. But I can't remember your name."

"I remember you." She broke out in a wide smile that revealed one gold-trimmed tooth. "My name's Tonya. Tonya Carson. Papa George is my second cousin."

Hellos were exchanged.

"Did you hear about the shooting?" Tonya asked.

"Noo," Pamela replied. "It wasn't anybody in the family, was it?"

"I don't think so." A man wearing a Kangol hat beside Tonya replied. "But I think it just happened. I heard some of the hotel folks say it was somebody with the last name of Valentine."

Shiri and Brenda looked at each other.

"Titan Valentine?" Shiri probed.

"I don't know the first name," Tonya replied. "Are there any Valentines in the family?"

"Not that I know of," Pamela replied. "But we know

some Valentines.'' She looked at Doris. ''I bet it's James's son they're talking about.''

''Oh, Lord,'' Doris said. '' Is he hurt bad?''

The man opened the door so Tonya and two preteen girls could precede. ''Don't know,'' he replied.

''I wonder where Essence is,'' Brenda said.

''Do you think she was with him?'' Shiri threw back.

''We've gotta find out.'' Brenda grabbed Shiri's arm. ''That girl doesn't need anything else to happen. Not a thing.''

''I'm coming with you.'' Pam started behind them.

''Me, too,'' Doris said.

''No. You all go on inside,'' Brenda instructed. ''It's no need to upset Grandma and Granddaddy. We'll let you know what happened,'' she assured them.

''All right.'' Doris gave in. ''But you two hurry up because I'm already worried.''

Shiri and Brenda rushed up the hall.

''Where is Building Four?'' Brenda asked once they got outside.

''It's can't be far,'' Shiri replied. ''But God knows these shoes weren't made for running.''

''Your . . . shoes,'' Brenda breathed heavily. ''There it is.'' She pointed.

They quickened their pace and entered the building. Brenda and Shiri ran down several corridors. They stopped when they saw a crowd of people standing in the hall. They tried to push their way to the front.

''Can you see who's in there?'' Brenda asked.

''No. Can you?''

''I can't see a thing. Essence,'' Brenda called.

''Essence,'' Shiri said even louder. ''Essence, are you in there?''

''Brenda! Shiri!'' They heard Essence's frantic voice.

''She's in there!'' Brenda pushed against the crowd. ''Let us through, please.''

''Ple-ease, let us through,'' Shiri echoed.

Slowly, the crowd gave way.

Anxious, Essence looked at the unfamiliar faces above her. She could hear Shiri's and Brenda's calls, but her thoughts were on Titan. Apprehensively, she looked for blood. There was none. Essence felt a threadbare sense of relief. She still couldn't believe what had happened.

Essence looked up at Vivian. She was shaking like a leaf and staring at the four of them on the floor. Vivian had been standing there like that ever since the gun had gone off.

"Essie," Brenda said, kneeling beside her.

Essence turned and looked back when Shiri put her hand on her shoulder.

"What happened?" Shiri asked.

Suddenly, Vivian screamed, "I didn't mean to shoot him. I didn't mean to shoot him. Oh, God! Oh, God! Please, God. I didn't mean to shoot him."

"Vivian shot Titan," Brenda said, shocked.

"Shut up!" Babette jumped to her feet. "You've shot my son! You and your craziness. You've had all that stuff bottled up in you for years. Now look what you've done. Are you satisfied now? Are the two of you happy?" Babette yelled at Cedric and Vivian. "Ever since James got involved with you it's been nothing but craziness."

"Babette," James called sharply. He put his index finger up to his mouth. "That's not going to do any good."

Babette turned on James. "Don't you say a word to me. You've known all the garbage that's been going on with them." She flung her arm toward Cedric and Vivian. "But you were always covering up everything." Her eyes narrowed. "So don't you dare tell me to shut up. Our son could be dying. And all you can think of is covering up for Cedric. To hell with you!"

Dying! Titan can't be dying! Tears streamed down Essence's face as she looked down at him. *Mama! Please, God! I can't take anymore!* Essence's tears fell onto Titan's face, and his eyes began to flutter. Slowly, Essence watched them open. "Titan," she said, softly. Excited, she looked up. "His eyes are open."

Babette dropped to her knees. "Titan! Can you hear me?"

Titan closed his eyes and opened them again. "Yes." His voice was strained.

"Thank God. Thank God," Babette repeated.

"Titan." James leaned over him. "You've been shot. An ambulance is on its way."

"Shot." Titan looked at Essence. "Are you okay?"

"Yes." Essence touched his face. Her tears continued to fall.

Titan shifted his weight.

"Lie still, son," James instructed. "Wait until the ambulance gets here."

"How do you feel, Titan?" Babette asked.

"A little dizzy. Winded." Titan leaned over and touched his side. "It hurts beneath my gun." He removed his hand and looked at it. "But I'm not bleeding. The bullet may have struck my gun."

"EMTs. Let us through," a man called. "Step to the side, everyone. We got to get through here."

"Come on, Essence." Brenda helped Essence get up as the ambulance worker knelt down beside Titan.

"What happened?" the EMT asked.

James motioned toward Vivian. "Her gun went off when she was waving it around." He looked at Babette. "My son was shot."

"All right. Give us some room so we can see what's going on here," the EMT said to the crowd. He leaned toward Titan. "Where does it hurt?"

Titan attempted to sit up.

"Take it easy." The technician put his palm up. "Just point. You don't have to move."

"The ribs beneath my gun hurt. I think my gun stopped the bullet."

"Is that right? What you doing carrying a gun?"

"I'm a private detective," Titan replied.

"I see." Gingerly, the EMT looked at Titan's side. "There's no blood. Why don't you remove the gun."

Titan did as he was instructed. He pointed to an indentation in the handle of the .38.

"Seems like you were right."

"I thought so." Titan swallowed. "After I was hit, I blacked out."

"Well." The EMT got on his haunches. "You're real lucky. This could have been worse. People have died from a baseball impacting the chest. If it hits just at the right moment between heartbeats, it can take you out of here."

"I didn't mean to shoot him. I didn't mean to," Vivian screamed.

"It's okay, ma'am," said a female EMT who was standing by. "He's going to be fine."

Vivian continued to shake and repeat, "I didn't intend to kill anybody."

"Maybe you need to see about her," the man advised the female.

"Ma'am"—the woman moved closer to Vivian—"he's going to be okay."

Vivian tried to hold her body with her hands, but it continued to shake.

"I'm going to give you something to calm you down." The EMT looked at Cedric. "Is this your wife?"

"Yes." Cedric tried to touch Vivian's arm. She yanked away.

One of the female's thick, arched brows went up. "Doesn't seem like she's too happy with you right now."

Cedric sighed. "No, it doesn't."

The EMT put her bag on the bed. "What I give her is going to work pretty quickly. Is this your room?"

"No," Cedric replied. "It's the Valentines' room."

"Do you have a room?" The woman stopped opening the bag.

"Yes," Cedric replied. He looked at Vivian, who looked away.

"I think we should go to your room. I'll give her the sedative there."

Cedric tried to take Vivian's arm again.

"D-don't touch me, Cedric." Vivian moved away. "Don't ever t-touch me again."

Cedric looked down. "Vivian, please. I—"

"Let me help you, ma'am." The woman gently took hold of Vivian's arm.

Essence could see the strain on her father's face. He looked much older than the day he walked around the Wyndham swimming pool, smiling and greeting everyone. Vivian's rejection, on top of everything else, appeared to be the last straw. Essence stepped back again as the EMT helped up Titan.

"You're going to be fine," the technician said. "Maybe a little bruised."

"It won't be the first time," Titan replied. His eyes met Essence's gaze.

"But I'd rest a few minutes, if I were you. Give your body a little more time to know it's out of danger." He shook Titan's hand and entered the hall.

Vivian and the female EMT were not far behind. Vivian spoke to Titan in a shaky voice. "I didn't mean for that to happen."

"I know," Titan said. "I'll be fine."

Essence touched Titan's arm. Vivian stared at her. There was a deep hurt and something else in her gaze. It tugged at Essence's heart. Essence heard herself say, "I wasn't trying to hurt you."

Vivian didn't reply.

Cedric followed with his head lowered. He didn't look at her. He didn't say a thing. It only sharpened Essence's pain. She watched him pass. Then he stopped. Cedric reached back and patted Essence's arm before he glanced at Brenda and Shiri.

"Cedric," Essence said.

His troubled gaze rested on her face.

She handed him the green box. "This is yours."

Cedric looked at Essence questioningly. He didn't seem to recognize the box. But the look on his face when he opened it said everything. It was obvious the cuff links struck a deep chord. Tears came to Cedric's eyes. He looked at Essence. "Thank you," he said softly and moved on through the thinning crowd.

"What in the world is going on?" Shiri asked.

Essence looked at Brenda and Shiri—her friends, her family. "There's something I've got to tell you."

"What is it?" Brenda looked apprehensive.

Essence looked past Brenda and Shiri at the two policemen who had turned into the hall.

"Is this the room where the shooting occurred?" the tallest officer asked.

"Yes," the three of them replied.

"I'm the one who was shot, officer," Titan spoke up. "If you come in, I'll tell you all about it."

The policeman looked him up and down, then asked suspiciously, "You were shot?"

Titan nodded.

"This should be interesting," he replied. The officers entered the room.

"You go ahead," Titan said to Essence.

"Wait a minute," the second policeman said. "Were any of you involved in the shooting?"

James pointed to Essence. "She didn't pull the trigger, but if she hadn't come here, it never would have happened."

"Don't blame this on Essence," Titan retorted. "I could as easily blame you."

James looked surprised. "She's just gotten to you, that's all."

"Yes, she has," Titan said. "But if you and Cedric weren't so eager to cover up the truth, none of this would have happened." Titan looked at the police officer. "The shooting was an accident. Vivian never intended to shoot anyone."

"Are you Vivian?" the officer asked Babette.

"No. I'm not. I'm Titan's mother." She looked at her son.

"Well, where's this Vivian?" the squat officer asked.

"She's in her hotel room," Babette replied. "One of the ambulance workers went with her to give her a sedative.

She was very upset. Like my son said, the shooting was an accident. Vivian was upset and the next thing we knew, she was waving this gun around. When Cedric tried to stop her, the gun went off."

"Cedric?" the tall officer inquired.

"Cedric's her husband," James said. "He went back to the room with them."

"So, you're all saying this was an accident?"

Looks went around the room, followed by a series of nods.

"We'll have to take a report anyway," the tall officer said.

"That's fine." Titan looked at Essence. He bent forward slowly and gave her a kiss. "Miracles do exist," he said softly.

Essence smiled. "Thank God, they do." She turned and linked arms with Brenda and Shiri.

"Come on. I've got something to tell you."

They started down the hall.

Chapter Thirty-seven

"What is it, Essence?" Brenda asked.

"Yeah. You've got me worried," Shiri pressed.

"I didn't know how to tell you," Essence began. "I still don't."

"What do you mean, you don't know how?" Shiri replied. "Just say it. We're your best friends. You can tell us anything."

Essence stopped and looked at them. "And no matter what I say, it won't change our relationship?"

Brenda put her hands on her hips. "If you don't tell us, I'm—"

"Okay. Okay." Essence took a deep breath. "Your uncle Cedric . . ." She looked in Brenda's and Shiri's expectant eyes. Essence forced herself to speak through her fears. "Your uncle Cedric is my father," she added softly.

Brenda and Shiri stood there with their mouths open.

"No way," Shiri finally replied.

Essence nodded. "Yes. He is. Mama told me a week before she died."

"Uncle Cedric is your father?" Brenda repeated. "I can't believe it."

Although Essence had expected their denials, to hear them was another thing. Brenda and Shiri couldn't believe Cedric was her father. At least, they couldn't accept it. "But he is," Essence said, with finality. "And all the denials in the world aren't going to change it."

Brenda and Shiri looked at each other, and Essence looked down. It was just as she'd feared. They would never be able to accept the truth. Brenda and Shiri had idolized their uncle for too long. Saddened, but ready to accept whatever came next, Essence looked up again. She was surprised by the slow smiles spreading across Shiri's and Brenda's faces.

"You're really my cousin!" Shiri threw open her arms.

"We said we were cousins, and we really are!" Brenda cheered.

"You mean you don't care?" Essence asked.

"Care? Of course, we care," Brenda replied. "We love it, and we love you."

Essence threw her arms around them. "I love you, too."

Finally, they stood back and looked at one another.

"That's why we've always looked alike." Shiri covered her mouth. "You're actually a Johnson." Then her eyes grew wide. "Oh, my God. Vivian! Was she trying to shoot Uncle Cedric?"

"No," Essence replied. "She was waving the gun around, like Titan's mother said, and actually"—Essence blew out a deep breath—"she was threatening me. But Cedric grabbed her from behind and when the gun went off, Titan jumped in front of me."

"You mean to tell me this man actually saved your life?" Brenda said.

"Yes." Essence looked back toward the Valentines' hotel room. "He could have been killed." A chill ran through her.

"That's some serious stuff, Essence," Brenda said.

Essence nodded. With her mother's death so new, she didn't know how she would have coped if Titan had died.

"This is wild." Brenda looked overwhelmed. "Did Uncle Cedric know? I mean, did your mother tell him?"

"She told him when she first found out she was pregnant," Essence said. "And that's when he stopped seeing her. But I think through the years he may have forgotten all about it. My mother never got with him again or asked him for anything after that." She looked to the side. "There was probably some wishful thinking on his part that my mother would have gotten rid of me, knowing he didn't accept the pregnancy." She paused. "And that he was married."

"God." Shiri looked disappointed. "I bet you're right."

"I'll be damned," Brenda said. "So Vivian was telling the truth in Grandma and Granddaddy's hotel room. Aunt Karen believes she was telling a bunch of lies. Boy, is she going to have a fit."

"What's Karen got to do with it?" Essence asked.

"I think I told you she and Vivian never got along. And I mean never. Even now, she's ready to fight Vivian over telling lies on Uncle Cedric," Shiri replied. "Wait until she hears this."

"Well, she doesn't have to hear it today," Essence said. "I've caused enough trouble by coming to this family reunion. I'm going home and letting the dust settle."

"You'll do no such thing," Shiri replied. "Now that we know you are a Johnson, you're coming to the dinner, and you're going to sit with us."

Essence held her head. "I don't think that's a good idea."

"Well, if you're worried about Aunt Karen and some of the rest of them, there will never be a perfect time for them to hear Uncle Cedric is less than perfect. To be honest with you, I'm still stunned by it all. But I love you. You've been my friend all these years and my play cousin." Essence saw Brenda's eyes turn bright with tears. "So what if we Johnsons aren't as perfect as we thought we were? We might as well get it over with in one fell swoop."

"I don't know," Essence replied, the scene with Vivian waving the gun and Cedric's drawn features stuck in her mind.

"You don't have to make a grand announcement or anything," Brenda encouraged. "Just go and see what happens. The news is bound to come out."

Shiri put on a comical fighting stance. "And if anybody got any bones to pick with you, we got your back. Don't we, Brenda?" Then she made a face. "I just hope it's not my mama or yours. There's only a certain amount of fighting you can do with your own mama."

Essence had to smile. "And I can't hide forever, can I?"

"Nope," Shiri replied. "And there's no reason for you to. You didn't do anything but be born."

Brenda smiled mischievously. "And we're glad you did." She gave Shiri the eye. "Gir-rl, Uncle Cedric has been cutting up sideways."

"Mm, mm. This will be a family reunion we'll never forget."

"You can say that again," Essence replied.

This time it was Brenda who locked arms with Essence. "So, let's go and face the family."

They arrived outside the ballroom. Shiri grabbed the door handle. "After you, cuz." She looked at Essence and opened the door. The untrained, but melodic voices of three Johnson girls singing "We Are Family" greeted them.

Essence looked at the room of faces that were all turned in their direction. She saw a hand waving them over. It was Mama Pam sitting at a table down front. As they made their way over to the table, Essence realized how nervous she was. Her case of nerves accelerated when the questions began before they could sit down.

"I was about to go find you two if you had been a second later," Doris said to Brenda and Shiri. She looked at Essence. "Was it Titan Valentine that was shot?"

"Yes, it was Titan." Essence could feel her heart beating.

"Lor-rd," Pamela replied. "Is he hurt bad?"

"No, he's fine," Essence said. "The bullet hit the handle of his gun. It was in a shoulder holster."

Rosie leaned across the table. "What's that boy doing carrying a gun?"

"He's a private detective, Aunt Rosie," Shiri told her.

"Ohh. So that explains it. Somebody he was investigating shot him."

Essence, Brenda, and Shiri looked at one another.

"Vivian shot him," Brenda finally said.

"Vivian!" Karen echoed much too loudly. "I told you that woman was crazy."

Mama Lela gave them a stern look from the other end of the table.

"Why did she shoot him?" Karen asked, trying not to look too pleased as she lowered her voice. "I hope they took her butt to jail and threw away the key. Cedric needs to divorce that woman. She's not doing anything for him. She's just going to bring him down."

"I didn't even know Vivian had a gun." Pamela looked stunned. "Do you know why she shot him?"

"It was an accident," Essence replied.

"She shot him because she's crazy," Karen reiterated. "There isn't any other reason. So, did Cedric have to come and get her?"

"Cedric was there when she shot him," Essence replied.

"And you were there, too? You saw her shoot him?" Karen asked.

Essence looked down. "I was there."

"Where is Cedric?" Doris asked. "Is he all right?"

"Uncle Cedric went with Aunt Vivian to their hotel room. Aunt Vivian was really upset, so the EMT thought she needed a sedative."

Karen huffed. "Her greedy butt needs to be upset. Telling all them lies." Karen's eyes brightened. "Here comes my baby brother."

All eyes shifted to the ballroom door.

"But oh, my goodness, he looks so bad. That woman is going to be the death of Cedric. You just wait and see," Karen declared.

Chapter Thirty-eight

Cedric stood by the ballroom door. Essence watched him look around the room. His gaze rested on various faces, including hers. He nodded. Essence nodded back. Suddenly, the door opened and Titan's father stuck his head inside. James said something to Cedric, but Cedric simply shook his head and walked away. To Essence the door closed slowly, almost reluctantly.

Cedric continued to search the room until he spotted Cedric Jr. With slow, deliberate steps he made his way across the floor. Essence watched Cedric lean over and whisper in her half brother's ear. Cedric Jr. spoke to his wife, got to his feet, and left. Cedric watched his son leave before he walked toward their table.

The Johnson girls were completing their song when Cedric stopped in front of Papa George and Mama Lela. He kissed his mother on the cheek.

"I'm going to give these back to you, Papa." He placed the green jewelry box in his father's hand. "I don't deserve them."

Papa George looked surprised. "They're yours now, son. Why are you giving them back to me?"

"They're a family heirloom, and I feel like they're safer in your hands right now than they are in mine."

"But I gave them to—" Papa George tried to give the box back.

Cedric wouldn't take the cuff links. "Trust me, Papa. I shouldn't have them." He turned away and walked to the front of the room.

"What did he give to Papa?" Doris asked, trying to see.

"Some kind of jewelry box," Pamela replied. "He said something about not deserving them."

"Wha-at?" Doris's eyes widened.

Karen looked totally confused.

"Hello, everybody." Cedric harnessed the room's attention. "I know I usually give a little speech or pep talk at the end of this dinner, but with all that has happened today"—he sighed—"actually, the last few days, I can't wait until the end. I have to speak up now before I lose my courage."

Low murmurs rose and fell, then finally came to an end.

"For years now I have been a member of this family that you have looked up to and supported, personally and politically," Cedric continued. "I have always appreciated your support and I always will. We are a strong, proud family because we have my mother, Lela Kincaid Johnson, and my father, George Johnson's blood flowing through our veins." Cedric looked at his parents. "Thank you, Mama and Papa. for the life you have given me. But there were times when I really didn't appreciate that life. Times when it seemed like it wasn't enough." He paused. "Wasn't big enough. Grand enough. But what you gave me was your hearts and your goodness, and if I couldn't see that was worth more than the money and the fame I sought, it wasn't your fault. It was a flaw in me." He looked down. "And now that flaw has come back to haunt me. So I just want to take this opportunity to personally prepare you, my family, before you hear it someplace else.

"Right now my wife, Vivian, is not feeling very well. She did something today that I must take the blame for, although it was her action. Vivian is a good woman. I know some of you don't believe that.'' Cedric looked at Karen. ''But when Vivian married me, she was a young, country girl who took on more than she could have imagined. Sometimes being a politician's wife isn't easy. Especially if you are my wife.''

The ballroom door burst open. Cedric Jr. stepped inside. He glared at his father.

''Cedric Jr.,'' Cedric called.

''How could you do it?'' Cedric Jr. exploded. ''My mother has been nothing but good to you. How could you do that to her?''

''Cedric. Son.'' Cedric took a couple of steps in his son's direction.

''Don't come to me now. You should have come to us before,'' Cedric Jr. retorted. He started walking toward his wife before he looked back at his father. ''She's no damn sister of mine.''

An appalled hush held the room in its grip while Cedric Jr. got his wife and children. They left the ballroom.

Essence could see the hurt Brenda and Shiri felt for their cousin. It hurt her, too. It hurt because she was the cause of her brother's pain, deliberately or not. Essence stared at the table. She couldn't bring herself to look at anyone.

''Well . . . ,'' she could hear her father say. ''As I was saying . . . I just want you to know I'm only human, and I have definitely made some mistakes. And as my family, as time goes by, I hope you can still find it in your hearts to support me. But most of all love me.'' There was an extended pause. ''Because I do love you.''

Essence looked up. Cedric turned away to hide his tears.

The room remained quiet. No one seemed to breathe or move. Finally, Papa George got up and went to his son. Slowly, he placed an arthritic arm around him, and patted his shoulder. ''It's going to be okay, son. Everything's going to be okay.''

''Well, I'll be dipped in dirt,'' Rosie said real low. ''Cedric's got a child by another woman.''

"That's what it seems like." Pamela's hand covered her mouth.

"He's not the first and he won't be the last," Mama Lela declared from the end of table. "So, there won't be no stones cast around here. I won't allow it."

Furtive glances passed around the table and beyond.

"Well, I don't believe it," Karen retorted. "I won't believe it until I see a DNA test. You know how these women are. All of them are gold diggers. They see a rising star and they try to latch on to him. I believe the woman who's claiming Cedric has a baby by her is lying."

Essence couldn't take any more. She couldn't sit quietly and let Aunt Karen belittle her mother—call her a liar, when she was a good woman who had accepted a fate with dignity and self-reliance.

Essence got up. "No. She's not lying. She can't. I know because I buried her one week ago today." She stepped away from the table and looked at Brenda and Shiri. "Love you."

"We love you, too, Essence." Brenda tried not to cry. It was already too late for Shiri.

Essence walked toward the front of the room. She could hear Karen say, "I don't believe it," and Mama Pam reply, "What part don't you believe, Karen?" Essence knew Mama Pam and Mama Doris would probably stand up for her, along with Brenda and Shiri. But suddenly it didn't matter anymore. It didn't matter what anyone said, about her, or her mother, because Essence knew the truth, and it seemed her father had finally accepted it. She joined him and her grandfather at the front of the room.

Cedric's eyes had almost dried. He tried to smile, but it only made the tears flow again.

Essence smiled for him. "I just want you to know, you're the only parent I have now, and if you want my support, I'll be glad to give it."

Cedric pulled Essence to him and hugged her. "I want your support, and maybe, eventually, I'll win your love and respect. God bless you, Essence Stuart Johnson."

Once again Essence cried. It was the first time her father had ever hugged her, and Cedric did it in front of the people who were most important in his life: the Johnson family. He patted her a couple of times before he let her go. Essence was surprised when she found it difficult to leave Cedric's arms.

Papa George shook his head. Then he placed Essence's hand in his puffy one. "I knew you were a Johnson. Nobody in this room looks as much like my mother as you do. You take care, child. I'll see you at the next family reunion, if God's willing."

Essence kissed her grandfather's sagging cheek and left the ballroom.

She didn't know how she found her car. Her mind surely didn't take her there. Maybe it was her mother who led her—glad to share the moment, glad that Essence had finally won, glad that she had found some peace at last. Essence unlocked the car door and prepared to climb inside.

"Hey, lady, your car smells like gasoline."

Essence turned. It was Titan. Immediately her heart beat faster and the roller coaster of feelings she had experienced since meeting Titan rushed through her. Memories of the attraction, the anger, the lovemaking, and the ever-present doubt of what the outcome of their relationship would be. In two days they had lived a lifetime of emotions, and Essence would continue to live because of Titan. He jeopardized his own life to save hers. How do you repay someone for that? What do you say? At that moment, all Essence could come up with was "Titan, what are you doing out here?"

"Searching for your car. Too bad you don't have any Giovanni rims, it would have made my job much easier."

She gave a short laugh before she walked over to his car. "Shouldn't you be resting?"

"I rested, but I had to make sure you didn't up and leave on me, which you were trying to do."

"Well . . . it got to be a little too much for me at the dinner." Essence looked down. "Being a Johnson can be tough."

"I can imagine," Titan said. There was a pause. "So, where you going?"

"Home. To rest. I'm done fighting."

"Sounds perfect. I had the same idea."

Essence crossed her arms. "Really?"

"Yep." Titan licked his lip.

Essence couldn't resist. "Tired from playing the hero, or is it the villain?"

He smiled and looked away. "A little bit of both, I guess."

Then Essence turned serious. "Thank you, Titan, for taking up for me with your father." She took a deep breath. "Things could have ended up quite differently if you weren't in your parents' hotel room. And for you to do what you did. I don't know what—"

"You don't need to thank me." He got out of the car and stood in front of her. "I think you're trying to say you like me?" He said softly.

Essence looked into his eyes. "I'm not trying to say it. I'm saying it. I *like* you, Titan. I like you a lot." But her eyes revealed much more.

"You like me, huh? Is that all?"

Essence's heart was beating so fast. She wanted to say more. To say that she loved him. She opened her mouth but nothing came out.

"What if I told you what I feel for you is much more." Titan put his arms around her.

"I-It is?"

He nodded. "From the first moment I looked into your eyes, it was more than that."

"For me too." Essence confessed softly. She watched his attention shift to her lips.

Titan drew Essence close and kissed her. Afterward he continued to hold her in his arms. "I would love to have the opportunity to show you how much more," he whispered in her ear.

"I'd like nothing more than that." Essence replied.

He looked into her eyes. "Let's go back inside. We'll have our own reunion and nobody will have to know."

"Our secret." Essence smiled.

They continued to stare into each other's eyes.

Finally, Titan said "I love you, Essence, and I'm so glad you showed up when you did. I was about to lose hope, but now I've got more than a man deserves."

Joy flooded inside her. "I love you, too." Essence replied with the brightest hope for the future she'd felt in a long, long time.

Dear Reader,

My, it feels good to sit down and write you a letter. It's been a long time. And now, once again, through Arabesque Books, we are together. I hope you enjoyed THE TIES THAT BIND. I enjoyed writing it, but I must share my excitement over my next novel. It is one that you have asked for for years. It's the conclusion to my Gemstone Series. First there was The Ruby, in THE PASSION RUBY, then there was The Emerald, in EMERALD'S FIRE, and now there is The Diamond, in A DIAMOND'S ALLURE. Sienna and Hawk are back! And because of them, I get to go to Hawaii to do research. Research on the island of Kauai, "The Garden Island" where much adventure and mysticism will take place. Thanks, Sienna and Hawk!!! And thank you, for continuing to read my books.

Remember, if you keep reading, I'll keep writing.

About the Author

Eboni Snoe has nine novels to her credit, novels that she hopes, opens the heart, mind and spirit. Her permanent residence is St. Petersburg, Florida, although she has spent the majority of the last year in Salt Lake City, Utah.

COMING IN OCTOBER 2002 FROM
ARABESQUE ROMANCES

__RHYTHMS OF LOVE
by Doris Johnson   1-58314-214-2 $6.99US/$9.99CAN

Modern dancer Brynn Halsted put her entire life into her art . . . until a devastating attack left her injured in body and spirit. But when quietly handsome jazz club owner Simeon Storey challenges her to try and recover her self-worth at his Poconos retreat, Brynn can't resist the offer—or the simmering attraction between them.

__STOLEN HEARTS
by Jacquelin Thomas   1-58314-347-5 $6.99US/$9.99CAN

Raven Christopher has found her soul mate in Andre Simon, a free-spirited yet intensely disciplined artist whose paintings have taken New York—and her heart—by storm. But when she confesses her involvement in the heist of a famous painting, Andrew vows never to speak to her again. But fate may have a different plan.

__IF I WERE YOUR WOMAN
by Robin Allen   1-58314-345-9 $5.99US/$7.99CAN

When Satin Holiday finds herself suddenly single again and living in a new city, she gears up for the challenges of her exciting new job at an Atlanta high-tech company. But is she ready for Drake Swanson, the irresistibly attractive advertising executive who clashes with her at every opportunity . . . and who is making her heart do a slow burn?

__AS LONG AS THERE IS LOVE
by Karen White-Owens   1-58314-369-6 $5.99US/$7.99CAN

An unexpected pregnancy in college brought Cameron Butler back home, but she still managed to start her own business and build a good life for herself and her daughter, Jayla. Yet Cameron's success has not erased the pain she felt from the betrayal of Jayla's father—or her memories of the passion they once shared.

Call toll free **1-888-345-BOOK** to order by phone or use this coupon to order by mail. ALL BOOKS AVAILABLE OCTOBER 01, 2002.

Name _____

Address _____

City _____ State _____ Zip _____

Please send me the books that I have checked above.

I am enclosing	$_____
Plus postage and handling*	$_____
Sales tax (in NY, TN, and DC)	$_____
Total amount enclosed	$_____

*Add $2.50 for the first book and $.50 for each additional book. Send check or money order (no cash or CODs) to: **Arabesque Romances, Dept. C.O., 850 Third Avenue 16th Floor, New York, NY 10022**

Prices and numbers subject to change without notice. Valid only in the U.S. All orders subject to availability. **NO ADVANCE ORDERS.**

Visit our website at **www.arabesquebooks.com.**

DO YOU KNOW AN ARABESQUE MAN?

1st Arabesque Man HAROLD JACKSON
Featured on the cover of "Endless Love"
by Carmen Green / Published Sept 2000

2nd Arabesque Man EDMAN REID
Featured on the cover of "Love Lessons"
by Leslie Esdaile / Published Sept 2001

3rd Arabesque Man PAUL HANEY
Featured on the cover of "Holding Out For A Hero"
by Deirdre Savoy / Published Sept 2002

WILL YOUR "ARABESQUE" MAN BE NEXT?

One Grand Prize Winner Will Win:
- 2 Day Trip to New York City
- Professional NYC Photo Shoot
- Picture on the Cover of an Arabesque Romance Novel
- Prize Pack & Profile on Arabesque Website and Newsletter
- $250.00

You Win Too!
- The Nominator of the Grand Prize Winner receives a Prize Pack & profile on Arabesque Website
- $250.00

ARABESQUE
A PRODUCT OF
BET BOOKS